THE

WHISPER

Ian Paul Power

Wolfpack Publishers

Wolfpack Publishers

Elphin Street
Strokestown
Co. Roscommon

Publishers Website: www.WolfpackPublishers.com

Published by Wolfpack Publishers 2013

First Edition

ISBN 978-0-9574994-1-6

Cover Image by Ian Paul Power

For kitten, Duck and Alpha,
Pack run together.

Acknowledgements

First and foremost, I must thank my wonderful wife Sarah. Before anyone else she was my editor, my beta reader and my inspiration. Were it not for her, one of the characters (who turned out to be most people's favourite) wouldn't even exist.

The hardest part of writing is delivering, every day. And so I thank my fellow writer Lora O'Brien for the encouraging and highly competitive communications which pushed me to make my initial deadline.

Without a publisher, a writer might as well be talking to himself. So my thanks go to John Sinnott of Wolfpack Publishers for putting so much effort into making this book a reality.

I also want to thank Alyssa Gilmore, whose keen eye spotted many errors and helped to soften the rough edges. Without her efforts, this would be a significantly less well written book.

I am extremely thankful to my beta readers. Heck, Shiv, Andrew, Janet, Fi, Kof, Coral, Ceara, and Dáire. Their input helped shape a lot of what you will read.

And finally I would like to thank my family. My mother, father and two sisters, who always knew I was talented, and were just waiting for me to show it (or so they assure me).

A lot of people have helped shape this book, but any and all errors are my own. If you find something you don't like, it is me you should blame…

… unless it's a semi-colon, those are all Alyssa's fault.

1

They would come gently at first, barely heard. I would often mistake them for the wind, slowly growing louder. But the wind did not travel around the room. The wind did not whisper in one ear, then the other. The wind was not full of half heard words lost in a maddening susurrus. Sometimes it wasn't so bad. There would just be one voice, or two. They would whisper softly to me, and it was merely harrowing. Other nights it seemed that the world was full of a thousand whispers, each trying to get my attention, each full of anger or fear or terrible emotions I didn't have words for. They filled the air and filled my head until I wanted to scream just to reassure myself that some other sound existed in this world.

That night was one of those nights.

I awoke with a start, searching the room, bleary eyed. Soft morning light filtered through the curtains. The night almost seemed like nothing but a bad dream. If only. I'd finally managed to sleep sometime around 4am, after hours of torment. It always got better with the dawn, that was something I'd realised. Daytime was no safe harbour, but at least it didn't make me want to scream.

I pulled myself from beneath the tangled covers and shambled as best I could to the bathroom. My arms and legs felt like lead, but I was used to it. I turned to the bathroom mirror and looked into the face of a zombie. Pale skin, dark circles around my eyes, short brown hair in disarray. Mum had blonde hair and blue eyes, but I took after my Dad. He'd died when I was young and I didn't remember him much, but I had his brown hair, and his eyes. They were black. Mum said that black eyes were impossible, that my eyes just had a lot of melanin, and they were very dark brown. But they always looked black to me.

Mum had already gotten up and gone. She worked in a department store and was working mornings that week. The house was completely quiet. Not a voice, not a whisper, not a hint of sound. It's like that sometimes, just after dawn. No sounds in the house, no sounds in my head, it's a little piece of bliss. Sometimes I wish I could sit forever in the post dawn light. I moved slowly, trying not to disturb the stillness as I made myself some toast and got a big glass of orange juice. It had to be big, to wash down all the pills. Five pills every morning, and again before bed. It could be worse, I'd been on more, and at least the current concoction left me relatively clearheaded. Every year or so there was a different doctor, with a different idea and, inevitably, a different set of pills. Some had been better than others, some had been a disaster. None of them had made me better, not properly.

Once I was done with breakfast I showered and dressed for school. My wrists were poking out past the sleeves of my jumper again. Mum wouldn't be happy. I'd tell her, "I've tried to stop growing, but it just won't work!" I was fifteen and at 6 foot I was the tallest in my class. I checked the mirror before I left. Black shoes, grey trousers, dark red jumper, haphazard tie, expression of existential dread… good to go.

That day at school was almost uneventful. I read once that the Chinese have an ancient curse "May you live in interesting times." A lot of people don't understand why that would be a bad thing. I get it, I totally get it.

Mr Egan's English class was the only upset. He was actually one of the better teachers. He tried not to draw attention to me too much, and always made sure I had a list of what we'd be studying. He'd figured out that I learn a lot better outside of the classroom. I took my customary seat at the back of the class and opened my book, trying to block out the wisps of sound that hovered at the edge of my perception.

Mr Egan was late. This was bad. A class of teenage boys

is like a pack of trained monkeys. While their trainer is present, everything is ok. Sure, some of the monkeys will act up, but the trainer keeps these individuals in line and a kind of tense peace reigns. Once the trainer has left, they start to act out only a little, testing boundaries, expecting at any moment to be corrected. But they're not. The longer they're left unattended, the bolder they grow, until chaos rules and peace is a distant memory.

I backed up into the corner, resisting the urge to grip my head in pain as a thousand voices chittered in my brain.

"What's the matter schizo? You look like you're gonna piss yourself."

The lead monkey smiled as the other boys smirked and laughed. Five of them surrounded the corner in a loose arc. The rest of the class looked on with bored disinterest, or at best, stared down at their textbooks. I wanted to scream. I wanted to lash out kicking and screaming until I was too tired to breathe. It was all I could do to keep my voice to an angry growl.

"Leave me alone Boyle."

"Me?" he said, his eyebrows rising. "I'm not doing anything Murphy, I'm not even touching you."

With that he threw a punch at my face, stopping it less than an inch away from my nose, making me flinch, and smirking when I did.

"Awwwww... poor scared little schizo!"

Laughter spread through the room, not limited to the five boys in front of me. My eyes burned, welling up in anger and frustration. My head throbbed as their laughter echoed through it, the whispers seeming to join in until my whole world was full of mocking laughter.

"What is going on here?"

Mr. Egan stood in the door to the classroom with a face like thunder. His jaw was set hard beneath his short greying beard. All attention in the room shifted to him. In that moment, there was silence, outside my head and in. In that blissful second of respite, I slumped against the wall.

"Declan?"

Mr Egan levelled a suspicious and angry gaze at my chief tormentor, who returned it with wide eyed innocence.

"Murphy is completely spazzing out Sir. I don't know what's wrong with him."

Mr Egan's features softened a little, but his tone remained gruff.

"That is not a phrase I wish to hear from you again Mr Boyle. Everyone, return to your seats and open your books to "The Road Not Taken.""

The chairs scraped and the books thumped as everyone fell in. I pulled myself upright and followed suit. Mr Egan strolled along between the desks, his hands clasped behind his back, looking around at the trained monkeys, making sure all was well. As he reached the end of the aisle, he spoke. His gaze remained roaming the room, but I heard him murmur, so softly that I almost doubted it was real.

"Are you ok Eoin?"

And so I whispered in return the lie that gets you through the day.

"I'm fine."

The rest of the class passed with relative banality. I tried to pay attention as much as I could with a wavering buzz in my ear. When the bell rang, I gathered up my things, threw my backpack over my shoulder and went to trudge into the halls.

"Eoin, wait a moment."

I looked up at Mr Egan as the last of my classmates left the room. He sat at his desk, a look of concern on his face.

"Eoin, if someone is picking on you, bullying you, you can tell me."

I let out a tired sigh and my gaze dropped to the floor in front of my feet.

"No Sir, everything's fine."

"There are things I can do to help Eoin, but I can't do anything if you don't speak up."

A flash of anger ran through me, and I lifted my head to look him in the eyes.

"I tried that once. Someone hit me, so I told on them. They got detention, and then the next day, they waited for me after school and beat me up on my way home."

My words were clipped. It was all I could do not to shout.

"So I told about that too, and do you know what the school said, Mr Egan? 'We can't discipline behaviour that happens outside school grounds'. They basically said that once I'm outside those gates, I'm fair game, and there's nothing they can do about it. So don't pretend that you have any more power over this situation than I do."

I didn't wait for a reply, just turned and stormed through the corridor to my next class.

This all happened on a Thursday. I know it was a Thursday because Thursdays are 'Doctor Days'. Mum picks me up after school to drive me there, and then spends a tense hour sitting in the waiting room, probably praying that somehow this session will lead to a breakthrough, and a different son will emerge. This Doctor was new; I'd only been seeing him a few months. He seemed to favour getting me to talk, like maybe if I told him everything there is to know about me then he could figure out why I was crazy. He made me lay down on his big leather couch and asked me how I felt about things. How did I feel about being different? How did I feel about missing school? How did I FEEL about being a fucked up kid who hears voices and can't sleep at night? As if my feelings about it could help, or were even a mystery. I hated it. I woke up every day hating it and I wished it would all just end. Only you can't shout that last part too loud or they put you on suicide watch. I learned that the hard way.

So I sat and talked in Doctor Hawkins wood paneled office, lying on the leather couch while he sat and wrote in the nearby chair.

"So, Eoin, how have you been?"

"Fine."

It's what everybody says when you ask how they are, and nobody ever is. I wasn't fine, my Mum wasn't fine, I'm sure even Dr Hawkins had some little not fine detail ruining his day.

"Have you been sleeping well?"

He was already writing in his little notebook. He always started writing as soon as I lay down even if I didn't say anything. It made me want to jump up and grab his little notebook off him. I was convinced that I would find it full of doodles and grocery lists.

"I've been ok, last night was bad, but mostly ok."

Dr Hawkins looked up from his notebook, reaching up to adjust his black framed glasses.

"What made last night bad? What was different?"

I dunno, they just, louder, angrier. It made my head hurt."

"Can you always tell the voices apart?"

I fidgeted on the couch. I liked this Doctor, because he filled me full of fewer drugs than the others, but I just couldn't get used to talking about things. It made me feel even crazier to say these things out loud.

"Yes, the … whispers, all feel different. So I can tell them apart."

"But still no words?"

"No, well, not really. Sometimes I'll think I hear something. It's like when you forget someone's name, or something else that you know you should know, and no matter how hard you think you can't bring it to mind, it keeps… slipping away."

He went on to ask me about school and home, same as always. I didn't see what he thought he could accomplish asking the same questions each week. School was fine, home was fine. Of course they weren't, but there was nothing I could do about it so there was no point talking, especially to him. He asked me about old memories and new memories. He asked me about my favourite animals and what kind of girls I liked (he was insistent on that one,

I think he was trying to make sure I wasn't gay, as if being repressed could explain all my problems away.) He finished up a little early, much to my relief, and I was about to grab my coat and leave when he called me back.

"Eoin, I wanted to talk to you about your medication. It certainly seems to have helped a little, but it's not helping you progress any further. There's a new experimental drug, called Cebocap. I think it might be helpful in your case."

I groaned at the thought of another pill

"Six pills now? Is it a big one?"

"No Eoin, I want to try you on just the Cebocap. Just one pill, twice a day."

"What, really? Just one pill, will that work?"

"Well, Cebocap can take some time to take effect, so I'd want to keep an eye on you. We'd have to have twice weekly sessions, Mondays and Thursdays. I've discussed this course of treatment with your Mother and she's agreed."

That's the problem with being a sick kid, all the decisions are made by other people and they never let you know. Still, one pill. I couldn't even remember the last time I was on that little medication. Best to count my blessings. Doctor Hawkins wrote me a prescription to give to my Mum, I thanked him and rose to leave. Halfway to the door doubt hit, my stride faltered and I turned to look at him.

"This will help, won't it Doctor Hawkins?"

He looked tense, but after a moments hesitation he offered a smile.

"There may be some initial adjustment, but I'm confident that this will help us progress."

For the first time in a very long while, I left a doctor's office with a smile on my face.

Mum and I went straight to the Pharmacy to get my new prescription. The girl had some trouble finding it because Dr. Hawkins had to order it in specially. I was happy on the drive home even though there was a constant sad little whisper in my head.

The Cebocap came in little plastic pills, half blue, half clear, with tiny blue and white balls inside. It looked no different than any of the other meds I'd been on, and yet, I was hopeful. I hadn't felt that way in a very long time. There wasn't a lot of hope left for me.

I took my first dose that evening. It was a good night, with just a few gentle whispers, and it didn't take me long to drift off. Was it the Cebocap, or just a quiet night? I tried not to think about it and gave thanks for a restful nights sleep, no matter what the source.

2

The Cebocap pill sat beside my orange juice the next morning. I was almost scared to take it. I'd taken one the night before, but the giddy rush of change had worn off a little. It seemed silly, I'd been popping whatever pill the Doctor Du Jour prescribed since I could remember, why be scared now? Part of me was scared that it wouldn't work, but another part of me was scared that it would. What would life be like without the constant unintelligible noise? Would it be like the dawn all the time, or did dawn only seem so perfect to me because it was a respite? Regardless, I swallowed the pill and headed to school.

It's hard to say when I noticed the change, but easy to pinpoint when it made a difference. As I arrived at school, the usual chittering started. I tried not to be too disheartened and just got on with my day. As the day progressed, the sounds in my head changed. At first I thought I was imagining it, but they started to get… clearer. I could hear little snatches of sound instead of a constant shushing. They also began to rise and fall more than normal, so I was able to tune them out more when I was concentrating in class, but they were even louder than usual in the corridor between classes.

The air seemed to be full of a thousand whispers as I walked home that day. They seemed, different. They weren't angry the way they usually were when there were so many. They were gentle. And yet still they remained infuriating and unintelligible. As I walked through the park on the way home the whispers thinned out, only a few remaining. I started concentrating on them as I walked. I tried to pick out one, and as I did I found it growing just a little louder. I swore I could hear sounds, not quite whole words but... there. There, it said 'look'. The whisper grew more insistent, it got a little louder. It was repeating itself now, short bursts over and over. My feet moved me automatically forward as I concentrated harder. A sharp pain shot through my temple as the whisper finally resolved itself into a shout, two words said with fear and warning.

"Look out!"

As I looked up to see Declan Boyle blocking the gate out of the park I thought...yes, I really should.

I won't write what happened, not in detail. I know I should if I'm telling the story, but it's not really relevant and I'd rather try to forget it if you don't mind. Just trying to write it out makes my breath catch and my hands shake. But if you've ever stood and had someone hit you and then stand and laugh at you, daring you to hit them back and knowing that you won't, then you have looked into the face of evil.

I cried when I got home. Does that make me weak? They were tears of rage, if that helps. I sat on my bed and thought of Declan Boyle and all the ones like him. I thought of all the people that looked at me like I was broken, like there was something twisted inside me that could never be fixed. I thought of them and cried, red hot tears of anger flowing down my cheeks. I took the pillow and buried my face in it and I screamed out my frustration, over and over, and still it wasn't enough. This world was broken. People like Declan Boyle got to live and act the way they did and suffer no repercussions. That was not fair, that was not justice. If I could see that, why couldn't anyone else? It was this world that was broken, not me.

When I finished crying I lay down on my bed, so tired that I could barely move. Though I hadn't left my room I felt as if I'd run a mile, and all I wanted to do was fall asleep. But I couldn't do that. Mum would be home soon, and if I fell asleep she would find me , tired, broken, with a tear stained face. She would make me tell her what had happened, and she would try to do something about it, and that would only make things worse. So I forced myself up and went to the bathroom. I concentrated on my breathing, taking deep long breaths, going slower and slower until I felt myself calm and my face was no longer flushed red. Then I washed my face and hands and looked at myself in the mirror. Just another fresh faced kid with eyes as black and bleak as my prospects. Life as usual.

Dinner was quiet that night. Who am I kidding? Dinner was quiet every night. We sat at the table, we ate our food and then left. That's how it always went, with my mother asking awkwardly polite questions every so often. As if she needed to prove that this was a happy family dinner. The questions were always the same, as were the answers.

"How was school today Eoin?"

"Fine."

"Have you done your homework?"

"Yes."

But today my mother had a new question. One she asked with a quaver in her voice and an unmistakable trace of fear in her expression.

"So, how is the new pill going?"

I hesitated, I almost said 'Fine' dismissing it like everything else, but it made me think.

"Ok, today was pretty bad, but my head is much clearer and Doctor Hawkins said it might take some time to adjust to it."

Mum's lips were small and white as she spoke.

"You know that you need to tell me if anything happens? We don't know how it will affect you. It's important that you be honest about it. And if you ever feel like it's making you... unhappy, we can always switch back to the other meds."

My mum had this talk with me, or something similar, every time I switched to a new treatment regime. But I didn't remember her ever looking this scared. I put it down to her being scared for me, this drug was experimental after all.

"It's ok Mum, I know the score. And I'd like to give this one a chance. Doctor Hawkins really seems to think it will help."

"Ok Eoin, I just wanted you to know, that I'm here, if, if anything happens."

She smiled, but it didn't reach her eyes. It made me uncomfortable in a way I couldn't explain. The rest of dinner passed in a tense silence. I finished my meal and asked to be excused, before heading up to my room to read.

I've always loved to read. If I'm reading a good book, like a really good book, the kind that pulls you in and drives you forward so that you're turning each page with anticipation, then the whole word fades away, even the whispers.

Unfortunately there weren't enough really good books for me to do nothing but read them every waking moment that I had, although if there were it would have seemed a perfectly reasonable treatment to me.

That night I was reading a new book Mum had picked up from a second hand book store about a psychic who solved murders with the help of the ghost of his dead sister. It wasn't the best thing I'd ever read, but it made me smile. I finished it about nine o'clock, and then I lay and stared at the ceiling. No whispers, not yet. But I felt weird. Like the air in my room was pushing down on me. My stomach felt strange and heavy. I didn't think this was going to be a quiet night.

I listened to the sounds of the house settling around me. I started at every creak, twitched at every sigh, constantly anticipating the arrival of the whispers. I was paying more attention than usual, trying to listen instead of just cowering in fear. Maybe that's why I heard it, right on the edge of hearing, so quiet I could believe it wasn't there, a plaintive whisper of "…please". Then it happened again, in a voice like the sigh of the wind. "Please". I sat in my bed, no longer hiding under the covers, sitting in my darkened room, straining to hear.

"Please… please… help."

Please help? Help with what. Was this my sub consciousness's way of telling me to help myself? Was the Cebocap making me hear voices? Was this separate from the whispers? Was this… oh God… was this a progression of my condition? Was I going to end up plagued by voices instead of whispers, driven to complete madness? I paled just at the thought of it.

I probably shouldn't have answered. I mean, they say the first sign of madness is hearing voices in your head and the second sign is answering them back. But what can you do when you hear a plea in the night? It's a human thing I guess. So, I answered, in a trembling voice of a boy trying desperately to stay calm.

"Help with what, what do you want me to help with?"

It was like I'd hit a switch, the voice grew stronger and more determined, it started asking over and over, continuously, the voice sounded small, like a child, but it was still fading in and out.

"Please… find… find my… man hurt… me away… please help…"

I couldn't make sense of it. I hesitated, but I'd started now, I couldn't exactly turn over and go to sleep, pretending there wasn't a plaintive voice in my head.

"Please, I can't understand you, can you speak up?"

The voice grew a little louder, but as it did a second voice joined in, talking over it. This one sounded like an old lady. Why was there an old lady in my head?

"You need to… *Don't listen*… it hurt… *not important*… I can't find… *you tell her*… it hurts… *best silver*."

I shook my head, it was too confusing, I couldn't separate the voices.

"Please, one at a time, I can't understand."

But there were three voices now, all sounding different, all mixing and talking over each other. They were getting frantic, sounding like they were shouting, and my head was starting to hurt.

"Bad man… *Kirsty never*… **I never meant**… please help… *her nana*… **I'm sorry**… why won't… *I wanted*… **please tell her**."

I shook my head, desperately trying to clear it, or to make sense of the jumble of words I was hearing. It had happened, I had finally gone insane. As the tears began to run down my cheeks, I consoled myself with the thought that I wouldn't have to face Declan Boyle anymore. I wouldn't have to face anyone, or anything, except maybe some padded walls. I rocked gently on my bed, sobbing a little as I cried. I didn't want this, I didn't ask for this, any of this. The voices kept going, they sounded frustrated now, almost angry, and there were… four… no… six… or were those two the same. I couldn't tell anymore. It was all dissolving into a cacophony of shouting, I couldn't understand anything. I crawled to the corner of my bed, where the walls met. I curled up in the corner, sobbing loudly, my pillow held around my head and over my ears, but it was no use. The shouts grew no softer and my head sang with pain as each second the noise grew worse, until I felt as if my head was too small to contain so much pain, and would soon burst, spilling it out into the world.

And then, I screamed. Or, at least, I thought I did. It sounded like my voice, I've screamed often enough to know. But my mouth was closed and I was still sobbing. And still I heard a scream. One long, impossibly loud scream that seemed to go on forever and silenced all the voices. In the blissful silence that followed I continued to cry, but these were tears of relief. My head still hurt but it was heaven compared to the pain of moments ago. I felt exhausted, drained. I curled up in the corner, in a sobbing ball, but I managed to get out some words.

"Thank…thank you… it hurt. Thank you so much."

And then, there was one last voice. It seemed familiar, but not in a way I could place. It said simply:

You're welcome Eoin, now sleep

.

3

I awoke with a start. The sun was shining through the curtains, I was curled up at one end of my bed and I felt… strange. I felt rested. As if maybe I'd slept straight through the night. I couldn't remember the last time that had happened. I sat up in bed and looked at my room. It didn't look any different than yesterday. There was my wardrobe, built into the wall above the head of my bed. There was my desk, a singled piece of wood running from one wall to another opposite my bed, my bookshelves on the wall above it and my door opening in the gap between desk and bed. It all looked as before, but it felt… different. There was something in the air, a quality that hadn't been there before. I wiped the sleep out of my eyes and got up.

I was the only one awake, it was Mum's weekend off and she generally tried to lie in. I sat at the kitchen table in my pyjamas and munched on a bowl of cereal, staring thoughtfully at the blank wall opposite me. As I sat, I wondered.

Did last night really happen? Or had it been a bad dream?

If it was just a dream, then how did I sleep so well?

Would it happen again tonight?

Yes, if you don't stop daydreaming and listen to me.

"Sorry, what?!"

I looked around the room, there was no one else there, but one of those thoughts definitely hadn't been mine.

No, it was mine, are you ready to listen yet?

I shoved my chair away from the table and sat, hunched down, my hands over my ears, slowly repeating the same thing to myself.

"It's all in my head. It's all in my head. It's all in my head. It's all in my head."

I may be in your head, but that doesn't mean I'm not real.

Why? Where had this come from? I'd never heard voices before, only whispers and fragments. I started to rock back and forth.

"This is it, they'll have to throw me in the loony bin now."

No one's throwing you anywhere, will you please just listen?

I sat up and stared at the empty room.

"Why should I? You're a delusion, who ever benefited from listening to a delusion?"

You could be the first?

"That's not funny!"

I'm not trying... never mind. Just, listen, please Eoin, it's very important, I promise if you listen to me then I'll stay quiet for the rest of the day.

"And how on earth do I know that you'll keep that promise."

I think you're just going to have to trust me.

"Trust you?"

Yeah, trust me. Or if you want, I could just sing ABBA at the top of my lungs until you give in.

I narrowed my eyes and glared at the wall.

"You wouldn't dare."

Wouldn't I? Why don't you just let me talk and listen?

I bit my lip. I was lost, to tell the truth. I was already crazy for having this conversation in the first place. I don't suppose listening a little more could hurt. But is that how you get crazy, in tiny little steps, with each one seeming not so bad? On the other hand, I really hate ABBA.

I let out a small sigh.

"Ok, I'll listen, but no more talk from you, ok?"

I promise, from when I finish, until you head to bed, not a word.

I had thought he would stay quiet until tomorrow, but I guess I didn't have much choice. I moved my chair into the corner so that I could face the room, as it felt weird talking to a wall, and then I assumed my best imitation of Dr Hawkins.

"Ok, what would you like to talk about?"

Well, it all starts with you, you're very special Eoin.

I gave the room an incredulous look.

I know sometimes you don't feel that special, but you are. You can sense more than you know, you can see into the heart of things, or hear rather. Imagine that the world is a room where the walls are really just sheets of cloth. Sometimes, if you listen hard, and you have very good hearing, you can tell what's going on... beyond the sheets.

I scrunched up my face.

"Hold on, I see where this is going, you're trying to tell me I hear dead people? You wanted to talk to me so you could rip off a Bruce Willis movie?"

I'm not joking Eoin, and no, it's not just spirits, it's... it's energy and flow and intention. Gods it's impossible to explain this in four dimensions. Okay, yes, part of it is that you can hear the spirits of the departed, if they're hanging around for some reason and if they want to talk to you. But you can also read places and people. Get an emotion from something somebody used or see the flow of somebodies thoughts.

I gave one quick short bark of laughter.

"I can read minds now? What, we've moved on to the X-Men?"

It's not as simple as that, you might be able to get words if you worked on your gift, but for the most part it's just emotions, feelings, hunches.

The chair scraped across the floor as I shot to my feet, finger pointing at the room.

"Don't you EVER say that again, this thing in my head is not a gift. It's made my life a living hell! There are mornings were I wake up and cry because I'm still alive, and I'm going to have to go through it all again. You are a figment of my imagination brought on by the new drugs, you're a lying sack of shit and you don't know anything!!"

My breathing was ragged, hot tears were running down my cheeks. It took everything I had to sit back down, to not break everything in the room because it hurt so much and the world wasn't fair. I focused on my breathing, tried to slow it down, taking deep breaths. The voice went on in the background.

*I'm sorry Eoin, I know it hasn't been easy for you, and if I could make any of this untrue I would, but this is what you face. I'm not brought on by drugs, I'm brought on by lack of drugs. The drug Dr Hawkins gave you is a placebo. For the first time in many years, you are completely un-medicated. That's why you can hear the voices clearly now. All these doctors, all these medicines, they've all been trying to block your gi... I mean your senses. They don't understand it, they think it's a disease, and if you let them keep trying to cure you, they **will** kill you.*

I looked up.

"Oh they're going to kill me are they? That doesn't sound like the paranoid ramblings of voices in my head AT ALL!!"

I'm sorry, I shouldn't have... the main thing you need to understand is that you are not crazy. You don't need the doctors, you don't need the medicine, but you do need help.

"Your help, I presume?"

Actually, yes. People with a... with senses like yours, are rare. And for spirits who want to connect back with the physical world you are like a miracle, burning bright in the darkness. Last night was what happens when multiple spirits try to contact you at once. You need to learn how to shield from them, how to keep them away unless you want them. Humans too, the more you're around or the more charged the atmosphere, the worse you'll feel. I can teach you how to block out what you don't need. If you'll let me.

I looked up through tear stained eyes.

"I don't believe you."

And I can understand why. This all must sound ridiculous, but it's true. I want you to do me a favour. Go research the drug, you'll see that it's a placebo. Then ask yourself, how on earth could a voice in your head know that when you'd never heard of the drug before you were given it?

I'm going to go, m... your mum is up, she'll go nuts if she sees you talking to yourself. Please Eoin, please think about this, I'll talk to you tonight.

And with that he was gone. I called out a couple of times, but there was no answer. I could hear my mum moving around upstairs. I went to the kitchen sink and washed my face, I didn't want her to know that I'd been crying. The cold water also helped to calm the red in my cheeks. You learn how to hide these things pretty quick.

I went to my room and lay on my bed looking at the ceiling. I felt as if the room was spinning as I tried to process everything I'd been told. Of course it couldn't be true. But if it wasn't true, then I was crazy, and what meagre happiness I had was going to be shattered. So I had to at least look into it, because if there was even a chance that I wasn't crazy, then I wanted to reach for it, grasp it with every bit of strength I had and hold on for dear life. You might not see why I would have considered believing the voice in my head. But if you've spent your whole life struggling to be normal, looking desperately for something, anything that will make it all ok, you'll turn to anything. Usually it was some new miracle drug, or a faith healer who promised people redemption. Desperate people will turn to anything if there's a chance, any chance, that they can be saved. My desperate chance came from a disembodied voice. Given all the crazy things people try when they feel like they've no way out, are you really surprised that I resolved to at least look in to it?

I decided to check out the Cebocap drug. I mean, it couldn't hurt, and it was probably a good idea for me to find out as much as I could about it, I was the one taking it after all. I headed downstairs and asked Mum could I use the computer in the spare room. She told me I had an hour and that she'd call me when I was done.

The computer was in the bedroom next to mine. The room held a long desk under a window, with an old guest bed to the right. It also contained the only computer in the house. I know, it's ridiculous, most kids these days have their own laptop and all we had was this desktop. But Mum wasn't big on gadgets and technology, besides, the bills for all my doctors and medication sucked up most of the spare income, so there wasn't a lot left over for such things.

I started up the machine and sat looking at the desktop. I pulled up Google and entered in Cebocap. I hit enter and was presented with a screen full of pictures. The browser must have been left on Google images. I went to switch back to web search, but before I did one of the images caught my eye. It looked just like the Cebocap pills I was taking. Half blue, half clear, with little blue and white balls inside. When I clicked it, it brought me to a website used to identify medications. It listed the pill description, but didn't give any of its uses or side effects, which was strange. But it was supposed to be new and experimental; there might not be much information about it released.

I switched to a blank web search. I must have sat there staring at it for five minutes. I knew what I had to do, the simple words I had to type, but I couldn't bring myself to. It was as if typing them would be actually admitting that I believed, and I'd be taking the first step on a slippery slope that would ruin me. Part of me wanted to just get up and run out of the room. But I forced myself to type "Cebocap placebo" and hit search. I froze as soon as I saw the summary text under the first entry. Right there, in black and white: "In fact, Obecalp and CEBOCAP are placebos -- fake drugs."

I felt sick. I tried to click on the link but my hands had grown thick and clumsy. There was a buzzing in my ears and my head was swimming. I tried to get a hold of myself. I closed my eyes and concentrated on my breathing. Slow, deep breaths. In and out, in and out. I kept it up until I was absolutely sure I was not going to pass out, then I opened my eyes. With trembling fingers I opened the first five links in separate tabs, and read through them.

It was true, it was all true. There was no official information, no industry website, but there were countless entries on forums, some from outraged doctors. Cebocap was a placebo. It was useless. It did nothing. I was unmedicated for the first time in my living memory. And I was hearing dead people. Which meant I was crazy, right? Except, how did the voice know Cebocap was a placebo? How could a voice in my head know something I didn't? I needed to think. I erased my browser history and then opened up some flash games so that when Mum checked the computer later (and she would) she wouldn't suspect anything. Then I went to my room and lay down.

It was a lot to take in. I was used to people lying to me, every time an adult looked at me with a fixed smile and said "There's nothing wrong with you Eoin, you're JUST like any other boy." But I wasn't used to Mum lying to me, or a doctor, not about important things. How could they? What the hell did Doctor Hawkins hope to achieve? More importantly though, what was I going to do about it?

I sat staring at the screen until my head ached and my vision blurred, all the options and possibilities spun in front of me. The way I saw it, I had two options. Either I went and told Doctor Hawkins that I was hearing dead people, and he put me in a straight jacket, or I listened to the voice in my head that wanted to help me with hearing dead people, hiding what was happening, until eventually someone found out, and put me in a straight jacket. They were not good options. I decided to go for door number two. Maybe it was crazy, maybe it would make me worse, but as long as the voice didn't tell me to do anything crazy (and I'd be watching) it couldn't hurt and I might learn something about what's going on in my head. Besides, door two might just lead to super secret, not to be thought about, door number three.

There was another subdued dinner. Mum asked if I enjoyed my computer time, I told her that I had and mentioned the flash games I knew she would have seen on the browser history. I headed to bed early to read. Mum kissed me on the head and wished me goodnight as I blushed. I thought I was getting too old to be kissed goodnight, but I didn't want to stop her. She smiled when she kissed me goodnight, and she smiled so rarely.

I sat for an hour, trying to read. I couldn't seem to concentrate, my attention seemed to waver before I could get to the end of a sentence. I tried calling out softly a couple of times. The voice had said it would return at bedtime. Where was it? I thought about the day, and realised that I hadn't heard a single whisper since it had left me alone. True, I usually didn't hear many whispers at home in the daytime, but there was usually something. This might just count as the quietest day I'd ever had, inside my head.

As I was thinking, the last of the light faded from the sky outside my window, and I felt a chill move across my skin. I shivered a little, wondering what it was, and then the voice came from nowhere.

Hello again Eoin.

I startled, looking around me. Strange that I'd been sitting here for an hour waiting to hear the voice again and yet still found it so surprising. I took a deep breath and tried to calm myself.

"H…hello?"

How was your day? Did what you learned make you ready to at least listen?

I bit my lip. This was it, step number two. I felt like I was cooperating with the enemy, but it didn't feel wrong, and as I started to speak, I did so with a little more confidence.

"Ok. I mean, I'll listen. But I'm not killing anyone or setting anything on fire."

I heard a bark of laughter.

Don't worry Eoin, I'm not going to make you crazy. Hopefully, I'm going to make your world a little less so.

"So, what now? Do you show me how to commune with the force or channel my inner chi or something?"

No, now you sleep.

"I sleep? Seriously? I tell you I'm willing to listen and you want me to sleep?"

This isn't going to be easy Eoin, and to be honest, I don't know how many nights of peace I can give you before you have to start shielding for yourself. We'll need to work most of tomorrow. It's best you face that well rested.

My face scrunched up in confusion.

"Wait, have you been shielding me? Is that why it's been so quiet today?"

I could hear the smile in the reply

I was wondering if you'd figure that out. Yes, I've been keeping it quiet. And for the most part, it's working. But I don't know how long it will be before the novelty and fear of my presence wears off. So get some sleep.

Even as the voice was speaking, I was stifling a yawn, turning my face away into my hand.

"Ok, but tomorrow, you've got some explaining to do."

I smiled as I lay my head down on my pillow, tiredness pulling at the edges of my mind.

Good night Eoin.

I let out a sleepy mumble.

"G'night. Wait… what do I call you?"

The room was silent, and the thought that the voice had gone away almost pulled me from the edges of sleep, but then I heard a soft little whisper.

Charlie. You can call me Charlie.

I smiled again, settling down into my pillow and yawning again before whispering.

"Good night Charlie."

My mind slid into a blissfully deep sleep, where I dreamed of mirrored smiles and happy tears, and I didn't wake until the morning, not even once.

4

As I woke to the lines of light framing the edge of my bedroom curtains, I felt happy. No, it was more than that, I was content. I had had two good nights of sleep in a row and it was warm and cosy beneath my duvet. It was a Sunday, with nothing to do but laze. Mum used to try to bring me to church on Sundays, but well, churches seemed to make me worse. Mum thought it was all the people, but now, I wondered.

I called out hesitantly.

"Charlie?"

I'm right here Eoin.

"Have you been here all night? Don't you need to sleep?"

Sleep is a biological function, I don't have a body so… no need.

"Oh… did you have a body once? I mean, what are you?"

I'm afraid that explanation would be complicated. We have a lot to do and not a lot of time to do it. So let's just say that I'm someone who wants to help, and leave it at that for now.

I raised an eyebrow. I wanted to push him on it, it was definitely a tick in the "voice is crazy" column.

"Ok, where do we start?"

With breakfast, a proper one, not just chocolate milk, then take a shower and we can begin.

The surprise was evident on my face.

"Gee Mom, wanna make sure I wash behind my ears too?"

I'm serious Eoin, you'll need energy for today's lesson, and the shower will help cleanse and ground you naturally until I teach you how to do it at will.

"Oh…emm…ok."

I hated unintelligible justifications delivered with confidence. There was always a little part of me that thought they're just making it all up. But I was hungry, so I went downstairs and got myself breakfast, it didn't take long to wolf it down. I realised that I had never taken my Cebocap the previous night. I pondered taking it that morning, but what was the point. It was a placebo. I took two pills upstairs and flushed them. As I watched them spin around the bowl before disappearing, it felt good. I felt free.

I was just pulling my pyjama top off for my shower, when I hesitated.

"Emm.... Charlie?"

Yes Eoin?

"Can you see me? Like, physically?"

It's not as simple as sight. But yes, I can see when you move and I know where you are and I can tell your pyjamas are grey. Why do you ask?

"Mmm... could you maybe... not see me... while I shower?"

Oh... well... I mean there's nothing that I.... I mean....

The room went silent for a second. A very awkward second.

Emm.. sure... yeah, I mean sure.

"Thanks."

I finished pulling off my top and reached for my bottoms.

"Charlie?"

There was no answer. Of course Charlie could be just staying quiet. I couldn't tell when he was here or not. Or, also, I could be going completely nuts, so much so that I was worrying about the voices in my head seeing me naked, but one problem at a time.

5

My head hurt. I felt like if I had to concentrate for even one minute more that my brain was going to melt and come dripping out my ears. It had been two hours since the beginning of Charlie's 'Lesson' and there was no progress that I could discern. I had told my mother that I hadn't slept well and that I was going to nap for the morning. She looked concerned (as always), but it wasn't unusual so she had left me alone.

Charlie's lesson so far seemed to comprise of him trying to get me to see things that weren't there. Not all that promising in the whole "I swear I'm not a figment of your imagination." department. I hadn't managed anything and I was becoming increasingly frustrated.

"It's useless! I can't see a thing! Maybe I don't have an aura?" I said as I lowered my hand from in front of my face. I was sitting on a pillow on the floor between my bed and desk. I had my legs crossed, trying to get comfortable, which would help with my perception, apparently.

I assure you Eoin, your aura is very real and quite strong. I think this is the wrong approach, you're trying too hard. Your conscious mind is getting in the way of your innate knowledge.

"....huh?"

Let's try this. Close your eyes, just sit and relax. Take long slow deep breaths.

I sat in the darkness behind my eyelids, focusing on my breathing as Charlie's voice grew softer.

In....and out... listen to the air flowing back and forth, let your mind settle. There are no thoughts, there are no problems, there's only your breath.

I felt my body relax and my mind empty. It was, relaxing, peaceful, and therefore very strange, but I tried just to let it happen. I don't know if I would have been able to relax into that wonderfully peaceful drifting mental place without the newfound silence that Charlie had brought. I felt my mind relax into a gentle mist, instead of the sharp stinging panic that it usually was.

In and out… breathing gently. Now Eoin, I want you to imagine that all around your body there is a layer of subtle energy, like a thick layer of barely there haze, from your head to your toes. Can you imagine it Eoin?

"Yes." I whispered, trying to hold on to my relaxed state while letting my imagination fill with the image.

Good… keep your breathing slow….. nice and relaxed… what colour is the energy Eoin?

"It's blue."

My answer was mumbled but confident. I knew that the energy was blue, except, I didn't quite know how I knew. As I tried to figure this out I felt the gentle mist of my mind begin to falter.

Don't think Eoin, the answer just is, it doesn't need a reason, just focus on your breathing, try not to think about the words, there is only air, in and out.

It was a struggle to let go of the puzzle, for a moment I hung on the edge, the gentle mist quivering, ready to disappear. But I forced myself to take a deep breath, and I listened to the sound of the air as it filled my body, and as I breathed out I listened to the contrast. In and out, over and over, until the gentle mist was restored in my mind.

Good. Now, you know the energy exists, you know its colour, imagine it surrounding your body, see it in your minds eye. How far out does it go?

"It's big… a big egg… around me… shimmery." This time it was easier just to accept the answer without needing its origin.

Well done Eoin, you're seeing your aura. Now, can you see how it's barely there, just a mist of energy?

"Yes."

I want you to imagine that the energy is pulling closer to your skin. Imagine that all that energy is coming together, until you have a tight shell of energy just above your skin.

It was surprisingly easy to imagine the energy growing

denser and denser, pulling down towards me until I could almost feel it, like a gentle humming all over my skin.

That's really good Eoin. Now, I want you to think about this feeling, the feeling of your energy pulling tight, hardening. I want you to think of this and in your mind, I want you to feed it energy. Imagine a line of energy running from you to the shield, filling it up, making it harder.

I tried, I could imagine the stream of energy, but it was shaky. I concentrated harder, willing the energy to flow. As the stream flickered and sputtered I grew frustrated. It was in my own head, how could I manage to fail at something completely imaginary? Anger came from the frustration and the stream of energy grew thick and dark. Like a pipe unblocking, the energy rushed into the shield making it thicker and harder, but it just kept going. Black swirls appeared in the shield and it started to bloat.

Eoin, calm down, you have to be calm, you can't le-

"Aaaaaarrrrrrggghhh!!"

I screamed at the top of my lungs as I felt all my anger, frustration and fear fuse with the unstable energy and explode out from me in a sphere.

The last thing I heard before I blacked out was the scream. So very familiar, but usually I only hear my own screams. This was like mine but didn't come from me. Charlie. Charlie was screaming.

I woke to late afternoon light turning the ceiling golden. I felt drained and weak, like I had the flu or something. I was in my bed, under my duvet and I was wearing my pyjamas. As I was trying to piece together my memories, the door to my bedroom opened and mum stuck her head in.

"Hey honey, how are you feeling?" She was smiling, but it was strained.

I wrinkled my forehead in confusion.

"Wha' happened?"

"I thought I heard a...shout, and when I came up you were on the floor with your pillow. Did you have a nightmare while you were napping?"

My mind felt fractured, it was an effort just to assemble enough pieces to articulate a sentence.

"I don't know... I'm....very tired... must have been something like that."

"Eoin, is it the new pill? I can call Dr. Hawkins, I know it's the weekend but if there's a problem?"

"No!" I was surprised at the energy in my shout, given how I felt.

"It's just, it's just an adjustment. I'll be fine, I just need to sleep. Anyway, I'm seeing him tomorrow. I can talk to him then."

Mum looked like she was about to argue, but she just sighed.

"Ok, ok, if that's what you want, but, just... just let me know if there's anything wrong, won't you?"

"I will Mum, I promise."

As the lie slipped out from between my lips, it felt like a knife twisting in my heart. But there was no point in telling. There was nothing she could do.

I waited until I was sure that she had gone back downstairs before I spoke again.

"Charlie? Charlie, are you there?"

The silence was deafening. I had never understood the phrase until that moment, when the great absence of sound roared in my ears like a hurricane.

"Charlie!?"

Everything was silent, everything was still, it was like dawn in the middle of the day, it was exactly what I wanted, and I was so scared.

"Please Charlie, I'm sorry, I didn't mean to. I don't know what I... please."

I strained and strained trying to listen for the slightest sound, and I heard it, barely detectable, the faintest of whispers.

It's ok Eoin, it's ok, just sleep. You did good. Sleep.

The world descended into peaceful darkness, and another night passed.

6

I woke before sunrise the next morning. The room was dark but the orange glare of the street lights crept in around the edges of my curtains. I checked my clock, it was just after 6am. I felt better. Another restful night's sleep, something I was beginning to get used to, I hoped it wasn't something I'd lose. The nights rest had washed away the bone weary fatigue from yesterday. But then, I had slept for nearly twelve hours.

I knew what I had to do, what I wanted to do, but I was scared. I took a couple of deep breaths, in and out. I realised that I was following Charlie's breathing exercise from yesterday. I concentrated on my breathing until I felt myself relax and my mind go still. I felt the aura of my energy like a tingle in the air and I drew it tight around me, hardening it a little until I felt safe and secure. It seemed a lot easier than the previous day, I just had to imagine what I wanted and I could feel it happen. I tried to ignore how crazy it felt and, finally, unable to put it off any longer, I whispered gently.

"Charlie?"

The answer came swiftly, nice and loud and sounding healthy, slipping out of the dark.

That was one hell of an outburst Eoin. If I didn't have such a monster headache this morning I'd congratulate you.

My brow furrowed in confusion.

"That was a good thing?"

Well... I wouldn't recommend you start pulling that trick at parties, but you threw out an explosive amount of energy. There's not a spirit left for a mile around. You drove away or evaporated them all.

My eyebrows shot up in surprise.

"I did that? So that means no voices today?"

Dude, no spirit in their right mind is going to approach you today. Don't get too psyched about what you did though. It drained you significantly, as you saw and, well, it wasn't too pleasant on my side.

My face flushed with guilt as I remembered Charlie's heart wrenching screams just before I'd blacked out. My voice stumbled as I struggled to apologise.

"Oh Charlie, I… I didn't mean, I'm so sorry, are you ok?"

It's not the worst pain I've ever experienced, but it was pretty bad. If we weren't linked, well… yeah… it could have been worse.

"Linked?"

Eh…yeah…see I'm sort of, tied to you. I can tell when you're upset or in trouble. I can reach you through your shield, which, by the way, is pretty impressive. Not as strong as yesterday, but then you are drained, but it's tight, good work.

I smiled, but something was bugging me.

"Charlie, why are you linked to me? I mean, don't get me wrong, I'm thankful, I feel better than I ever have, but… why are you helping me?"

Em, well, that's a reeeeealy complicated story. Let's just call it a twist of fate, I was joined to you and I want to make sure you're ok. Maybe once we have you settled and secure I'll tell you the crazy background stuff.

I listened to Charlie's words, but I also tried to, feel them I guess. I tried to see them in my mind like I could see the shield. They quivered. They shook, and there was some pain in them, but they shone true. I had a split second where I was almost looking down at myself and the crazy things I was accepting, but I tried to push it away.

"Ok, but you owe me that story."

Oh I look forward to it, just as soon as we have more time.

"So, what's the plan for today?"

I want you to get up and be ready for school before your Mum wakes up.

"What? Why?"

Because we need her to see how well you're doing. If she sees that you're coping well and acting normally when she knows you're on a placebo then we can work on keeping you off the medication.

"So, what, she'll just assume I was over medicated the whole time and now I'm magically cured?"

It sounds ridiculous, but she wants you to be better, more than anything in this world. She'll believe anything that will mean it's true.

I thought of Mum's face, always smiling, but with eyes that worried, and a voice that caught.

"Ok, I guess you're right."

I got up, showered and changed. Mum always left my uniform hanging on the outside of my door on Sunday night so that it was ready for Monday morning. By the time Mum got up at 7am for work, I was sitting at the kitchen table, eating a bowl of cereal and reading a book.

"Morning Mum!"

She let out a yelp as she gave a startled jump.

"Jesus Eoin! You scared me, what are you doing up? Is everything ok? Were there noises? Does your head hurt?"

By the end of the sentence she was across the kitchen on her knees beside me, her palm on my cheek and her face a mask of worry as she looked into my eyes, searching for an answer.

I smiled warmly at her.

"I'm fine Mum, I just woke up early because I slept so much. I feel much better today, there's nothing to worry about."

Mum looked at me, confused.

"You're ok?"

"Yes, I'm really ok. I think I've finally adjusted to the new pill."

As I saw the flash of guilt shoot across her face, any doubt that Mum knew that I was on a placebo melted away. Her brow furrowed.

"Oh, that's good then. Do you want me to make you anything special for lunch?"

"Do we have ham? Ham sandwiches would be nice."

She smiled happily.

"Ham sandwiches it is then."

As Mum busied herself at the kitchen counter, I saw something different in her, it was in the way she stood, the soft humming she made as she cut and buttered and arranged. As she handed me a packed lunch box, she smiled, all the way to her eyes, and I realised what it was. It was hope.

Charlie waited until I was walking to school to talk again.

Well I think that went quite well.

"She definitely seems happy." I felt a guilt pang of my own at deceiving her. But I had to, I wasn't ready to give up my newfound clarity, however crazy it may be.

"Were you keeping quiet on purpose?"

Kind of, yeah. I'm going to try and avoid talking to you while you're with people unless I have to, less chance of you answering me absentmindedly and looking crazy.

"Good plan." The thought of it made me look around, but I was crossing the park and it was pretty empty, no one was close enough to hear.

"So how do we handle school, treat the day as normal?"

No, I am very much hoping that today will be far from what you are used to. I'm hoping today will be extraordinary.

I laughed.

"Isn't that a little ambitious?"

Aim high Eoin, shoot for the stars.

That day in school, Charlie taught me how to harden my shield to block out the energy of my classmates. The teachers sent out stuff too of course, but it was nothing compared to the buzzing cacophony of thirty young minds crammed into a room together. As I sat, my shield carefully hardened, I was able to block out the babble almost completely and listen to the teacher. I wondered how I'd ever coped with just drugs to dampen the chaos. It was like I was a different person. I could follow the lessons and even contributed to discussions. My classmates gave me a couple of confused glances, but it was the teachers who really noticed. Mr Egan stopped me as I was leaving English again.

"You seem different today Eoin, is everything ok?"

Typical teacher, if something's changed then there must be something wrong.

"Yes Sir, everything is fine. I'm feeling good today."

"Oh…well, long may it continue."

His smile was genuine, so I offered him one in return as I left. With every new experience I was determined more than ever not to go back to the way I was. At that point I didn't care if Charlie was a figment of my imagination or not, he was bringing me peace, and possibly a bit of happiness as well. And I was not going to give that up.

7

"A Meta Analysis by the Royal College of Surgeons in Ireland found that, in a series of 19 separate studies, an average of 17% of 9 – 12 year olds reported hearing voices or sounds that no one else could hear. This falls to 7.5% in 13 – 18 year olds. So you see, Eoin, it's not that unusual. You're not alone. This is more common than you think."

Dr Hawkins finished walking back and forth in his office and stood by his chair.

"But I don't hear voices."

Good answer

"I know but you do hear whispers. How have the whispers been lately, have they become any clearer?"

"No, and shouldn't you be asking if they're going away?"

"Are they?"

"No."

"And have they become clearer?"

Why do I feel like he's trying to trap you? Hmm, just stick to the story.

I sat and stared at Doctor Hawkins for what seemed like an eternity.

"No. No, they've just become quieter. They're a lot easier to cope with now."

"Your mother says that you've been having nightmares, struggling to cope."

"Yeah, em, at first, they were bad, like really loud, and the dreams were really bad. But Sunday was a bit better and today is good."

"Do you hear any whispers now?"

I tapped my fingers on my knee in a slow rhythm as I cocked my head to the side.

Tap-tap-tap-tap

Tap-tap-tap-tap

This was the signal to Charlie that I wasn't sure what to say.

Hmm. Tell him that you can hear something, faintly, but you're not sure.

I frowned in thought and pretended to listen. "I think so, I can hear... like wind, as if it's in the next room."

"And what are they saying?"

"Nothing." The answer was instinctive and sounded a little defensive, or was that my imagination?

"How do you know they're saying nothing?"

"Because they never say anything, they're just whispers."

"Sometimes we can know the answer without actually perceiving anything. Do you know what I mean?"

Yes, I thought, I know exactly what you mean. I know your aura is green and you're more than a little nervous.

"I think so."

"So, without trying to hear them, what do you think the whispers are trying to say?"

I looked out the window, frowning in thought.

Tap-tap-tap-tap

Tap-tap-tap-tap

I'm sorry Eoin, this is in depth psychobabble. I'm not sure what will get him off your back. Try sticking to the truth but... I don't know... vague it up a bit.

"I think... I think different whispers want different things."

"Really? Different how?"

"Well, some feel angry, like when they get really loud and my head hurts. And some feel, soft and, emmm, I dunno, pleading I suppose, and then..."

I cut myself off and bit my lip.

"And then? Go on Eoin, it's ok, this is a safe space." His words were careful, soothing, but he wasn't looking at me, he was looking down at his notepad where he was writing feverishly.

"I... I don't know... every now and then I hear... something that makes me feel happy."

At this he looked up at me.

Careful Eoin.

"Something that isn't a whisper?"

"No." I amended, "Just a whisper, a happy whisper."

As I left Dr Hawkins office I couldn't shake the feeling that something was wrong. Dr Hawkins talked with my Mum, said he was pleased with my adjustment, and that he would see us on Thursday.

On the drive home, Mum looked relieved, like she'd dodged a bullet.

"Is everything ok?" I asked.

"What? Of course." she replied, giving me a quick, brittle smile. "Everything's fine. I'm just really glad you're adjusting so well."

It was hard, watching Mum lie to me. But I took comfort in the fact that she was so very bad at it, and that I knew she thought she was doing it for my own good. Dr Hawkins had convinced her that he could help me without drugs, except I wasn't supposed to know. The hows and whys of the situation spun around my head. I kept quiet for the rest of the car journey home, so did Charlie.

I palmed my Cebocap pill and flushed it down the toilet before bed. I suppose I could have just taken it, I mean, it didn't do anything. But it felt good to flush it, like I was rejecting the lie being fed to me, or rejecting all the pills that had come before, I don't know. But when I watched the pill spin in the bowl and disappear, I felt calm, I felt at peace.

That night, before I slept, Charlie dropped the bombshell.

"What do you mean you're not going to help me anymore?"

I didn't say I wouldn't help you, I said I can't protect you anymore. I was keeping spirits away mostly on bluff, and any bite I had left is gone since you let off the mind bomb yesterday.

"So what? You're just going to leave me to them, until I go to sleep screaming again? I'm not going back to that Charlie!" I felt my face begin to flush and I struggled not to shout.

Calm down Eoin. I'm not going anywhere, and you will be fine. The shielding I've thought you should give you enough peace to sleep. Especially for the next few days, spirits will be a bit scarce after that blast you let off.

"But what happens when I go to sleep and stop thinking about it? Won't they wake me up?"

The shield doesn't go away just because you stop thinking about it, if you build it up properly, if you feel it solid around you, then you shouldn't have to think about it at all. It should remain there, protecting you, ready to respond to you if necessary.

I scrunched up my face in confusion.

"But if that's the case, why do I have to do it every day? Why can't I just do it once?"

The dawn weakens it. As the light of the new day moves across the land, it wipes it clean. It disperses spirits, weakens shields, and does a whole lot of other things. But the main point is that your shield would only last a day or so if you didn't renew it.

"So that's why it's always quietest first thing in the

morning?"

Yes.

"So, if I travelled around the world, and I was constantly in the light of a new day, I'd never hear voices?"

I don't know, I suppose so, though as a solution it's a little clumsy.

"But I'd still hear you, right?"

You'll always hear me Eoin, just so long as you want to.

Charlie talked me through some breathing exercises. He got me to imagine everything that I was pulling inwards into a tight ball inside me, then a line linking me to the earth, and finally a shield, nothing spectacular, just a good thick solid line between me and the world, keeping out all that wasn't me.

Good, now, get some sleep. Tomorrow, we start on the harder part.

"What's the harder part?" I mumbled as I turned on my pillow.

People.

§

Tuesday was surprisingly bright. The sun felt good as it warmed my skin on the walk to school. As I imagined that warmth cleansing me, freeing me, it made me smile.

"So, why are people hard?" I whispered. I had begun to worry about people seeing me talk to myself. If I was supposed to be getting better, I needed to avoid that.

Spirits are easy. They don't have much energy in this plane and, to be honest there aren't that many of them, comparatively speaking. With people, they're everywhere, with minds full of energy, and though they're not sending any of it directly at you, if you're surrounded by too much of it you can be overwhelmed.

"Ok, well, how would that happen?"

Oh, it would have to be a very specific occurrence. You'd have to be surrounded by a lot of people, all in a very agitated state, and they'd have to have strong auras, people like you, or very emotional teenagers, and you'd probably have to be stressed or worn down as well.

I raised an eyebrow.

"So I'd have to be in or near a fight or other major occurrence in school when I feel tired or run down?"

Well… yes.

"Something that happens about once a week?"

I did think that might be an issue, yes.

"And what exactly happens if I get overwhelmed?"

Well, If your shield doesn't hold, then you'll probably just black out while screaming in pain, probably. There's a small chance of brain damage, but that's like, teeny. Teeny, tiny chance.

I froze in place, rooted to the spot as the wind gently moved the grass around my feet.

"… Brain damage?"

An infinitesimally small chance, negligible really.

"And how come this has never happened before?"

The drugs the doctors gave you dulled your perception. They were a buffer, so while you were tormented, you were never in danger.

"Score one for the drugs, remind me why I'm not taking them?"

Because on the drugs, you can't shield, so you will be tormented. And of course, on the drugs, you can't talk to me.

I felt a slight pang of guilt.

"I was only joking Charlie, I wouldn't really go back to the drugs. I feel better than I ever remember. Thank you."

You're welcome. And don't worry, we'll soon have you practiced enough to shield your way through anything. Just, you know, avoid confrontation for a few days.

Famous last words.

Have you ever had an epiphany, a completely life

changing event? They say it occurs in an instant, one second you see things one way, the next, boom, the world looks completely different. I don't know if this counts as an epiphany, after all I'd been changing slowly for days, but the world was different.

My shield turned the daily torture of noise and pain into a barely audible whisper. Charlie was right, I didn't have to concentrate on it, but I could feel it there whenever I wanted. It felt like a positive version of that feeling you get when you know someone is standing too close to you, even if you can't see them. A warm, blanketed, protected feeling.

In class after class I was able to pay more attention. I was even answering questions, though I stopped answering quite so many when I realised some of my classmates were shooting me puzzled looks. I felt normal. I should have known not to relax.

Lunch was always the riskiest time. Forced out into the yard for an hour with nowhere to hide, I generally ate fast and found a crowded corner in which to fade into the background. People think they need to hide in dark, secluded corners, but to be truly hidden you need to be where everyone else is, but be too boring for anyone to notice. I'd gotten quite good at it, which is why there was no excuse for me walking about on my own with a goofy grin on my face, revelling in the sunshine beating down on me. I couldn't help it, I felt wonderful. I'd never known such peace.

I was staring at the sky, watching a cloud drift across it, when a football connected with the back of my head, almost knocking me to the ground. I turned around to find Declan looking at me with an evil smirk on his face, a few other boys were walking up behind him.

"Watch where you're going schizo, you just wrecked our game."

I gritted my teeth.

"Sorry."

I tried to walk past him, but he grabbed me and shoved

me back out in front of him.

"Not so fast schizo, where do you think you're going?"

I looked Declan right in the eye.

"Back inside, if that's alright with you?"

I could see confusion flash across Declan's features. This wasn't how things were supposed to go. Usually by now I would be holding my head in pain. I shouldn't be able to stand up straight, never mind look him in the eye, but today I was fine. I could feel the sting of their hate on the other side of my shield. It was horrible, but it couldn't get me, not today. So I stood and looked him right in the eye. He didn't like that at all.

In a rush of movement Declan dove forward, grabbing the front of my jacket and shoving me up against a wall. I kept looking him in the eye, refusing to look away, refusing to cower. Yes I was probably going to get a beating, but for once I would make him see me.

"I'm going to bash some sense into that addled brain of yours, you filthy little schizo."

I reached up to grip his fists where they bunched my jacket, my hands trying to pull his away, pulling at his wrists. And as I gripped him, looking into his eyes, feeling his hate beating down on my shield, I felt my shield begin to crack. I panicked, I couldn't lose it, not now. I did not want all of Declan Boyle's hate inside my head. I tried not to think about the psychopath in front of me and instead concentrated on my shield, trying to reinforce it and hold it in place, but even as I did I felt the crack open and a sharp hot bolt of hate and anger and darkness shot straight into me.

And suddenly, I wasn't there anymore. I was looking up at a tall unshaven man, big and burly, but getting fat as he aged. His face was a picture of disgust as he screamed down at me.

"I'm gonna beat some sense into you, you filthy little ingrate!"

The man raised his fist. I tried to stop him, but his punch landed, knocking me across the hall onto the bathroom floor. I could hear his shouting as I tried to get up, my ears ringing, my head spinning.

"You're nothing but a mistake, no use to anyone. I should have left before your mother had you!"

I pulled myself up to the sink and looked in the mirror, watching hot angry tears run down Declan's face.

And with a flash I was back in the yard, with Declan's fist winding back to punch me, his friends in a semi-circle egging him on.

I stared into the eyes of the guy who was about to punch me, the guy who had made my life a living hell for years, and I felt sorry for him.

"Hating me won't stop him hitting you, Declan."

I kept my voice low and soft, I don't think anyone but Declan heard me over the shouts and jeers.

He froze.

"What are you talking about?"

His face was screwed up in anger, but there was fear in his eyes.

"It's not your fault Declan. You're not worthless. It doesn't have to be this way."

I looked at him, not with hate, but with concern. The buzzing stinging hail against my shield faltered. Declan lowered his fist, but threw me to the ground with his other hand.

"Shut up! You don't know anything! You're crazy anyway, you're nothing but a crazy schizo!"

He was standing, screaming down at me, but I could see tears welling up in his eyes. He ran off then, barrelling through the gathered crowd, just as the bell rang to call us back into class. The crowd quickly dispersed. I got up and dusted myself off, staring at Declan's disappearing back.

Well.

Charlie whispered in my head.

I'd call that a success.

9

Declan stayed away from me for the rest of the day. Everybody pretty much left me alone. I desperately wanted to talk to Charlie about what had happened, but we'd agreed not to talk much during school. There was too much of a risk of someone seeing me talking to myself. I got through the rest of the day and headed home. Mum was still in work, so I had the house to myself. I made myself a ham sandwich and sat at the kitchen table.

"You there, Charlie?"

Yep, I headed out to the Caribbean earlier to catch some sun, but I'm back now.

"Ha ha…wait, are you serious?"

No, I can't just pop wherever I want, most spirits are pretty limited in their range, and mine is very specific.

"Huh, nice to know you're always near."

I finished my sandwich and looked up at the air.

"What happened with Declan today?"

Well he totally didn't hit you, so like I said before, win.

"No, something happened, it was weird."

I told Charlie about what I had felt and seen, the crack in my shield, the bolt of emotion, the vision. I tried to remember all I could.

Wow, that's some serious mojo. You got a flash of his memories.

"Is it going to happen again?"

Not likely, I think you just got lucky. It's usually very difficult to see inside a person's head.

"Well good, 'cause that was creepy."

I don't doubt it. But it did stop him from hitting you.

"I suppose."

I sat and read, well pretended to read at least. I couldn't stop thinking about what had happened, about what I'd seen. Those were Declan's memories, that was his life. No wonder he was so angry all the time. It was difficult to stay angry at him when I knew where his darkness came from. I guess it's true what they say, we would all get along a lot better if we could understand each other more. Then again, my understanding him wasn't necessarily going to stop him beating me to a pulp. The thoughts spun round and round in my head until it hurt.

I gave up and lay down to enjoy the silence. It was wonderful. It wasn't even just the lack of whispers, I never really noticed before how just trying to get through the day left me feeling drained and worn out. But now, shielded and grounded, I felt whole. I felt as if the world could throw anything at me and though it may be hard, and might even break me, I wouldn't feel as if I was spending every day bleeding away pieces of me.

10

Wednesday started well, which seemed to be a theme. Maybe the dawn wipes everything clean, including people, and it takes until the afternoon until they become their normal, crappy selves again. Who knows, maybe it's my fault for going around smiling so much, some people just can't stand to see others happy.

Declan caught me in the corridor after Maths, just as the home bell was ringing. He shoved me into a corner as the other boys surged around us, eager to get home as soon as possible and to completely ignore what was happening in the corner.

"Who told you, schizo?"

As he leaned in, speaking in a vicious whisper, I realised his aura was agitated. I could feel it all around me, it was murky red with streams of black and it was churning like a storm. I hadn't learnt how to interpret colours much, but I could tell that his was not very nice at all.

I tried to remain calm as I replied.

"Who told me what, Declan?"

"Who told you about HIM!?" He screamed, bouncing my back against the wall.

I could feel myself getting angry. I couldn't believe I had spent last night feeling sorry for this moron. I grabbed his arms and shoved him away from me.

"No one told me anything you idiot, now get the hell away from me!"

I was yelling now, I couldn't help it, this was the first fight where I was in a position to do anything other than cower.

Declan jumped forward knocking me to the ground and started hitting me wildly, his punches didn't even hurt that much. He just seemed to want to hit me as fast as he could.

"You'll shut up, I'll make you. I'll kill you, shut up, shut up, shut up!!!"

I felt my anger burning brighter, some of it was leaking in through my shield from him, but that was just the start. His anger touched something inside me and made it flare. I felt my own anger answer the call. It burned hot and dark inside me, remembering every name, every prank, every punch. It remembered every time he and others had made me wish I could just die. It was angry about every memory, and it let it all out now. I felt my anger surge up inside me like a twisting roaring blast of fire. It hurt to have it inside me, it hurt more than anything I had ever known, so I screamed and let it out, not in a wave like with the shield, but in a beam. A hot burning lance of rage that I screamed right into Declan's face, and as I blacked out I heard his scream join mine as he held his head in pain.

I opened my eyes to see the ceiling of the corridor framed by a ring of confused faces. I wanted to sit up, but I couldn't persuade my body to move. I lay, paralysed, and began to slowly freak out. Had I fried my own brain? Charlie had warned me that I could hurt myself. Was this it? But no, feeling was slowly coming back. There, I'd wiggled my fingers. I could hear distant shouts, by the time they had gotten through the crowd of muttering boys I had managed to pull myself up onto my side facing the ring of legs. I was breathing in and out slowly, trying to focus on not throwing up. No one was helping me of course. They all just stood there like they were on a field trip, watching a particularly strange exhibit. The legs parted to reveal brown loafers with black trousers.

Oh dear. Only one person at school wore brown loafers with black trousers. With my head swimming, I managed to turn my face up to see the scowling mouth of Principal Hume. His eyes looked down at me through his thick black rimmed glasses with all the disgust I usually only got from my peers.

"What is the meaning of this?"

I remember thinking: Seriously, do they teach that line on the first day of teacher school? "Now prospective educators, when faced with students quite obviously engaging in typically unruly behaviour, it is vitally important that you question its meaning, for only through forcing them into philosophical thought can we hope to curb their wild actions."

I may have hit my head while unconscious.

At this point I lost my battle with nausea and threw my lunch up all over Principal Hume's shoes.

It turns out Declan wasn't much better than me. He woke up screaming that his head was split open. He curled up holding his forehead and wouldn't let any of the teachers near him. Eventually we were both brought to the principal's office. We sat side by side in stiff uncomfortable chairs, on the other side of the desk from Principal Hume's scowling face.

"Well Mister Boyle, fighting again I see? It seems no amount of punishment will persuade you to act like a human being."

Declan practically jumped out of his seat. "He hit me Sir! He's a lunatic! Attacked me for no reason, he nearly split my head open!"

"Is this true Mister Murphy?"

I sat with a sullen expression as I listened to the familiar tirade. It was always the same way. Someone would attack me for no reason, or for evil little sadistic reasons, and when it came to face the music, I was crazy, or I'd insulted their mother, or called them names. Against such vehement lies, the truth was but a sputtering candle in an endless darkness.

"I didn't hit Declan, Sir."

"He's lying Sir! He nearly killed me!"

"Really, Mister Boyle? Strange then that I see no injuries about your person?"

Declan actually looked confused. He stopped and felt around his head.

"But... he hit me... he must have... it felt like my head was exploding."

"Indeed. Well since neither of you actually seem injured in anyway, we'll just called it rough behaviour and blocking the corridors. But I'll be calling both your parents to come pick you up."

Declan actually paled.

"No. No Sir please, can't I just have detention?"

Principal Hume looked unmoved.

"I've made my decision Mister Boyle. You can both wait in reception."

We sat in reception, as far away from each other as we possibly could, the level of silence reaching hostile proportions.

Mum showed up first. She looked tired and worn out, she must have come straight from work. I didn't meet her eye as the principal greeted her and took her into his office for a 'talk'.

As I sat seething at Declan, but still too drained and sick to do anything about it, I listened to the silence. It was completely still in the reception area. I couldn't hear anything, not a whisper. I wanted to call out for Charlie, but I couldn't with Declan still in the room. I thought about my shield and felt for it with my mind. It was there. But it seemed… thinner… weaker. I didn't have anything left in me to strengthen it, so I left it as it was. Where was Charlie? I mean I knew we'd said he'd try not to talk to me during school, but checking to see if I was alright or saying something reassuring would have been appreciated right then.

Before I could worry anymore, the door opened and Mum came out.

"Thank you for coming, Mrs. Murphy. I'm sorry to have bothered you."

"No, it's fine." She smiled weakly "Thank you for calling."

She turned to me and let out a sigh that broke my heart.

"Come on Eoin."

I stood and followed her out, turning as I did to steal a glance at Declan. He sat hunched with his head in his hands. Maybe it was an after effect of whatever it was that I did to him, but to me he just looked scared.

I sat in the front seat of the car, waiting for my lecture. I've heard several variations over the years, "Why can't you stay out of trouble? Don't draw attention to yourself."

Mum turned in her seat to face me.

"Eoin… violence is wrong."

"Yes Mum."

"You should never solve issues with violence if any other option is available."

"I know Mum."

"But, that doesn't change the fact that I'm proud of you."

"Yes M- Sorry, what?"

As I turned to look at her, there were tears in her eyes. I was extremely confused.

"Principal Hume said that the other boy was on the ground when he got to you, that it seemed that you came out on top of whatever happened."

She wiped at her eyes.

"Of course fighting is wrong, and I do NOT want to get another call like this." She reached over and gripped my hand. "But part of me is just so very happy that you stood up for yourself."

I looked up into my Mums happy tearful eyes. I always thought I had hid most of what I went through each day, but maybe there was a part of Mum that knew nonetheless. I stared at her, in utter confusion at the two conflicting sentiments I was getting, and I said the only thing I could.

"I love you Mum."

She smiled wide.

"I love you too son."

II

When we got home, I hugged Mum and told her that I was tired and going to lie down for a while. She kissed the top of my head and smiled at me. Sitting on my bed, staring at the books on the shelf opposite, I felt lost. I mean, I felt good, Mum was proud of me, and I'd finally stood up to Declan... but how? What had I done to him, and where was Charlie? As if on cue, I heard his soft whisper in my mind.

We need to talk Eoin.

"Finally! Where have you been? Do you have any idea what I've been through?"

Oh I do Eoin, though I don't think you do. Just... just sit and listen.

Charlie sounded strange, not quite himself. He sounded sad, but more than that, tired. I sat back on the bed.

"Ok, I'm listening."

The reason I wasn't around earlier is that I was summoned, because of what you did to Declan.

I raised an eyebrow, but kept silent.

You used your, abilities, to harm a human. That's a giant no no. To be honest, I'm surprised you managed to do it. I mean, it's theoretically possible, but actually managing to black out another human with just your mind? Incredible. But wrong, so I got summoned by, well, just think of them as the bosses. They're not happy, Eoin. See I'm not really supposed to interfere, not officially. Some of them wanted to block me from contacting you again, it was a close thing. As it is we're on thin ice, one more incident and I'll be pulled away forever.

I sat on the edge of the bed, my hands gripping the duvet. "What happens to you if you get pulled?"

Well, it won't be pleasant, but it will be worse for you Eoin. If they see you as a threat, you'll be… neutralised.

"Em, dramatic much? What the hell does that mean?"

Honestly? Send spirits to hound you, make you want to run from your abilities. Make your life far worse than it's ever been.

I felt my face flush as I replied "Seriously? I was defending myself! This is the first time in my life I've had a way to stand up for myself and they're going to condemn me for it?"

This isn't about you Eoin, it's about preserving the balance and maintaining the division of worlds. Your abilities were never meant to interfere in human affairs, they were certainly never meant to be this strong. I know it's been hard, bu-

"You know it's been hard? How can you know? You've been in my life for five days! You don't know what I've had to live through, you don't know how many times I've cried myself to sleep, you don't know anything Charlie!!"

The sound of a mug smashing stopped me in mid rant. I froze. I knew, I knew and I didn't want to turn. If I didn't turn I could pretend it wasn't real, but it was inevitable. I turned my head to look at the door of my room, to look at the hot chocolate splashed out over the wooden floor, staining the white porcelain pieces, to look up at the face of my mother, twisted into an expression of pain and heartbreak.

I think it would have hurt less if she would have stopped hugging me. She just held me for ten straight minutes, telling me over and over that it was going to be ok, and that she was sorry. She was sorry and she should have never lied to me. But it would be ok, she'd make it all better. I tried to talk to her, but I don't think she was listening, she just kept repeating the same sentences over and over, hugging me repeatedly. Eventually she stroked my head and told me she'd be right back before running to the bathroom.

Well... crap.

"My sentiment exactly."

You don't know the half of it.

I raised an eyebrow but Mum stormed back into my room, almost slipping on the spilt hot chocolate.

"Oh, I'll get that later. Here Eoin, take these, it's ok, everything will be ok."

In her hand were the five pills that had ruled my life up until last week. The five pills that had dulled my mind and stolen my spirit.

"No! Mum! You have to listen, I don't want to take them. I've been happier, I really have. I know it must have looked weird, but I was just... It's hard to explain, I just-"

"Eoin, it's ok, everything will be ok. I know you don't want to take them, and I'm sorry, but it's my job to look after you and I need you to take them for me. Please Eoin, trust me, it's the right thing to do."

Her words came out in a forced calm tone, gentle and persuasive, but for her benefit or mine? I looked down at the pills in her palm. I knew it couldn't last. It had been horrible and painful, confusing and hard. It had been the best week ever and I knew it couldn't last.

I'm sorry Eoin, I don't think there's any way out of this.

"I know."

Mum smiled a little and moved her palm closer to me, a glass of water in her other hand.

I took the five pills and swallowed them, washing them down with water. I contemplated trying to hide them in my mouth, but I knew Mum would check, and she did, gently. I took another drink of water. I knew the pills had gone down, but I still felt a lump in my throat. I was scared. I didn't want to go back. I didn't want to live life in a soft haze filled with pain. Mum made me take a sedative as well. I took it in a daze. I felt broken, like everything was off track somehow. She got me to dress for bed and tucked me in. She hadn't done that since I was ten. And it was still light out. It was all wrong. Everything was wrong. It wasn't supposed to be this way. She was supposed to understand. The world was full of crap and evil and it hurt, even just walking in it hurt, but she was supposed to be there, she was supposed to understand. But she didn't understand. Why couldn't she understand?

I felt drained and sleepy. It wasn't just the sedative. It was all too much, the fight with Declan, shouting at Charlie, seeing that haunted look in Mums eyes. I just wanted to close my eyes and welcome the darkness. But I held on, there was one important thing I had to do first.

Once mum had left I rolled my head up off the pillow to look around the room.

"Charlie, are you there?"

Maybe it was just my imagination, but his reply seemed a little fainter than usual.

I'm here Eoin.

"Don' go 'way Charlie, it's important. Don't wanna lose you."

Don't worry Eoin, I'm right here. I'm not going anywhere. Not this time.

With Charlie's reassuring words running through my head, I drifted off into the dark.

12

I woke with a headache and an overwhelming sense of dread. The sun was just up and a gentle light seeped around the edge of my curtains. My head felt funny, like I'd just forgotten something very important and I was constantly on the edge of remembering it.

I thought about last night. Mum, she'd freaked out, made me take the pills.

"Charlie? Charlie, are you there?"

There was no answer, just the stillness of the dawn. But Charlie had been quiet before, it didn't mean that he was gone, right?

I tried to keep calm, I found myself automatically controlling my breathing, concentrating on breathing slowly in and out, thinking about each breath. I felt myself grow calmer. Good, Charlie might be silent but his lessons were still with me.

I closed my eyes and reached out my thoughts to strengthen my aura… and failed.

I shook my head, maybe I was too sleepy, I just needed to concentrate. I started the breathing over and tried again. I couldn't see my aura in my mind. There was… something, but it was, chaotic, scattered.

I couldn't shield. I was open, vulnerable. I felt, naked. I'd only been shielding for three days and yet now that I couldn't I felt lost. I don't think I realised how safe and secure the shield had been making me feel until that moment of panic.

I sat on the edge of the bed, my fingers digging into the mattress, trying to stay calm. My head was spinning and I felt nauseous. That's how Mum found me when she slowly opened my door.

"Eoin, are you ok?"

"I'm not taking them Mum, I can't fe… I'm not taking

them, I don't want to."

"You don't have to baby, I called Dr Hawkins. He wants us to come right in and he said not to give you anything until we got there."

I gritted my teeth as I felt my face flush. Dr Hawkins was the last person I wanted to see right now, but no pills was good, maybe there would be time for the ones I took last night to wear off.

"Fine. Can I get dressed please?" I hadn't even looked up, my eyes locked on the grain of the flooring.

I waited until she had closed the door before moving. I got dressed slowly, carefully. I felt like I was teetering on the edge, all I wanted to do was scream as loud as I could. But that wouldn't help and might even land me somewhere worse than Dr Hawkins office. I had to stay calm. There had to be a way out of this, I just had to wait and figure it out.

As we were getting ready to leave the house, I could see Mum flinching a little whenever I moved unexpectedly, so I made sure to sit as still as possible during the car journey so that we didn't crash.

Dr Hawkins waiting room seemed smaller than before. The walls were closing in, but the door was still open so I could breathe, that was good. They must have known the walls were moving, that's why the door was kept open. I don't think I'd spoken at all since Mum had found me this morning. I was too inside my own head, desperately trying not to lose it.

Mum went in to talk to Dr Hawkins first. His office door was carefully made not to let sound out, important I suppose, but I still heard raised voices. Shouting, unintelligible, angry… like angry painful whispers.

Eventually the voices lowered until I couldn't make them out at all, and I was left alone in the waiting room with the ticking of a clock to keep me company.

I heard a voice, and I thought it was calling me. I closed my eyes and concentrated hard, trying to pick out the words, trying to hear like I had before.

"Eoin… Eoin? Can you hear me? I'd like you to come in now."

I opened my eyes and looked up to see Dr Hawkins looking down at me, his hands open and at his side, his body language carefully non-confrontational.

I stood slowly and slouched my way into his office. I'd been listening so hard I was starting to get a headache, and I hadn't picked up anything, not even one of the old whispers.

Mum was sitting in one of the two chairs in front of Dr Hawkins desk, her mouth was set in a grim line that softened into a brave smile when she looked at me.

"Take a seat Eoin." Dr Hawkins said, gesturing at the remaining chair. "We have a lot to talk about."

"I don't see that we do." I replied sullenly.

"Now, Eoin." Mum said as she looked at me. "Be nice, Dr Hawkins is only trying to help."

I might have been more reassured if she hadn't sounded like she didn't quite believe that last part.

"Eoin, your mother tells me that there was an incident yesterday evening, that she found you talking to someone that wasn't there, is this true?"

I resisted the urge to shoot Mum a dirty look. I tried to focus on the fact that she was only trying to help.

"No."

Dr Hawkins looked surprised.

"It isn't true?"

"No, it was before six o'clock, so it was afternoon not evening."

"Eoin!" I knew that scolding tone in Mums voice, but it didn't seem to have much effect today.

"What!? He asked!" This time I did shoot her a look, it wasn't my fault that she couldn't get her times right.

Dr Hawkins cleared his throat to get our attention.

"What I'm trying to establish Eoin is that it happened at all, but I would like to hear about the incident from your perspective."

He looked at me, as if waiting for an explanatory

monologue. This was it, this was what I'd been dreading. What to say? I could have told the truth, and looked forward to a new wardrobe of coats with long sleeves that tied at the back. I could have tried to explain it away as a game, or rehearsing for a play. But that had about as much chance of success as me breaking out of there with some killer kung-fu moves. In the end I did the only thing I could. I denied everything.

"I don't remember what Mum is talking about, I remember coming home from school and then I woke up groggy this morning." I tried to keep my expression as neutral as possible.

Dr Hawkins looked sceptical. "I... suppose it's possible that the medication your mother gave you along with the sedative could be making it hard to remember."

I sat and played dumb. Dr Hawkins leaned forward and steepled his fingers.

"Eoin, can you tell me who Charlie is?"

Out of the corner of my eye I saw Mum flinch when he said Charlie's name.

"Nope, don't think I know anyone by that name, does he go to school with me?" I was seriously going for an Oscar.

Dr Hawkins leaned back and lifted a large bulging folder on to the desk. "Eoin, do you know what this is?"

"A folder?"

"It's your file Eoin, it has all the reports from all the doctors you've ever seen. Your mother has been very meticulous in ensuring that nothing is lost."

I kept quiet, unsure where this was going.

"I mention your file Eoin, because Charlie is in it."

"What?" I looked at Mum who was staring down and her hands as she wrung them in her lap.

Dr Hawkins opened the file and began looking at pages.

"He isn't mentioned recently of course, but in your earliest diagnosis, it mentions that you heard a voice that you called Charlie. You were only five at the time, so of course it could have been put down to an imaginary friend, were it not for the other symptoms."

I sat, my hands gripping the arms of the chair, struggling to remember how to breathe. I couldn't speak.

"There were the nightmares of course, leading to sleep deprivation, but then there were auditory hallucinations during the day time also, voices, asking you to do things." He picked up one of the pages and began reading.

"The patient hears many voices but he only names one, Charlie. Charlie protects him from the other voices and tells him that he is special. I suggest that the child has constructed Charlie as a defence against his psychosis. This is why Charlie 'protects' him and tells him he is special."

Dr Hawkins dropped the paper back in the file and looked up at me.

"Has Charlie come back Eoin? Is he talking to you? It's important that you tell me. I know that you won't want to. Charlie probably tells you that you're special, that you have the power to stop all the bad things that are happening to you, but you have to understand that that is just a deeper delusion that can only harm you in the long run."

I turned to look at Mum with tears in my eyes only to see that they had already escaped hers. She looked at me with love and pain.

"I'm sorry Eoin, I'm so sorry, but you see we had to come straight in, we can't go back to that. I thought you were doing so well, and I wanted to believe, I'm so sorry."

I opened my mouth to speak but all that came out were the shattered pieces of my heart.

I sat in the chair, staring at the floor, trying to spy the broken pieces of my world that were now strewn around me. The world was reduced to whispers. Dr Hawkins and Mum were talking, but their voices echoed like I was underwater. On the edge of hearing, there were other sounds. I knew them all, I knew them well. The whispers were back. Charlie was gone, or perhaps had never been, yet the whispers were back. I think I cried, I remember my eyes feeling itchy and hot and my cheeks feeling as if they were burning. But I didn't move and I didn't speak. The whispers were soft, unintelligible. I thought I heard my name.

One of the whispers was crying, another was all hard and sharp and sickly green, one of the whispers was scared, oh so scared, and shouting. Was I shouting? It sounded like me, but when I concentrated I could feel my lips and they were closed tight. Still, I heard the shouting, the warning, it was all wrong, but it was my voice telling me it was wrong. No, Charlie. It was Charlie's voice. I'd always thought it was familiar. It was my voice, not the voice I hear when I speak, but the voice I hear if I'm recorded. That's why I didn't recognise it. Charlie's voice is how other people hear me. Charlie wasn't real, he was just my voice. Yes. There were definitely tears. I remember.

My memory gets a little hazy then. I remember a bright light in my eyes, it hurt, and someone was trying to move me. I let them, there was no point in resisting. There was no point in anything. I felt gripped, my body pressed in on all sides by everything. Everything? That didn't make sense. If everything was pressing, then what was it pressing? Nothing. I was nothing. I was nothing.

And so nothing was moved and nothing was touched. People whispered and nothing was said. The ceiling lights were bright and moved and nothing was flat. The sound of the crying hurt, because even in nothing there is pain.

The two loud bangs heralded the bouncing and the bouncing lasted forever. At the end of forever came the jostling and the careful whispers. So careful. So measured. So controlled. Nothing hurt with a short sharp stabbing pain, and then in the nothing there was darkness.

13

When I woke up, my head hurt and my tongue felt like it was made of carpet. I opened my eyes and saw the wall. The wall was grey and that seemed wrong because my wall has striped blue wallpaper. The bed felt wrong and the air felt wrong and my mind felt wrong. After about ten minutes I persuaded my body to move. It didn't want to, it wanted to lie there and cry forever. It wanted to be nothing because in nothing there was at least a measure of peace.

My muscles felt sore and worn out as if I'd been exercising too much. I groaned as I rolled over. The stiff bed creaked as I moved. I was in a room smaller than my bedroom. There were grey walls and a metal bed frame. The bed had white sheets but grey woollen blankets. To my left was grey wall, to my right another, but that wall held a sink and a bare metal toilet. I felt like I should be panicking, but I'd only just managed to persuade myself to move. Panicking would take a while.

I pushed myself up in the bed to see the stark metal door, with a small sliding letterbox shutter at eye height.

Was I in prison?

I couldn't remember anything I'd done that would get me arrested.

I wondered what time it was. The light coming in through the high frosted window opposite the door seemed bright enough for mid day.

Wait, my clothes, I wasn't wearing my clothes. I looked down at what I was wearing, it was like a hospital gown but in plain blue fabric. A quick check confirmed that I was still wearing my own underwear, thank god. And I still had my own socks, though the coldness of the wooden floor was starting to seep through them. My thoughts were interrupted by the sound of the metal shutter clanking open on the door. A familiar set of cold grey eyes looked in at me.

"Ah, Eoin, good. I was hoping you'd be awake."

There was further clanking as the door opened and he stepped inside.

"Where am I?"

Dr Hawkins had his calm reasonable session face on, his tone matched it. "You're at a special care facility. I'm sorry about the sparse accommodation, we will hopefully be able to move you to a more comfortable room once we get started."

"Get started? Am I… am I in a mental hospital?" I could feel my stomach twisting up in knots even as I asked the question.

"Not as such, no. This is a special care facility that I have set up to help patients who might not be able to afford specialist private care. The building is pretty basic, but we have some top psychologists donating their time."

I tried to get my head around my situation.

"So, it's a charity hospital?" I hated charity, but I'd take charity hospital over mental hospital any day.

"Yes. It was plain that you were going to need a lot of help and there was no way your mother was going to be able to afford it. She is struggling just to cope with your current needs, as I'm sure you know."

More stomach knots, of guilt this time. It seemed that Dr Hawkins wasn't above a little emotional blackmail to ensure my cooperation.

"How long am I going to be here?"

"Well, that remains to be seen. Why don't I see about getting you some clothes and then we can have our first session?"

I was given a light blue t-shirt along with matching sweatpants. They were stretchy at the waist and didn't have any string to draw them tight. No shoes though, so when Dr Hawkins came for me I had to walk with him in my socks. I looked around as Dr Hawkins ushered me along, there seemed to be a number of rooms on this corridor. It was closed off at one end, but the other end had a set of sturdy double doors with a bored looking but burly orderly sitting behind a desk off to one side. Dr Hawkins nodded at the orderly, who reached a hand under his desk. A buzzer sounded and Dr Hawkins pushed through the door.

"Am I a prisoner?"

Dr Hawkins turned his head to smile reassuringly at me. "No, of course not Eoin, we just have the standard security you would see in any medical facility."

I tried to remember the last time I had seen a hospital with bars on all the windows. We didn't have far to go. Two corridors away he led me into a small room. There was just a desk, some chairs, and a bookcase, all against grey walls on cheap grey carpeting. Oh, and there was the couch, always the couch. It looked identical to the one in his office, maybe he bought them in bulk.

"Take a seat Eoin."

His tone was warm, friendly. I took a seat and tried to think. That sounds weird, but that's literally what it felt like. Ever since I'd woken up I had felt like I was just walking along, not thinking properly at all. As I sat in front of Dr Hawkins desk I tried to sit up and pay attention, and it was hard to do. My mind kept trying to drift, it just wanted to float. I could think about something, but not for long.

"Eoin, Eoin are you with me?"

"Sorry, what?"

"I know it might be hard to concentrate right now. Unfortunately we had to give you a little something when we brought you in, but don't worry, it will wear off soon."

Of course. I was broken when they brought me in. They had probably given me something in case I freaked out. That made sense. But there was something irritating about his sentence, something was wrong there.

"Eoin. Eoin?"

I looked up as Dr Hawkins clicked his finger at me. That wasn't nice. Wasn't it rude to do that?

"Eoin, do you want to wait and do this another time?"

"What? No! No, I'm just a little, fuzzy. I'll be fine, just need to concentrate. Please tell me why I'm here and how I can leave."

That seemed a little blunt. But that was ok, because you're supposed to be honest with a doctor, right?

Dr Hawkins laid his hands on the desk in front of him and smiled. "You're here because you're not well, Eoin. I'm hoping that with some intensive therapy, some of it quite innovative, we can help you uncover the source of your problems."

I tried to focus on his words, and I could, though it would have been easier without that niggling feeling that was back again.

"So, when you cure me, I can go?"

"Broadly, yes. Though we're not looking for a miracle cure here, we're looking to understand why you are the way you are."

"That doesn't make sense. I'm crazy, that's why I'm like this. I'm just nuts." It was only when I felt my lips stop moving that I realised I'd said all that out loud. I squinted, trying to keep track of my words.

"We don't like to use those words here Eoin, and it's not always as simple as that. Sometimes the cause can be quite complicated, but once we understand it, I think there will be some amazing breakthroughs."

He was smiling at me again, but there was something wrong with it, it was a painting of a smile, all the bits were in place but it wasn't really there.

As he led me back to the room, he said that he would give me time to settle in and we would start properly tomorrow. I should have been looking for the exits, if only in case there was a fire, but it didn't even occur to me. I just followed beside Dr Hawkins like an obedient puppy.

He swiped a plastic card over a rectangular reader beside a door and I realised we were back at the ward where I'd slept. He just about had time to usher me through and close the door behind us before the screaming started.

The orderly's desk was empty and the screams were coming from an open door at the far end of the corridor. They sounded high pitched, they sounded female, but most of all they sounded terrified. They echoed down the corridor, over and over, along with bangs, crashes and other sounds of struggle. I looked up at Dr Hawkins. He seemed to hesitate, hovering between moving forward and going back. Finally the screams slowed, grew quieter, until it was just the occasional heart breaking sob. Two orderlies came out of the room, one of them was limping. The other one gave Dr Hawkins a curt nod before locking the door behind them.

Dr Hawkins seemed to ignore the fact that we had just come in to a corridor filled with screaming, and waved me down the corridor.

"Is she ok?"

"Hmmm? Is who ok Eoin?"

"That girl, the one who was screaming."

"Oh, yes, quite ok, probably just a bad nightmare."

His explanation twisted in my head, but I couldn't make it straighten out, so I nodded and walked back into the room where I'd woken up.

Dr Hawkins stood in the doorway before he left, his doctor smile firmly in place.

"Why don't you lie down and get some rest Eoin? I'll have some food brought along shortly."

I lay down and listened to the sound of the bolts sliding home. Food. Why wasn't I hungry? How long had it been since I was in his office with Mum? Why was I not freaking out about being locked in a room? I hated being locked away. I should be screaming too. Why wasn't I screaming? Was I broken? That must be it. Whatever had happened in Dr Hawkins office had broken me, I remembered now, it had shattered me into a million painful pieces that had all been sucked into a great big hole of nothing. That's why I couldn't feel anything, because I was nothing. With that mystery solved, I was able to settle down and sleep.

14

When I woke my head felt a little clearer, but the edges of my thoughts were still a bit fuzzy. I did feel well rested though, and the light coming in through my frosted glass window was bright. Was it the same day? No clock, no way to tell. I could end up locked in here forever and there would be no one to tell, and no one to come find me. Would Mum come looking if they never let me out? Surely I'd been more trouble than I was worth. Why she hadn't just dumped me in a mental hospital sooner I didn't know.

I realised I was hitting the wall when my knuckles started to bleed. The pain was sharp. Hot and cold at the same time, as a trickle of blood ran across my hand. I stared at it as its brother ran down my cheek, but the rivulets on my face soon outnumbered the ones trailing down my hand. I curled up on the bed and let my eyes bleed out everything. Bleed out the pain, bleed out the anger, and above all else, bleed out the fear. I kept crying, but there just weren't enough tears. Maybe it was an hour after I woke up, maybe it was ten minutes. No way to tell, but it wasn't long before the weight of all my tears dragged me back to sleep.

It was darker when I woke the next time. Not dark, but not as bright. Something woke me. The clank of the door, Dr Hawkins was coming inside. I pulled myself up into a sitting position on the bed, my legs folded up against my body, hiding me. I wiped at my face, worried that I was still crying, but my cheeks were dry. I must have run out of tears while I slept.

Dr Hawkins had his clinical, almost smile on as he

slowly approached the bed. He was carrying a tray. The smell made my stomach growl. I looked down at the noise, then back up.

"Yes, I thought you might be hungry. You've slept quite a while. I thought it best to let you rest, I think you needed it."

I went to speak, but I just made a croaking sound. The inside of my throat was sore. Had I been screaming? I swallowed and tried again.

"W… what day is it?"

"It's Friday Eoin, about six in the evening."

"I think I dented the wall a little, I'm sorry."

Dr Hawkins gave me a lukewarm smile. "That's quite ok Eoin, I completely understand. This is all very scary for you, it's completely natural for you to lash out."

I opened my mouth to reply but a loud gurgle echoed its way up my throat instead, my hand flew up to cover my mouth in embarrassment.

"Of course, let me leave you with your food. After you've eaten, I'll come get you and we can get your hand cleaned up."

I looked down at my right hand, the knuckles were caked in blood.

"Thank you." I said, still staring at my hand.

Dr Hawkins left the tray at the other end of the bed from me and opened the door. Just before he walked out, he turned to look at me.

"Everything will be ok Eoin, I promise."

With that lie, he ducked out, and I heard the harsh scrape of the metal lock.

On the tray was a bowl of thick beef stew, two dinner rolls, a plastic cup full of water and plastic cutlery. Luckily the stew wasn't too hot else I would have burned myself with the speed that I ate. I honestly don't know if it was any good, but it tasted like heaven. I wiped out the bowl with the last of the bread, then sat on the edge of the bed, staring at the sink with no mirror, sipping my water. There was nothing else to do. Was that the point? Was I supposed to have time to think? I didn't know if that was going to do any good, because my thoughts sure weren't getting any saner.

With a deep metal clank the door opened up once more, revealing Dr Hawkins standing in the threshold, his hands in his pockets, smiling down at me.

"Did you enjoy the food?"

"Yes, thank you." I mumbled.

"Good, now come with me and we'll see to that hand."

I rose from the bed, and he walked off, leaving me to follow. We followed the same route, out past the buzzing orderly and down one corridor, then another to the same office.

"Lie down on the couch please." he said, closing the door behind us.

I lay out on the couch, moving slowly. I felt a little sore, like I had been running too hard for too long. Dr Hawkins went behind his desk and opened a drawer, taking out a first aid kit. He walked back, pulling a chair with him so he could sit down beside me.

"Don't feel bad about it Eoin, I've seen people do much worse. When you're angry and alone, sometimes you need to hurt to be able to feel."

Something rang out in his words, like the barest hint of a bell in them. I don't think I'd heard that in his words before.

There was a snap as Dr Hawkins put on latex gloves, a tear as he opened an antiseptic wipe, and a stinging pain as he began to wipe my knuckles clean. It wasn't so bad once all the blood was cleaned off, just splits across my top knuckles, but Dr Hawkins wrapped a bandage around them anyway. Maybe it was to cushion them in case I freaked out again. Once he was done, he tidied away the first aid kit and grabbed a writing pad.

"Now, why don't we get started, if you feel up to it?"

"I guess so."

"Do you remember what we talked about in my office before we brought you here?"

Whenever I thought about that moment, the moment my world shattered, I wanted to thrash about and scream. I felt my left arm jerk a little, my fingers twitching. I'm pretty sure Dr Hawkins noticed because I saw him scribble a quick note before I answered.

"... Yes."

"Can you tell me what we discussed?"

I felt like I had a lump in my throat, but swallowing just made it worse. "Do I have to?"

"I understand that this might be hard for you Eoin, but it is important that you come to terms with this, talking will help with that."

I lay back and closed my eyes. I felt raw, like every part of me was too sensitive, I didn't want to speak about it, didn't want to think. So I did what I'd learned to do in such a situation, I started to centre and ground. I could imagine my centre, I remember how it looked, but I couldn't feel it with the certainty that I'd had before. Focusing on my breathing helped though, and as I went through the motions, I started to calm. I assumed Dr Hawkins knew I was trying to calm myself as he didn't interrupt. Eventually I started speaking.

"You asked about Charlie." Slow breath. "I tried to deny everything" Another breath. "You brought out my file."

It became easier as I continued. I still wanted to cry, but I felt that I was in control.

"You told me about my first diagnosis... about Charlie... that he's been there from the beginning. That... that he's a lie."

Dr Hawkins voice was as gentle as mine was heartbroken.

"Go on, do you remember anything else?"

"You... you said that Charlie was someone I'd made up to protect me from the crazy parts of my brain."

"Not quite, one of the first doctors that diagnosed you said that Charlie was a protective construct. That is a distinct possibility, but I try not to be constrained by previous diagnoses. We're here to figure out what's wrong and how I can help."

That seemed, refreshing somehow. I mean, he'd still decided I was crazy, but at least he was willing to be open-minded about how I was crazy.

"So how do we do that?"

"Well, for a start, tell me about Charlie. Do you remember him from when you were little?"

"No, but then I don't remember much from back then. Before we got a balance of meds that worked, life was a bit, hazy."

"So when is the first time you remember talking to Charlie?"

"Em, Sunday morning. I mean, Saturday night, I think, but like, properly on Sunday morning."

"And what did he say to you?"

"That Cebocap was a placebo and that you were trying to fool me."

That sounded so rude, but if I was going to take this seriously, if was going to get better, I had to be honest. Dr Hawkins stopped his writing and looked up.

"I was worried that a smart boy like you would figure it out, the name is practically an anagram. I didn't like deceiving you Eoin, but I felt you were being over medicated, and the only way you were going to be able to face and tackle your problem was to get you completely clean."

"But I'm medicated again, right, my head is fuzzy round the edges, like before, you've... it was in the food, right? You gave me an injection yesterday and put it in my food today?"

It actually sounded a little paranoid once I said it, but I was a little fuzzy, and the food was the only thing I'd had.

"Yes, that's true. We're going to take you off them over the next few days, but you had such a bad reaction yesterday that we had to put you back on them for the moment."

"When can I stop?"

"Well this session is going well, you certainly seem

willing to face up to the problem, and you're not in denial. If you want we can stop now and see how you feel tomorrow. Just remember that you may have to go back on them, or some other regime as part of the therapy."

I nodded. "Ok, I... I want to get better Dr Hawkins."

The session went on much longer than a normal one. I went through the past week, explaining how Charlie had gotten me to shield, how the other voices had gone away. He seemed very interested in the fact that Charlie had been the only voice I'd heard, and also in the incidents with Declan. It was growing dark outside the window by the time we were finished.

"Thank you Eoin, I'm glad you felt you could be honest with me about your experiences this past week."

It hadn't been easy, and I'd started twitching more than once during the session, but Dr Hawkins hadn't commented. He'd just allowed me time to calm down and carry on.

"I'm glad too. Thank you Dr Hawkins."

It had actually felt good being able to talk to someone about everything that happened. It made me feel less crazy, which is weird. I stretched out on the couch and yawned.

"We should get you to bed. I'll phone ahead and make sure they have some supper waiting."

He had a quick conversation on the phone, before wrapping up the session.

"Ok, I think we can safely come off the meds, but it's important that you tell me about any changes, and especially important that you tell me if Charlie comes back."

I nodded meekly. "Yes Doctor."

"We'll have another session tomorrow and see how you are."

"Oh... you work on Saturdays?"

"I'm here every day Eoin, this project is very important to me."

And there is was again, something about the way he

said those words.

There was a plate of sandwiches and a plastic mug full of milk waiting on a tray in the room when I was brought back. Dr Hawkins told me to just leave them on the floor when I was done with them. They tasted good, all the better for being unmedicated, I hoped. But no, Dr Hawkins wouldn't have lied to me, he wanted me unmedicated, he wanted to find a solution. I settled down for a restful night's sleep.

Unfortunately, that was the night the whispers returned.

15

I was sitting in class, when the boy at the next desk turned and whispered to me. I couldn't hear what he said so I leaned in closer. His lips moved, but all that came out was the softest of sounds. I shook my head, telling him I couldn't hear him. He turned to the boy in front of him and tapped his shoulder. Then they both turned back to me and whispered together. I turned from one to the other, trying to read their lips, but it was no use. I couldn't understand anything they were saying. I raised my hand to ask to be excused from class. The teacher turned to look at me. It was Mr. Egan, but when he opened his mouth it was just another whisper. Now three different whispers washed over me, like the sound of wind in the trees. I shouted, but no one could hear me. Suddenly the rest of the class started turning towards me. Each one opened his mouth to let out another sinister whisper, the volume building until it was impossibly loud. It seemed impossible that something so loud could still be so maddeningly unintelligible. My classmates stood in unison and began moving towards me. I fell off my chair, scrambling into the corner as they surrounded me. Their expressions were blank, their arms hanging against the side of their bodies. But all of them whispered, the many threads weaving together and covering me in a blanket of sound, confusion and pain. As I huddled in the corner covering my ears, I felt their hands grip me, taking my arms and legs and pulling at them, until I could feel my flesh begin to tear.

I woke screaming, my head gripped tightly in my hands as two orderlies tried to wrestle me out of my foetal position at the end of the bed. My muscles felt like they were cramping all at once, my head felt like someone was trying to split it with an axe. I couldn't scream fast enough, the pain was building up and I couldn't get it out. One of the orderlies pulled my stretchy bottoms down and stabbed something into the outside of my thigh. There was a sharp pain and then I felt the world slip away into darkness.

My eyes felt crusted together when I woke. The light through the window was grey and there was a tray of cold buttered toast and orange juice on the floor. My body felt sore, like I'd been hit all over.

It must have been not long after dawn, because it was still quiet, unless whatever they shot me with in the night had made the whispers go away again. No, my head was clearer than before, around the edges. Foggier in the middle, but that was from the rough night, that was a familiar feeling. Why didn't they give me more drugs if I was screaming? I had thought I'd be doped up, that Dr Hawkins wouldn't want to try taking me off the meds. Unless I'd spent days sedated and didn't know it?

The room looked like it had the last time I'd seen it. The cold toast didn't tell me much. I lay looking at the ceiling trying to figure it out. I rolled over away from the wall and felt a stab of pain in my leg. Sitting up, I pulled down the side of my bottoms to look at the tiny pin prick where they'd shot me. There was a spot of dried blood and it was quite tender. I checked my body for other injection sites but couldn't find any. So, it was probably Saturday, which means there was only one thing for me to do. I ate the toast.

With nothing else to do, I lay on the bed for what seemed like forever. I knocked on my door and eventually an orderly came, but he wouldn't open the door. He said I'd have to wait until Dr Hawkins came. I think it was an hour before the whispers started, but there was really no way to tell. I heard a gentle shushing like a running tap, and I looked to the little sink. But of course there was no water, because the sound was in my head, because I was crazy. This was important. Dr Hawkins said I had to accept the problem before I could face the problem. And so I sat on the bed as the whisper grew.

"You are in my head, you are trying to be a voice but you are just in my head."

"You are not real, I will not listen to you! I will only listen to real people."

"You are a symptom, all you can do is help me find out what's wrong, that is your only purpose."

The whisper softened, it was pleading. Before, I used to wonder how I could know that. Now it was obvious. The whisper only existed in my head, so of course I knew what it was doing. It was begging for my attention, which was a lot better than screaming at me until it hurt. I kept repeating the thoughts over and over. The whisper wasn't real, I didn't want it there, I wanted quiet. I thought to myself over and over again, until the words just filled my mind leaving no room for anything else.

I jumped when the door lock scraped, shocked out of my mantra. Dr Hawkins opened the door but didn't step into the room.

"Good morning Eoin. How are you feeling?"

I paused before I answered, cocking my head to see if there was a trace of the whisper remaining, but there was nothing. I broke out into a smile.

"Better actually! Last night I was… it was bad, but this morning is better. Do we have another session?"

Dr Hawkins smiled. "If you feel up to it?"

"I do, I want to get better Dr Hawkins."

He gently ushered me out of the room and past the buzzing orderly. As we walked the two corridors to his office, I looked up at him.

"Dr Hawkins, why am I locked in that room?"

He became sombre. "Hmmm… well Eoin, I'm sure you can understand that there might be some concern that you would harm yourself, or someone else. Some of your outbursts have been very violent. Really, the locks are there for your protection."

I tried not to look disappointed.

"Do I have to stay in the room all day?"

"Oh lord no, I'll make sure you get to use the shower room later today, and we'll be having daily sessions."

His voice was warm and sincere, but I needed more in the day than just showering and talking.

"It's just, well it's kinda boring, there's nothing to do."

"That's the point Eoin, you have time to think about our sessions, about how to make the next step in your recovery."

I nodded, trudging along beside him.

"Would you like me to see if I can get you some books?"

"Oh! Yes, that would be great. Could I call Mum and ask her to bring some for me?"

"Hmm, we'll see. I think as little contact as possible is better for you right now."

I stopped in the middle of the corridor and stared at his back. He took a couple of steps before he turned to look at me, eyebrows raised.

"You mean Mum isn't coming in to visit me?" I don't know why, but I just assumed I'd be seeing Mum, if not today then at least tomorrow. I knew I was being treated but even prisoners got visits.

Dr Hawkins went still. His smile didn't go away, but it wasn't moving anymore.

"I'll tell you what, I was going to call her to let her know how you're doing. Why don't we call her together, and you can ask her to send some books, would you like that?"

As I thought about hearing Mums voice it hit me just how lonely and lost I felt, and I wanted to cry.

"Yes, I'd like that, please. Can we do it now?"

"Let's have our session first, if it goes well we can call her straight after, ok?"

I deflated a little, but nodded.

"Ok."

As I started walking again he waited, making sure to keep me at his side all the way to his office. When we got there, he let me go in first before following, closing the door behind us.

It was a productive session, I thought. I told Dr Hawkins about the whispers in the night, about being drugged, and about the other whisper today. I told him how I persuaded myself that it wasn't real and I was a little surprised at his reaction.

"You didn't listen to it?"

He scooted forward in his seat.

"What it was saying?"

"No it was just a whisper, like before, I couldn't hear any words."

He stopped taking notes and sat staring down at his pad for a moment.

"Eoin, I think these voices could tell us more about your condition. They are a link to your subconscious. I want you... I would like you to try and listen to the voices, to find out about them. Will you do that for me?"

This didn't make sense, it sounded like the opposite of what I should be doing.

"But, when I listen, there's too many. It hurts so much, and I can't understand them."

"But Charlie, he taught you to," He flicked back through his notes. "shield? Yes, do you think you could still tell if someone was trying to speak to you if you're shielding?"

I sat up and turned to face him.

"But, you said Charlie was just a deeper delusion, that it wasn't real, that he couldn't help."

"Yes, of course, that's true, but it's also true that the Charlie voice was able to bring you calm through this shielding. We may still be able to use that as a tool to better understand the other voices."

"But will the shielding even work if Charlie isn't in my head?"

"Why, has he tried to contact you?"

"I don't know! I've only heard whispers!" My face was flushed and I was trying not to raise my voice.

Dr Hawkins coughed, and let the silence that followed ease the tone.

"It's ok if you hear Charlie again, it's even ok to humour him, as long as you remember that he is just a facet of your illness."

He walked to his desk and took something from a drawer. It was a plain red notebook, about the size of a paperback, with a sleek black pen resting inside the spiral binding.

"I want you to have this, Eoin. When the voices come back, which no doubt they will as the medication wears off, I'd like you to write down what they say, your conversations with them. This way I'll be able to review them and see what light they shed."

I stood, taking the notebook from him.. "Thank you Dr Hawkins." Truthfully, it would be nice to have something to do while sitting alone in the room. Looking down at the notebook made me think of my books.

"Can we call Mum now?"

"What? Oh! Of course, yes. Why don't you pull one of the chairs round and we'll do it now."

He was smiling again, the one that didn't move. He sat down at his desk, picked up the phone, and started dialling as I pulled the chair around.

"Mrs. Murphy? Yes, it is, I just wanted to phone you with an update."

"Yes, he is feeling much better, he is up and about and we are beginning his sessions. In fact, he'd like to say hello."

I could hear Mum's excited reply from where I sat. I took the receiver from Dr Hawkins and put it to my ear carefully.

"Mum?"

"Oh Eoin! It's so good to hear your voice. How are you doing? Are you eating ok, are you alright?"

I smiled as I tried not to drown under the avalanche of questions. "I'm fine Mum, I'm feeling much better, Dr Hawkins is helping a lot and I'm eating fine."

"Oh, good. Is there anything you need? Do you need extra pillows? Or do they have those?"

"Em, could you bring me some of my books? Anything from the bottom shelf is fine. About ten of them?"

"Of course darling, I'll bring them tomorrow. Will I be able to see you?"

I turned to where Dr Hawkins had sat down at his desk watching me

"Can Mum see me tomorrow Dr Hawkins?"

He nodded with his fixed smile.

"I'm sure we can schedule a short visit, about half an hour, say at 2pm?"

"Did you hear that Mum?"

"Yes, that's no problem, it will be good to see you."

"I love you Mum."

"I love you too Eoin."

I handed the receiver back to Dr Hawkins, who double checked the time with Mum before hanging up.

"Well, wasn't that nice? Shall we get you back to your room? I think your lunch should be waiting for you."

I went to check my watch but of course it wasn't there. There weren't any clocks in his office either.

"What time is it?"

"It's just one o'clock. Come on, let's get you back."

I walked back along the corridors, the notebook held against my chest, Dr Hawkins at my side. There was something I wanted to know, but I didn't know how to ask without sounding defensive.

"There won't be any medicine in my lunch, right Dr

Hawkins?"

"No, I want to see if we can tackle this alone, just me and you, figuring it out."

He made it sound like it was an adventure, or some kind of fascinating puzzle.

"You know Eoin, we do have a recreation room here. It's nothing special, but if you don't have any more incidents before your mothers visit, I'll make sure you have access from tomorrow afternoon."

"Oh, that would be great, thank you Dr Hawkins." I knew if I had to spend all day cooped up in the room it was only going to increase my level of crazy.

He swiped his access card as we reached the door to the corridor and walked me to the room. As I walked in, he held the door and looked at me at me, hesitating.

"Eoin, I'm going to leave the door unlocked."

"… Ok."

"You can come out and get the orderly if there is anything wrong, or if you need something, and I'll be sure to knock before I enter in future."

I felt myself smile.

"Thank you Dr Hawkins."

He nodded.

"You're welcome Eoin, enjoy your lunch."

As he shut the door, I turned to find a tray of chicken sandwiches on my bed, with a plastic mug of milk. I sat eating in silence. It was actually quite nice. I began to think how thankful I had been for the peace that Charlie had brought in the past week. This was even more peaceful than that, with Charlie gone. Is this what it would be like, to be cured? An endless expanse of peace?

When I was done, I opened the door and left the tray in the corridor outside, like a hotel or something. Just being able to do that made me feel a whole lot better about being here. I lay back on the bed, staring at the ceiling, and thought about the session. Dr Hawkins wanted me to listen to the voices, listen to Charlie even, if he came back. He wanted me to shield, so that I could listen without being overwhelmed. Except the shield wasn't real, it was all in my head. But if the shield was in my head, and the voices were in my head, would the shield work on the voices? It all began to spin around until my head hurt. I decided to centre and ground. That wasn't shielding, but it always made me feel better, calmer.

As the high window in the room darkened, I closed my eyes and tried to relax on the bed. There was nothing to distract me, so it was easy to concentrate on the sound of my breaths, to listen to them but not change them, to let the sound of them fill my mind. Then I imagined everything that I was, everything that mattered, spinning around me. It was discorded and spiky. I imagined slowly pulling it all together into a small sphere in my chest. The surface wouldn't stay smooth though, there were pieces that just wouldn't fit. It was good enough. I then imagined a line sliding down from this center, through the bed, through the floor, finding the earth. Once the line had found the earth I was grounded. I felt calm, I could feel all of my body. I could hear everything in the room, from the dripping tap to the softest rustle of the blanket under my body as I breathed. And I could feel them. I could feel them across the hall in the room of screams. I could feel their anger, and I could feel her fear. They were killing her.

16

I jerked up on the bed, my head spinning. I heard her screams, the same ones I'd heard yesterday. She was so scared, and no one was listening. I slowly opened the door to the room, expecting to see the orderlies rushing down the corridor, but the corridor was still and silent. She wasn't screaming anymore, or was she? I concentrated, and I could hear it, as if it was just on the edge of hearing. The more I concentrated the louder it got, a series of ragged screams, over and over, scarcely a gap between them. They were terrible. I felt my heart begin to tear just listening to them. They were definitely coming from that same room at the end of the corridor. I stuck my head out of the door and looked back towards the orderly's desk. He was facing away from me, looking down at something, a book probably, and I could see wires from his earphones.

Was that why he couldn't hear the screaming? No wait, the screaming was in my head. That was important. Why was it important? And if it was in my head then was it really happening? If it was only in my head, then she wasn't really screaming and I should stay in the room. But if she was screaming and I only thought it was in my head, then I should tell the orderly. But they'd just sedate her, they wouldn't make the things that were hurting her go away.

Maybe the things that were hurting her were in my head and her screams were real and she should be sedated. But that didn't make sense, either it was all in my head or it was all real, yes, that made sense, simpler.

So either she was in the most terrible pain I could imagine, or everything was fine.

No harm in checking it out then.

I crept down the corridor, checking back over my shoulder every now and then, but the orderly didn't so much as twitch. The screaming grew louder as I approached the last door on the opposite side of the corridor. It tore through my heart and made me stumble, it was all I could do not to fall down and cry out in sympathy. I covered my ears with my hands, but it didn't make the screaming any quieter. That was the giveaway. I was hearing the screaming in my head, not through my ears. But I was almost at the door, and she was in so much pain. It felt like she'd been screaming forever. I leaned against the door, my forehead resting against the metal, tears running down my cheeks. I wanted to help her, I wanted to make the pain go away. I thought of all the pain I'd felt, how lost and alone I'd been, how much worse the pain had seemed because I had suffered in the dark. That's when I knew what I had to do. I whispered my words against the metal, and I felt them slide from my mind as well.

"You are not alone."

Silence, but not an empty one. It lasted for just a few seconds, and it swelled. It was practically bursting with the weight of attention on me. I could feel their eyes, burning into me, angry eyes, but distracted for a second. Then they pounced. It felt like a rushing wind roaring towards me. I could hear a screeching in my head, and it was full of hate and anger and malice. The screeching wanted to tear me apart until there was nothing left of me but screams. It terrified me, because I knew as soon as they got me it would be over, I would scream and scream until I was no more. I dropped to a crouch, cowering, knowing I was going to die, and there was nothing I could do. In the end, it was Charlie who saved me.

Or at least, his training did. As I crouched low to the ground, I felt myself instinctively reach with my mind for my aura. I felt it there, trembling, but present. Without even thinking, I poured energy into it, hardening it and pulling it tight around me. The first few slashes tore into it, and it hurt. I could feel it like a pulling in my stomach, it made me want to throw up. But I knew what I was doing now, I hardened my shield further and the slashes stopped hurting. I could still feel them, but they were like claws scratching at metal, annoying, but harmless.

I rose from the ground, and as I stood facing the door, I let my hands fall to my sides and a slow determined smile slid across my face. They couldn't hurt me, Charlie had made sure of that. They couldn't hurt me, but I could hurt them. I imagined all my pain and frustration, the utter chaos I'd been going through, I imagined it welling up inside of me, ready to explode. I could feel myself trembling with the effort of not falling apart. I slowly raised my arm, and pointed my open palm at the metal door. I imagined the surface of my palm growing thinner and thinner until all of that emotion came rushing out. I blasted it through the door and let it fill up the room beyond, burning up every slashing screeching thing inside. I felt elated, like I'd won a marathon. I was invulnerable to their attacks and they would run from my power. My vision went grey and I could see the darkness creeping in from the edges, but I didn't care. I felt wonderful. Just before the darkness took me, I thought I heard the voice of the smallest mouse in the world say:

Thank you.

17

I remember my dreams, I remember standing on a mountain top with a giant sword, screaming my defiance at the sky. I remember feeling my body explode, energy streaming from every pore. I remember Charlie and I lying out on the grass beside a river, watching the world go by, except Charlie was me and I was Charlie. I remember a different place full of blinding light, and the feel of lips pressed against mine. They were soft and warm and they tasted like cotton candy, and that kiss felt so good I thought I might die.

I've never had a hangover, but if it was anything like the way I felt when I woke then I don't know why people drink. The first thing I noticed was my head pounding repeatedly, as if someone was beating a massive drum inside my head. When I sat up the room started to spin and I had to lie down again. I lay very still until I was absolutely sure that I could move without falling over. The smell of food was not helping, I could smell tuna. I tried taking deep breaths to still the nausea but the smell was too much, so I settled for shallow breaths and not moving. It must have been a few minutes before I slowly sat up and looked around. I was back in the room, the light was fading through the frosted glass and there was a sandwich on a plate inside the door. Supper I suppose. I tried to puzzle over what had happened and the dream that had followed. Had the events in the corridor actually happened? They seemed almost as fantastical as the dreams that had followed them. Had it been a dream as well? I supposed I could always ask the orderly, I was sure he'd know if I'd been found unconscious in the corridor. I tried to turn the handle on the door, but it was locked once more.

I took that as a yes to having been found in the corridor. I felt drained. Whether the blasting those things was a dream or not, I hoped I didn't have to do that again, because I really didn't think I could keep it up. But did I do it? It was all in my head right? It was just another symptom. Well if it was a symptom, I knew what to do. As I sat and ate my sandwich, I took the notebook that Dr Hawkins had given me, and I wrote out everything I could remember about the corridor. As I read back over what I had written, I was glad that I already knew that I was crazy, otherwise I might have worried.

I finished my meal and read over the notebook twice to make sure I hadn't missed anything. I couldn't shake the tiredness and I wondered if they'd put a sedative in the sandwich. Dr Hawkins had promised no more drugged food, but that was before I started playing spirit blaster in the corridor. Maybe it was just the blasting that was making me tired. If it was drugs I should fight it, but if it was from the blasting there was no point. Actually there was no point fighting a sedative either. My mind was actually unable to think straight. I brushed my teeth and washed up, there was a toothbrush, wash cloth and toiletries in a neat pile by the sink. They must have brought them with the food. I placed the tray by the door and curled up under the blankets, letting the darkness take me once more, though somewhat more gently this time.

I stretched as I woke up, yawning. I felt warm and content. Another good night's sleep, I could start to get used to that. The light coming through the frosted glass was dim. I thought maybe it was overcast, but last night's tray still inside the door implied early morning. After I'd washed and brushed my teeth, I made the bed and then sat crossed legged on it. I focused my breathing until it was calm and regular. I centered and it felt a little smoother than yesterday. I grounded myself, feeling that sense of surety when it locked, and then I reached for my aura to shield. I could see it in my mind, brighter than yesterday, smoother, calmer, but thin. It pulled around me with ease, a feeling of being held.

Once I was ready to face the day, I tried to see if I could sense the girl from yesterday. It was difficult. It took me about ten minutes to realise that my shield was blocking out everything from the outside. I sat for a while trying to figure it out. I considered giving up, that it was enough crazy for the day. I knew Dr Hawkins wanted me to shield and that he thought that it would help, but I didn't know if he meant for me to go this far. But I wanted to check on her, even if it was just in my head, her screams had been in my head as well. I was worried about her. So I thought, what would Charlie do?

I imagined my shield turning clear, like a crystal. Still hard, still protecting me, but allowing me to see through it, then I tried to focus on the room at the end of the corridor. I couldn't quite keep it in my mind, but I couldn't hear any screams either, the only thing I could get was gentle buzzing, like static.

Sighing, I relaxed my concentration. My head was beginning to hurt anyway. I was sitting on the edge of the bed, writing in the notebook about it when the metal door clanked and opened. Dr Hawkins stood there with my breakfast tray, all smiling and cheerful.

"Good morning Eoin, it seems you had a little

adventure yesterday. How are you feeling?"

I took a deep breath, resisting the instinctive urge to lie.

"I'm feeling better Dr Hawkins, I wrote all about it if you'd like to read?"

I saw him smile. It wasn't the fixed one, this one was genuine and excited.

"That's good Eoin, I'll review it before our session today. Why don't you eat your breakfast and then we'll get you a shower?"

I remembered that I hadn't showered in four days. There's only so much you can do with a wash cloth at a sink.

"And my Mum, I'll see her today?"

"After our session Eoin. Eat up, I'll be back in a bit." He left the breakfast tray and took yesterdays.

I sat and thought as I ate. Dr Hawkins didn't want me to hide from my problems. I suppose that made sense. But I didn't know how shielding and fighting invisible slashing things was supposed to help cure me if none of it was real. I thought in circles until my head began to hurt.

I was all done when Dr Hawkins returned. He'd left the door open while he was gone, I wondered if it was going to stay like that after my little trip yesterday. He carried my tray to the orderly's desk, then led me out the door as it buzzed, turning right instead of left.

"From now on you can shower everyday. There will be someone to escort you each morning. I'm afraid you can't wander the facility unattended, for security reasons."

Yep, as in they wanted to keep me securely where they could see me. But I put on an understanding smile to match his concerned face.

"I understand Dr Hawkins, will I have to have an escort to the recreation room?"

"Hmm, oh yes, you can go for an hour each afternoon, just ask the orderly to get someone to bring you if you want to go."

It wasn't far until he pushed through a door into what looked like a locker room.

"There should be towels in a pile over there and toiletries in the shower cubicles. Oh and here are some clean clothes."

He opened a door to reveal shelves of light blue clothing. T-shirts, sweatpants, even underwear, all in the same light blue. He assembled a bundle, one of each plus a pair of white socks.

"This should all fit, I'll be right here if there's anything wrong, just shout."

I wondered if it was ethical for him to be alone with me in a room while I showered, but there wasn't exactly anyone around to complain to. I showered quickly, a little on edge, but Dr Hawkins stayed around the corner out of sight. I dried off with the cheap thin towel and got dressed. It felt good to be properly clean again. I remembered what Charlie had said about water naturally grounding me and I closed my eyes to check my shield. It sparkled a little, clean and strong.

When I walked back around the corner towards the door, Dr Hawkins was sitting reading my notebook, which I'd left on a bench. I stopped for a moment, shocked. It felt wrong, but it shouldn't have. I knew he was going to read it, I'd written in it to help our sessions, but it still felt like I'd caught him reading my diary. He looked up and gave me the fixed smile again.

"Ah Eoin, good, just put the old clothes in the blue hamper, the towels in the white one."

I shook my head and did as he said, trying to dispel the sense of unease I was feeling. Once everything was tidied away, he opened the door and waved me out, still holding on to the notebook. Seeing it in his hand as we walked along made my palms itch. We walked back to his office and I lay down on the couch. Dr Hawkins sat in his usual chair, steepled his fingers and seemed to consider me.

"Eoin, I've read your notes, and I want to thank you for writing them. I know it must have been hard, and you certainly seem to have been thorough in your descriptions."

"I thought it was important to be honest, if I'm going to get better."

I got the fixed smile again.

"Now, tell me about the, things, that slashed you. What did they say?"

"Say? Em, nothing. I didn't really hear voices from them. I just got this terrible impression of hate and violence."

"Hmm, and you haven't heard any voices, words specifically, since our last session?"

"No. Well, just before I blacked out, I thought I heard a voice say thank you, but that's it."

"Thank you? What where they thanking you for?"

"I don't know, I didn't exactly get a chance to ask them."

"Of course, of course. And there's been no sign of Charlie?"

"No. Is that bad?"

"Oh not at all Eoin, your mind is trying to process your new environment, but once you've settled, perhaps Charlie will return and we can talk to him."

I raised an eyebrow.

"You want to talk to Charlie?"

This got another smile. "Oh yes, very much so."

The phone on Dr Hawkins desk gave a short, warbling ring.

"Excuse me Eoin."

He went to the desk, lifting the receiver and speaking softly. When he was done he hung up and looked to me.

"It seems that your mother is a little early, what do you say we cut our session short rather than keep her waiting?"

I jumped up from the couch.

"Yes! I mean, yes please, I'd like that."

As he looked down at me, eager and excited to see my mum, his smile turned true, just for a second. I almost went to run to the door before I realised there was no point, as I had no idea where we were going. So I let Dr Hawkins lead me down the hallway, even further away from the ward. He seemed to walk so slowly, I practically jittered beside him, so eager to see Mum.

An orderly was standing at one of the doors up ahead. Dr Hawkins nodded to him and he stepped away. Dr Hawkins placed his hand on the door handle, but paused, looking back at me.

"You have half an hour Eoin. I'll come and get you when the time is up, but otherwise I'll leave you two alone."

He opened the door and waved me in. I shook a little as I walked into the room. There was a part of me that thought that all the nice parts of my life were in my head, that Mum would turn out to be just a dream as well. But there she was, sitting on a battered old black leather couch in front of a chipped wooden coffee table. She was wringing her hands together with a watery smile on her face. I could practically see her trying not to jump up and grab me. She stood slowly not wanting to startle me. I could see it was killing her to be still but she was doing it because she thought that's what I needed. Every thought I think I couldn't love Mum any more, well.

"Hi Eoin." she said, with only the smallest quiver in her voice.

"Hi Mum, are you ok?"

Her smile grew a little more genuine at that, and her eyes watered.

"Yes, I'm fine."

I walked over and gave her a hug before she shook herself apart with the effort of not seeking one. She held on to me as if she was never going to let go, stroking my hair. Eventually her grip loosened enough for me to breathe. She pulled back a little to look down at me and tears were running down her cheeks.

"I've missed you." She said, her fingers reaching to stroke my cheek.

"I've missed you too Mum."

She had a big bag of books for me, including new ones and some puzzle books. I told her I was glad to have them as it was a little boring here. That was her cue to ever so gently grill me about how I'd been and what had been happening.

I didn't tell her everything, obviously. I couldn't see a conversation that started with "Well yesterday I blasted imaginary spirits to stop the screaming in my head." ending well. But I said the food was ok, and that I had been very confused at the start, but that Dr Hawkins was working really hard with me, and we had sessions every day, and I was... hopeful.

"Oh! I never brought your meds, do they have you on the same ones here?"

"Mum, I'm not on any meds."

To call the look she gave me sceptical would be wasting a prime opportunity to use the word incredulous.

"And you're... ok? There haven't been any..."

"No voices so far, but that doesn't mean there won't be. I have to accept the problem before I can solve it, and it's not going to be easy."

She looked confused.

"You seem so, together."

"It's amazing what you can accomplish when you're not doped out of your mind."

I regretted the words as soon as I saw the hurt flash across her face.

"Mum, I didn't, I mean. What you... you did the best you could. I don't think anyone thought the best way for me to get better would be to take away the medicine."

She sat holding my hands, welling up. As she spoke, her voice breaking, another tear escaped and rolled down her cheek.

"If...if I'd just known, I'm so sorry Eoin. I'm so, so sorry."

I leaned forward and hugged her tight.

"You don't have to be sorry Mum, you didn't do anything wrong."

I pulled back so I could look her in the eye.

"You did everything you could and I love you, I

wouldn't be doing this well if it wasn't for you."

She sighed and her shoulders relaxed a little, and she looked a little less like she could fall apart at any minute.

"It's just, it was so scary, walking in and seeing you talk to Charlie, just like you used to. I thought that was it, that there was no way I could help. And it hurt as well. I mean it always hurt, like keeping a picture of a painful memory, but I didn't medicate you just to make Charlie go away, I didn't. Please believe me Eoin, I really thought it was for the best."

She talking so fast I could barely keep up. It was like these words were all repressed inside her, and as soon as she let one out the rest came pouring along with it.

"It's ok Mum, I believe you."

I wasn't sure what it was that I was saying I believed, but it was obviously what she needed to hear as she calmed down a bit and just sat, looking at me and biting her lip.

There was a double knock at the door and then it opened. Dr Hawkins stuck his head in before entering.

"I'm afraid we'll have to cut it short Eoin, but your mother can come back next weekend."

Mum turned, eyes wide. "Next weekend? Can't I visit sooner?"

"I really do recommend as little contact as possible while we begin Eoin's treatment, Mrs Murphy. Why don't we arrange a phone call for Wednesday evening, say around eight? Then you can come back next Sunday and we can see how he's doing."

Mum hugged me tight and then pulled back to look at me "Is that ok with you, Eoin?"

I smiled and tried to look as calm and reassuring as I could "Yes Mum, it's for the best."

She nodded, biting her lip.

"Ok then."

She kissed my head and hugged me some more before she left. Dr Hawkins told her the orderly would show her out. Once she was gone Dr Hawkins turned to me.

"Good visit?"

"It was good to see her, yes, I think she worries that she's abandoned me. I tried to tell her how much better I was feeling here."

"Good, good." He patted my back and moved me towards the door.

"Well, let's get you back to your room."

I carried the big cloth bag full of books as we walked back down the corridors. Dr Hawkins didn't lock me in the room, which was a good sign. I killed some time lining the books up against the wall under the window, arranging them until I found an order I was happy with. It was a lot of books. I was going to be here for some time.

18

That afternoon I asked to be brought to the recreation room. I was a little worried I wouldn't be allowed after the incident in the hallway, but the orderly just picked up his clipboard and checked something before nodding and picking up the phone on his desk. He asked for an escort from 'A ward' to the rec room. He listened for a second, then hung up and looked up at me.

"He'll be here in a minute, just wait there." His voice was gravelly. He had a stony look all over actually, from the angles on his bald head to his lumpy, muscly arms.

"I want to go too."

The soft little voice startled me, but that's nothing compared to what it did to the orderly. He almost jumped out of his skin as his eyes went wide and locked on to something behind me.

"Now Miranda, what are you doing out of your room?"

"The door was unlocked. I want to go to the recreation

room."

Her voice was soft and gentle, like she was singing a little song to herself and not talking to us at all. I turned slowly and saw her standing behind me, a lot closer than I thought she was. She was just a little shorter than me, but really thin, like she'd been stretched out. Her hair was a black, tangled mess hanging half way down to her waist. The curtain of darkness contrasted against her skin, which was pale in a highly unhealthy way that would take a goth girl two hours and a lot of makeup to achieve. The crumpled, pale blue t-shirt and sweat pants were the only real colour on her. She was just standing there. She had a faraway look in her eyes, even though she was staring right at the orderly. Her hands hung limply at her side, and when I looked at her I could almost see her swaying slightly.

The orderly didn't even look at his clipboard, he just held his palm out to her as if warding her off.

"Now, Miranda, you know you're not cleared to go to the rec room."

"How would I know that? I've never asked for a wreck before." She smiled and giggled a little. Her smile was beautiful. It was the smile of someone discovering ice cream after a lifetime of only bread. It was a smile of utter joy.

"I never asked… oh! But I can now, so I am, can I go to the wreck room please?"

She swung her hands gently back and forth as she made her request in her little sing song voice.

I saw the orderly's brow furrow.

"What? Look, I'll ask Dr Hawkins. Why don't you go back to your room so that everyone's nice and safe?"

He still had one hand stretched out towards her and he was slowly moving out from behind his desk.

"Why don't you just call Dr Hawkins and see if she's allowed?"

It actually took me a second to realise I had spoken. I didn't know why I'd spoken up, it had just kind of come out.

"Look kid, just stay calm and everything will be ok."

He was talking like a bomb was about to go off, but it was just me and this strange girl. She must have been half my weight, she definitely couldn't have been older than me, and she was just standing there looking like a Wednesday Adams limited edition mental hospital action figure. I couldn't understand what had him so spooked.

"Why don't you just call him? I will if you won't." I took a step towards his desk

"Don't!" He waved his hand at me "No. Sudden. Moves."

This was really beginning to weird me out.

"Ok Miranda, I'm going to call Dr Hawkins and we'll get this all sorted, ok?"

Miranda smiled at him as if she knew something he didn't, then giggled. "Ok!"

She turned to me and her smile warmed. "You're so blue, I like you."

I looked down at my blue clothes and then at hers. "You're pretty blue yourself."

She giggled and blushed, holding her hand up to her mouth. It was actually nice to see a little colour fill her cheeks.

"Dr Hawkins? It's Earl Jenkins. Miranda is out of her room. She's stationary at the moment but I don't know for how long...what? ... No she just asked to go to the rec room... No, with the Murphy boy, she wanted to go with him... Seriously?... Well I can ask Frank to take them both but I can't say he will, I know I wouldn't... what? ... No Sir, I'm sorry Sir, yes I'll let Frank know."

Jenkins looked at the phone receiver as if it had just transformed into a miniature Bolivian folk singer before putting it back down and turning to Miranda.

"Dr Hawkins says you can go to the rec room Miranda. Just one hour though, Frank will be here in a minute to bring you."

"Yay!" Miranda jumped up and down and clapped her

hands. I could have been wrong, but I thought I saw Jenkins flinch. Just then the door buzzed and another orderly walked in. He was a little less bulky that Jenkins, same shaved head, but a close cropped black beard. He stopped dead when he saw Miranda.

"What the hell is she doing out?"

"Don't know, but Doc Hawkins wants you to bring these two to the rec room for an hour." Jenkins eyes didn't move from Miranda as he talked. She was twisting her head, as if listening to something, and she was grinning from ear to ear.

"You have got to be kidding me, he wants me to leave the boy alone with her?"

"No you idiot, stay with them for the hour."

"But what if she… you know?"

"Well I guess you'll have to keep a close eye on them."

"This is crazy!"

"This is what we've been told, you wanna call the Doc and tell him 'No'?" Jenkins picked up the receiver of the phone and held it out to Frank without looking at him.

"Fine… but I'm not happy."

"If you were happy Frank then you'd be in the wrong job."

Both of them kept their eyes on Miranda as Frank went to the door and held it open.

"Ok you two, out and to the left, stay ahead where I can see you."

Miranda skipped out the door, humming to herself. I saw Frank move back as she passed. He spoke without looking at me.

"You coming, boy?"

Part of me didn't want to. This was seriously freaking me out. I mean, they were acting like this girl was a psycho killer. She didn't exactly look like she was playing with a full deck of cards, but I didn't get a sense of danger off her, not like with some, not like with Declan. Eventually it was curiosity that made me step through the door. There really wasn't that much to do here. Even if

Miranda was a psycho, I might as well see what happened.

The journey to the rec room was an unusual one. It involved Miranda skipping ahead, waving her hands from side to side then standing and giggling to herself. Occasionally she would bounce up and down a little as she waited for Frank and I to catch up. Sometimes I would watch her waiting and I'd see her swaying gently to herself, as if she was listening to music that only she could hear. I turned to look back at Frank.

"Is she always like this?"

He answered me, but like before, he never took his eyes off Miranda.

"No, this is new."

His hands were down by his side, but he was making fists and then relaxing them, over and over. He kept behind me at all times, which effectively meant he kept me between himself and Miranda. This seemed like something I should be concerned about. Ahead, I heard a fractured giggle as Miranda took a left turn.

"Is she even going the right way to the rec room?"

"What? Yeah, she's heading straight there."

"But I thought she'd never been before?"

"Look kid, I don't know, maybe she just got lucky, maybe the fairies are telling her where to go, let's just get there and get through this and maybe we can both keep our noses."

I scrunched up my face. Wasn't I supposed to be the one who wasn't making sense? As I followed Miranda around the corner Frank hung back. Maybe he was waiting to see if she jumped out and killed me, but when I turned the corner she was just standing there, about ten feet away. She was looking right at me, smiling with a look of pure joy, her eyes sparkling. It made me stop and stare at her. At first I thought she must be smiling at whatever crazy things she was seeing in her head, but she was looking me right in the eye. That smile was just for me, and that made me more than a little uneasy.

I thought I might stand there forever, caught in the light

of that smile. But she bit her lip and giggled, the spell breaking as she turned and skipped to a door at the end of the hall. It was a secure door with wire glass filling the top half. She just stood at the glass, stroking it, smiling as if it was the most beautiful thing it the world, then she spotted something through the glass.

"Oh! They have checkers! Can we play checkers?!"

She spun, addressing the last part to me. I looked to Frank for guidance but he was wearing the stupefied expression of a man not only watching a dog walk on its hind legs, but also operating a microwave and get itself a ready meal.

"Emm… yeah… I guess so."

"YAY!!"

Miranda's voice screeched so high that I'm surprised my ears didn't bleed. I heard a scuffle behind me and when I turned I saw Frank with his hands held out in front of him as if he was about to wrestle.

"Aren't you going to let us in Frank?" she asked in her sing song voice, looking at him with her eyes lowered, a creepy smile on her lips.

"Ok, just… get in the corner, both of you, and I'll unlock the door. I'm going to be at the orderly station keeping an eye on you both in case… well, I'm going to be right there."

I retreated to the corner. Miranda followed me, trailing her fingers along the wall as if it were a summer stream, then she leaned into the corner, staring at me with her joy filled smile again. I watched Frank fumble with a set of keys. Initially he tried to find the right one while still looking at us, but then he looked down at the ring hanging at his hip and started sorting through them.

"What's your name?"

Her voice was barely a whisper. I almost questioned if I'd heard it at all, but I turned to her nonetheless.

"Eoin, my name is Eoin."

I had thought that her face was lit with all the joy there was in the world. I had been wrong, because when I told her my name it was like a star burst beneath her skin and a pale light suffused her features. She leaned in swiftly and kissed my cheek. The sudden feel of her lips against my skin froze me in place. Her lips were dry and cold. She pressed them against me all pursed up and then pulled back, as if she wasn't sure how to kiss, or if I would fight her. It was quick and perfunctory, but when her lips touched me, a shock ran through my entire body. I felt like she'd taken a live wire and slid it straight through my shield, brushing it against my core. It was electrifying and rejuvenating. It made me feel so alive that I thought I might die. It lasted less than a second and it left me panting. I looked into her eyes, the palest I had ever seen, a blue so pale that they almost blended into the white surrounding them. I stared into those eyes and I was lost.

"Thank you Eoin. Thank you so, so much."

As the whisper of her voice filled my ears, I remembered where I had heard her voice before, and I knew exactly who Miranda was.

"Yay!"

She dashed off and through door just as Frank got it open. He reeled back, desperately trying to stay out of her way. He stared after her, shaking his head. It took him a few seconds before he remembered I was there and turned to beckon me through the door. I tried to remember how to walk and stumbled through the door, not knowing what I was going to face. In truth it was a bit of an anti-climax. It was a large room, maybe twice as long and wide as the classrooms in school, with a large desk bolted to the floor in the corner beside the door, and multiple sets of tables and chairs around the room. I smiled as I saw that one wall was full of bookshelves. In the corner opposite the desk Miranda was throwing boxes out of a cupboard. They landed behind her, dice and pieces scattering everywhere. After about four more smashes, she crowed victoriously and bounced out of the cupboard waving a box.

"Checkers!" She set her face in what I thought might be

a stern expression and her voice became deadly serious. "I'm red."

Miranda set up the checkers board on one of the tables. Her hands jerked back and forth in a hurry, rushing to finish. Frank sat behind the desk in the corner by the door, but he didn't relax. He sat, ramrod straight, hands fidgeting on the desk, watching us. When I turned back to Miranda she was seated at one side of the board, bouncing impatiently.

"Come on! This is when we play!"

I walked towards the table and went to pull the chair out, but it wouldn't move. It was bolted to the floor, so was the table. They really didn't trust us much. I slid awkwardly into the chair and looked across the board at Miranda.

"You go first, but I win." she said.

"Em... I think either of us could win, that's the point of the game."

She almost collapsed in a fit of giggles.

"You're so funny. Sometimes you win, but I've seen this one, and in this one I win. You go now."

Trying to follow a conversation with her made my head hurt, as I tried to twist my brain into a space that wouldn't fit, so I settled for moving my piece instead. She moved hers almost before I'd finished moving mine, her hand darting out to move the piece before pulling quickly back to her side of the board. I thought for a second and then went to move another piece. As I did Miranda's hand darted out to move one of her pieces beside mine. Her little finger trailed along the edge of my hand, and it made me shiver with goosebumps. I jumped a little, which only made her laugh. I could feel myself blushing.

"Miranda... your room is at the end of the hall, isn't it?"

She cocked her head to the side and looked at me.

"You know it is. You were outside it when you rescued me."

She took one of my pieces but left herself open, I quickly took two of hers.

"You remember me? I... I thought you were screaming, but I don't think anyone else heard you, so it must have been in my head."

She moved again. She didn't seem to have any tactic, her moves were too quick, without thought, maybe she was just moving randomly.

"It was in your head, but it was in my head too. Thank you for making them stop."

"Your wel...hold on, how can you scream inside my head? It was just in my head, it wasn't real."

"Just because you're the only one who knows something doesn't make it not real, it makes it a secret."

She took another piece. I sat and stared at her for a second, wondering if none of this was happening and it was all an elaborate dream. I was really still asleep in my room a few corridors away, no, it was all a dream and I was asleep in my real room. But when did the dream start? If I woke up, would it be any better? I felt a great big hole start to open up underneath me and start to drag me down.

"Don't get lost!"

Her shout of alarm shocked me out of my thoughts.

"Sorry, what?"

"You're getting lost, we are here and this is now, don't get lost. Also, it's your go. You move that piece now."

I looked down at the board. That was actually the best move for me. I moved it, slowly.

"Miranda, why were you screaming?"

She froze. With her hand still on the checker piece, she became a statue, not a muscle twitched, not a breath of air moved between us, and then I heard her whisper.

"They hurt me. They always hurt me. Thank you for making them go away. I don't know if this is a dream, I haven't had one in so long, but even if it is a dream, we are here and this is now, and now is when I'm happy."

She looked up from the board, and tears flowing down her cheeks and around her smile as she spoke.

"Thank you for making me happy."

"Oh... em... you're welcome. I just... you're welcome."

I look back down at the board to hide my embarrassment, making my move. Her hand darts out, moving one of her pieces back.

"Would you, I mean, I'm very grateful, but, will you be keeping them away tonight?"

I looked up. She sat there biting her lip, looking for all the world like a puppy that is expecting a kick.

"Miranda, I… I don't really know if I can, my door might be locked and… I really, I don't know ho-"

She interrupted me with a shake of her head and quickly looked down.

"It's ok, it was greedy of me to ask. I should be happy for this gift, and I am."

She looked back up, her tear stained face full of joy again.

"Besides… I win the game!"

I looked down at the board, and as I did, her hand darted out and moved one of her pieces in seven quick jumps, back and forth across the board, taking every one of my men. And then there was only the claps and the giggling.

19

We played another game. That one was quieter as I tried to pay more attention to her moves. It turned out she was really good at checkers. I won the second game, she won the third. She clapped and giggled at the end of each game, even the one I won. I snuck a peek at Frank every now and then. He stayed behind the desk, eyeing us like animals in the zoo, occasionally scratching his stubbled chin in thought.

"Miranda." I said, as she smiled and giggled her way through a fourth game. "Do you know how to shield?"

"Is that when you put your little man in front of your big man to stop me jumping over them?"

"What? No, I mean, it's a way to stop... things, from hurting you."

I almost didn't go on. I was supposed to be getting better, not pandering to my delusions. But Dr Hawkins did tell me to use what Charlie had thought me. But if it was all in my head, what was the point of telling Miranda about it, and if it was all in my head, why did Miranda think I'd saved her? In the end I decided to talk to her about it anyway.

"It's like a mental exercise that helps...calm you."

"Oh I don't like running too hard, they always catch you anyway."

"No, it's not that kind of exercise... it's in your head and it helps keep it quiet."

She smiled and shook her head, staring down at the board.

"You can't put anything in your head, your brain's already in there, although I suppose if you put something in there instead of your brain it would get very quiet indeed."

I ducked my head down, trying to catch her eye.

"No... you're not understanding me!"

I heard a slight rustle as Frank sat up straight, ready to jump towards us. I didn't know if he was worried that I'd raised my voice or moving in anticipation of how Miranda would react. Miranda just sat and gave me a new smile, this one was sad and knowing.

"Oh my poor knight, I think you'll find it's you who does not understand me."

"Knight?"

"Yes, you came at night, to end my plight, my timid knight."

Her voice moved up and down as always. Usually it seemed out of place, but now it was like everything gently slipped into where it should be. Her words were beautiful, delivered as they were by a voice that sang.

"Beautiful." It took me a second to realise I'd said that out loud, but Miranda just looked up and held my gaze for a time that should have been uncomfortable, but wasn't. When she spoke I almost jumped in my seat.

"Yes, you were. The most beautiful thing that I can still remember."

"No, I meant… never mind."

I thought about her words and an idea struck me.

"Miranda, when I banished the dark could you… see my light?"

"Oh yes, it filled the room and made me feel whole."

"Ok, good, could you see my-" I thought about how to describe my shield "My armour, could you see my armour?"

"Mmhmm, it was the most beautiful blue, a blue that was truly you."

"Ok, well, my armour stops the dark from hurting me. Would you like me to teach you how to have your own armour?"

She stopped moving her piece and reached forward to take my hand. She gripped so tightly, but it didn't hurt, instead I felt my mouth go dry and I started to tingle all over.

"Oh surly knight, if you could teach me how to shroud myself I think I would love you even more than I am going to."

"Eh, steady on."

I would have taken my hand from hers if my body had let me, but it had very definite ideas about not moving away from her.

"Ok, I'll try to teach you."

Maybe it would help her, maybe it was crazy, but what was there to lose?

"How shall I shroud myself in light, my knight?"

Her smile lifted a little further on one side. I would have accused her of making fun of me, had I been able to keep up with what she said. As it was, I was starting to zone out on the words, listening only to the way her voice sang them.

"Mmm… I mean, yeah ok. First of all sit with your eyes closed, try to be as relaxed as possible."

Miranda bit her lip and shook her head.

"If I close my eyes I'll get lost."

"Why will you get lost?"

She leaned forward and whispered.

"I will not know the here and now, I will get lost in the dark behind my eyes."

This was not going to be easy.

"But, I'll be talking, all the time, and you'll be able to hear me, and I'm in the here and now, so… if you hear me, you can't be lost. Right?"

The logic seemed tenuous even to me, but she seemed to consider it and then nodded her head happily.

"But you'll have to hold my hand so I don't get lost, my mom always said I wouldn't get lost if I held her hand."

As she talked, she squeezed my hand a little, and I realised how her grip had become gentle without me knowing.

I thought about how best to do this.

"Right, sit up, relax your shoulders, and close your eyes. I won't let you get lost." I said, squeezing her hand back.

I watched her take a deep breath, before she let her eyelids close. Her hand gripped mine tightly as she did, but relaxed a little as I kept talking.

"Concentrate on your breathing. Don't try to change it, just listen to it, listen to the sound the air makes as it enters and leaves your body. Listen to it as it moves, in and out, over and over. With each breath you should feel more and more relaxed, each breath, in and out, over and over."

I watched her shoulders lower a little and her face start to soften. I hadn't realised how tight all her muscles were. She sat smiling dreamily.

"I want you to imagine that all around your skin is a layer of light. Like wisps of fog, barely there, but covering you from head to toe, can you see it in your mind Miranda?"

"Mmm, yes. It's like a fluffy cloud, but it's all icky, it's not a happy cloud."

"What colour is your cloud?"

"It's grey. Oh… that's sad, but it's not supposed to be grey, it's grey because it's tired. There's bits of… oh… yes, there's bits of bright yellow, swimming in the grey, like little fishes. Oh, they're so pretty!"

"Ok, don't get lost Miranda, listen to my voice. I want you to imagine the mist coming in close to your body, pressing in tight, like a blanket. Can you do that?"

"Mmhmm. Oh Eoin it's lovely and warm, oh and the yellow bits like it, they got brighter!"

"Ok Miranda, hold that blanket tight against you, this is the important part, I want you to ha-"

"Times up, and stop holding hands, there's not supposed to be any touching." Frank reached down and gave me a rough tug at the elbow, pulling my hand out of Miranda's grip.

"No! We're doing something, it's important!"

Frank pulled me up by the arm "Yeah yeah, I'm sure it is, but it's time to go back to your-"

Miranda's scream made us both jump. She bent over the table, her face buried in her hands.

"Can't see! Lost! No it's not… that came before… I don't like that part… Eoin!"

I turn to go to her but Frank pulls me back.

"I knew it was only a matter of time. Stay back kid, she's dangerous."

I pushed against Frank but he held me back with ease.

"Eoin! I can't find me, where's the here, please, don't leave me!"

"Miranda, it's ok, listen to my voice, I'm right here, you can be too, just... just follow my voice home. Can you do that? Just like, a thread, just follow the thread home Miranda, I'm right here."

Miranda twisted and thrashed on the chair, banging her elbows on the table, her hands still gripping her face.

"It's ok Miranda, it's all ok, we are here and this is now, this is when you are happy, remember? It's after the one where you win, do you remember Miranda?"

Frank started pulling me towards the door but I was pushing against him.

"Eoin? Oh... I... yes... it's after I win but before it hurts. I don't like it when it hurts, is it much before it hurts? I hope so."

"Frank, please, stop, she's ok now. Look at her... look!"

Frank stopped pulling me long enough to turn and look at Miranda. She sat, her body heaving a little as she breathed, but her breaths were slowing. As we watched her breathing settled into a steady rhythm, her arms relaxed and she looked around in confusion, until her eyes caught mine and she broke out into a smile.

"Oh! Found you!"

Frank stopped trying to push me out the door. The only sound from him was a confused "Huh."

"She's fine now, can we finish what we were doing?"

"What? No, no canoodlin'. Besides, time's up, back to your rooms."

Frank unlocked the door and stood to one side, waiting for us to exit. I wanted to refuse to leave, I stood there with my arms crossed, staring him down. He had just raised an eyebrow at me when I felt a shivery touch on my shoulder. I turned to look into Miranda's eyes. They looked less pale than before, a few tiny flakes of blue standing out against the white. She held my gaze before blushing and turning her head, hiding behind a fall of her midnight hair, peeking at me through the tangles.

"It's ok, we were never going to have time, but it was nice to try. We leave now, or possibly then... but whenever we do, it will be ok Eoin, it really will."

With that confusing pot of wordage, she walked out. She wasn't skipping anymore, she just walked quietly, staring down at her hands clasped in front of her. Frank seemed more at ease now than with her earlier behaviour. He was more relaxed as we walked back, though he still let her go ahead. I went to catch up with her.

"Miranda, I'm sorry, maybe we can try again tomorrow?"

"We will, he'll insist on it. It's strange though, I've spent forever in the burning dark, one day as painful as the next, and I thought all I wanted was to be saved by the light. But if the dark will just come to tear me once again, then I wish I had not known today. To have loved and lost is not always better."

Sometimes I wasn't sure if she was talking to me or just reciting poetry, it was difficult to follow the winding path of her words to find the meaning.

"You'll be ok Miranda, just get to tomorrow."

"Oh I will, and I am ever so happy tomorrow. I just wish there was a way to tomorrow that wasn't through tonight."

20

When we reached the door to our ward, we stood back to let Frank swipe his card, then went in as he held the door open. We walked in to find Dr Hawkins standing there, his hands in the pockets of his brown suit trousers, his tie a little loose against his white shirt, looking at us over his glasses.

"Eoin, I see you've met Miranda. You two certainly seem to be getting on well."

"I won!" Miranda said brightly.

Dr Hawkins smiled like a blank page.

"Of course you did, dear."

Miranda gave Dr Hawkins a puzzled look.

"Do things have to go before they can be talked about?"

"Speaking of talking, since you're up and about why don't we go and have a little talk? We can talk about how things went, would you like that?"

Miranda covered her mouth with her hand.

"Oops! That was the when, but… yes. I'm here, so yes."

"Right, well, let's go have a chat then. It's quite alright Frank, I'm sure we'll be fine. Eoin, I'll see you tomorrow, enjoy your dinner."

Dr Hawkins walked to the door as it buzzed, waving Miranda out as she chattered.

"Do you like my yellow fish? They're getting bigger. Eoin gave them to me, they get eaten all up but I'm hoping to win some more tomorrow and then I'll be officially yellow… hehe… oh-fish… I'll be oh-fishally-"

The door closed on her giggles. Jenkins looked at me over the desk.

"Right kid, dinner's in your room, leave the tray outside when you're done."

I walked down the corridor and into my room, but instead of going for the tray, I stood at the threshold and listened.

"Well? How did it go? Did she try to eat the kid? Is the room still in one piece?"

"Earl, it was the weirdest thing. I took them both down there and she was skipping like a schoolgirl, freaked me the hell out. She spent the whole time laughing and giggling."

"That crazy giggle she does between screams, the broken one?"

"No man, this was different, she sounded happy. I don't know what drugs he has her on but long may it last."

"She didn't cause any trouble?"

"Well, she freaked out a little when I made them leave, but no biting or scratching, the kid talked her down."

"Seriously?"

"Yeah, I think she has a crush on him, had to stop them holding hands."

"Poor boy, he's lucky he kept all his fingers."

I stepped over to my bed and looked at the tray there. A metal cover hid mashed potato, carrots and a mystery meat. There was a plastic mug of milk and plastic cutlery. Looking at it all made me feel twelve. I ate dinner on autopilot, my mind too busy processing the events of the day to pay attention to the food. Why did the orderlies think Miranda was so dangerous? I suppose if she spent most of her time as crazy as when Frank made us leave, I'd be scared too. I didn't know if she had a crush on me or it was just hero worship, she did keep calling me her knight. But there was that kiss. I replayed the kiss over and over in my mind. Whenever I tried to think about something else it would pull me back, the feeling of her lips on my cheek, but more importantly, the feeling of my entire body tingling with electricity. I liked that feeling and couldn't help but want to feel it again. But was the feeling real or just in my head? And did I really want to get involved with someone who might be incredibly unstable? It wasn't enough that I was crazy and that my doctor wanted to cure me with my own delusions, I had to go and fall for a girl even crazier than me.

It must have been only six or seven when I placed the empty dinner tray on the floor outside my room, but when I lay down on the bed, I felt myself drifting off right away. Before I slept, I reached out with my mind to touch against my shield. The solid feel of it all around me was comforting, even if it was a delusion. Just before the darkness took me, just before I slipped into a blissfully restful sleep, I thought... how did Miranda know my aura was blue?

21

The sea crashed against the cliffs, sending white spray up into the air around me. My horse stood making soft harrumphing noises beneath me, far too well trained to react to the crashing waves, but restless to be off. One hand released his rein to steady the pommel of the sword at my hip, and as my arm moved I heard gentle clinks as bits of armour moving against each other. I looked down at my metal covered arm, gleaming brightly in the sun, with the tiniest hint of blue in its sheen. I looked around me at the desolate, rocky land atop the cliffs. The wind blew across rocky outcrops and patches of scrub, carrying the clean scent of life. I turned my naked face to the wind, letting the new scent mix with the salt of the sea, and that was wrong. Didn't knights wear helmets? But then how would people see my face, which was important, wasn't it? Behind a mask I could be anyone, and it was very important that I be me, yes, that much I knew. With a sudden turn of its neck my steed whinnied, looking towards a distant hill. I shaded my eyes against the sun, the steel of my gauntlet cooling my forehead. There was a tree at the top of the hill, all alone, a tiny black stain against the blue sky. A black tree? Yes, a black tree with black birds, I could see them, little black... No... not little, huge, with wings as wide as the tree, three of them swooping around the tree, before diving down as if to attack it. Why were giant black birds attacking a tree? And then the scream reached my ears. It spoke of pain, it spoke of torment, it spoke of never ending terror. It was a scream I'd heard before, but it had a new note now, for now it screamed of loss.

"Miranda!"

I kicked my heels against my steed and he seemed to

explode forwards, one moment standing on the cliff top, the next galloping across the rocky terrain. The scream continued as we rushed toward the hill, on and on without end, until no human lungs could possibly have supported it. My heart wrenched within my chest to hear it, my chest filling with pain, I slumped forward in my saddle. Pulling myself up, I gritted my teeth. I could not falter, I could not fail, I was her knight and would prevail. The words flowed through my head liltingly.

My steed stumbled, his hooves becoming bogged down in the suddenly muddy earth. He slowed and then stopped, trying to free himself. I dismounted, pulling him forward by his reigns, urging him, but he fell to his knees. I desperately tried to pull him out, but my armour weighed heavy on my arms and made it hard to move. My steed whinnied in fear as the mud began to take him, sucking him down. He twisted his body but only sank quicker. His whinnies seemed to turn to screams that mixed with Miranda's. Twisting around each other until they were both screaming the same word. They were screaming my name. I turned to see Miranda on the hilltop. She was tied around her waist to the tree, dressed in her blue ward clothes, and I could see long slashes across her arms and legs where she had tried to defend herself. She was surrounded by a grey mist. It kept moving towards her, wrapping around her, but then one of the … oh God they were dragons. Black as night and as big as a house. As soon as the mist started wrapping around Miranda, one would swoop in and slash at her with its claws, leaving a fresh spatter of blood on the rocks, scattering the mist once more.

I turned back to my steed, his body deep in the mud now, his neck thrashing. I reached for him, looked into his eye, and then I heard him.

Eoin! Eoin wake up! It's important please wake up!

Charlie?

Charlie was my steed? And he was screaming at me just like Miranda was. Why was Charlie scared? I looked down into the horse's eyes, and the light darkened around me as his eyes filled with fear, and changed into human eyes as black as mine. Darker and darker, the light leeching from the world, until I looked up to see the shadow of a dragon above me, eclipsing the sun, plunging me into darkness.

I woke screaming with the feeling of claws slicing open my stomach, tearing me open and spilling my insides out. I screamed in agony, it was pain unlike any I had ever experienced. I curled up in a ball on my bed but the pain went on. As I filled the air with pain I could hear other screams answering. There was one of terror and one of pain and more of malice. When I took a breath to scream some more, I felt like I would drown in them.

There were words in the screams, or at least in some of them. I felt claws rip open one side of my leg, leaving a long line of burning agony from my hip to my knee. It was unbearable.

Leave h... *Eoin!...* **not his...** *stay...* **Please!..** *sorry!*

The words screamed through my mind, but they were nothing compared to the pain tearing through my body. I tried to breathe, I tried to focus on the words and pick them out from amongst the screams of rage and evil.

Eoin! Just hold on. You can do it, try to sh-

I screamed as acid spread across my face, I could feel it burning my flesh away. I held my head in my hands and screamed until I felt my throat go raw. I clawed at my face, trying to get it off. I rolled, falling off the bed. Pain shot through my back as I landed on the floor but I didn't notice, because the burning acid was crawling down my throat. It was burning me from the inside out, and no matter how long or how hard I screamed, it wasn't enough to let the pain out.

The metal door smacked against my head as it opened, and then there were hands, more hands to hurt me. I thrashed and kicked. I felt an arm go around my neck and I arched my back trying to bite it, everywhere they touched burned more. I kicked and screamed and punched, trying to get away. The tiny stab in my leg was lost in all the other pain, but it was the last thing I remembered.

22

I woke with a horrible feeling, a feeling I knew well. It's the one you get deep in your gut when you've woken up and realise you have to face another day of pain. I groaned softly. Before opening my eyes, I did a quick mental checklist. I could feel all my limbs, nothing was in actual pain, though my back was really tender. I opened my eyes and squinted against the morning light. It took a minute before I could open them fully. My clothes were stuck to me with sweat, though it was a little chilly.

I lay staring at the ceiling wishing I was dead.

Morning sunshine.

I tried to speak but only managed a croak, so I swallowed and tried again.

"You're back? I thought I might have imagined you."

No, I'm really here, and boy what a mess you've made since I was gone.

"Seriously? I'm lying here feeling like death run over and you're giving me shit?"

You bet I am, you really don't know the trouble you're in.

"Let me guess, I've attracted the attention of whatever spirits or demons were preying on Miranda and they've decided I'm much tastier, so I can look forward to a life of pain and torment?"

Eoin, this really isn't something to joke about, we're both in some serious trouble here.

"Wait... why are you in trouble?"

I'm not supposed to be here Eoin, I was um, warned away I

suppose. It's-

"Let me guess, it's complicated?"

Yeah.

I sighed and fell back on to the bed, closing my eyes.

"Go away, Charlie."

What? I-

"I said go away. In case you didn't notice, I'm exhausted and sore, so I'm really not in the mood to talk to you right now."

Right, I'll see you after lunch then?

I was tempted to tell him to go away for good, that I didn't want to hear him or his cryptic answers ever again, but with the words on the tip of my tongue my heart clenched in my chest and I couldn't.

"Just... yeah Charlie, after lunch."

I lay on the bed, enjoying the peace of the morning light. I couldn't tell if Charlie had actually gone away, but I didn't care. It was quiet and that was all that mattered. I tried not to think about what I'd gone through during the night, but it was coming back in stomach clenching flashes. As I remembered each slash, each cut, I could almost feel them happening again. I started concentrating on my breathing, trying to hold it together. Was this what life was like for Miranda, spending each night in a world of nightmares and every day reliving the wounds? No wonder she was broken.

Of course there was always the chance that this had nothing to do with Miranda and it was all in my head. I didn't know what to think, didn't know what to do. Either this was real and I was doomed to torment, or I was crazy, and doomed to imagined torment. And at this point, was there really any difference? I'd managed the strange things that had happened to me before, with Charlie's help. Whether it was all in my head or not, it led to me being happier, better able to cope and in no pain. Maybe I should listen to him. It was worth a try. After all, it was that or drugs, and I just didn't think that was going to work anymore.

The metal shutter shot back on the door and a pair of eyes looked in on me.

"You're awake then, you able for breakfast?"

I recognised Jenkins' voice.

My stomach turned a little at the mention of food, but I had to eat. If I had another night of screaming ahead of me, I'd need all the strength I could muster.

"Sure… why not… thanks."

I pulled myself into a sitting position at the edge of the bed and looked up as the door opened. Jenkins stood there with a tray in one hand. He moved carefully, leaning down to place the tray just inside the door, but keeping his eyes on me the whole time. He was looking at me like he looked at Miranda, oh God.

"Earl?"

He froze, looking at me warily.

"Yeah?"

"I'm sorry, if I hurt you. I mean, I don't know if you were on last night, but… not that I'm not sorry if I hurt someone else, just, aw God. I'm just… sorry."

He looked at me, inquisitive, calculating.

"Don't worry about it kid, part of the job. I wasn't on myself but I heard about it, no one was hurt."

I felt my shoulders drop and I let go of a piece of stress I hadn't realised I'd been holding on to.

"Good, thank you. I'll… try not to let it happen again."

That earned me a raised eyebrow.

"Sure, well, you do your best."

He went to close the door but stopped and looked me up and down instead.

"You want to head to the showers after breakfast?"

I looked down at my sweat stained clothes, then looked up and smiled.

"That sounds like a good idea, yeah."

"'K, just give me a shout when you finish and I'll get someone to bring you."

"Thanks Earl."

"Yeah, you're welcome."

He shook his head and closed the door. The scrape of metal as it locked made my head ache.

23

Breakfast this morning was toast and milk. I wondered if that was on purpose, if they knew I wouldn't be able for much. Maybe if I saw Miranda later I'd ask her what she'd had. Miranda! What happened to her after the dragons attacked me? Nothing if it was all in my head. I tried to ignore my thoughts long enough to eat breakfast. It was a struggle, but I managed it.

After breakfast I shouted through the door that I was finished. There was no answer. I sat on the bed. Maybe Earl wasn't there. He wasn't supposed to leave the ward unattended though, right? Or maybe he'd just changed his mind.

A heavy knock landed on the door.

"Step away!"

I scrambled back towards the toilet. The voice was deep, angry and unfamiliar. When the lock scraped and the door opened, a monster appeared. He was six foot and muscled, with close cropped hair, a squashed face and a broken nose. This was not a face that you wanted to make friends with.

"Shower time kid, move it."

He stood back to give me room to exit and followed me as I walked down towards Earl's desk. Earl gave me a nod and a smile but didn't say anything as he buzzed us through the ward door. My new companion was silent on the short walk to the showers. I took clean clothes from the cupboard along with a towel and headed to the shower cubicle, leaving Mr Grumpy broken nose leaning against the wall with a scowl on his face.

There was shampoo and shower gel in little pumps mounted on the shower wall. I was getting used to the scent of them, not bad, just different. Then I stood under the hot water with my hand jammed against the button that kept it going. I breathed slowly, in and out, focusing on the sounds of my breaths. I could feel the warm water sliding over me, through me, cleansing me, connecting me. I took all the different parts of me, who I was with Mum, who I was with Charlie, the part of me that felt so close to Miranda, I took every aspect of me and pulled them in tight to my center. It was a beautiful, smooth centred ball. It fit, it all finally fit.

"Hey, what you up to in there? I don't got all day. Out in the next minute or I'm coming in."

I let the water turn itself off as I finished grounding, and then raised a hard tight shield just against my skin. It wasn't as bright as I'd like it, but it was there and it slid easily into place. As I quickly dried myself off I realised that centering grounding and shielding today had been easier than ever before. Maybe I'd try doing it in the shower every day.

I'm sure it was more than a minute before I came round the corner to see Grumpy Face looking bored and restless, but I didn't mention it. He walked me back to the ward, scowl fixed and unchanging, and disappeared almost before the ward doors closed behind me.

"Is he always that cranky?"

Earl looked up and gave me a smile.

"He just doesn't like coming to 'A' Ward, not his favourite place."

It was then that something Frank had said clicked in my mind.

"Earl, did… did Miranda do that to his nose?"

Earl paused, scrunching up one side of his face.

"Eh, yeah, I wouldn't mention it though, he doesn't take it well. Anyway, Doc called. He'll be picking you up for a session before lunch, so he should be along in a few minutes."

"Oh… thanks."

I wandered in to my room and sat staring at the wall. I thought about Miranda, about the screams I'd heard my first day here, about how the orderlies seemed to fear her. Was she really dangerous? I mean they wouldn't have let me sit with her for that long if she was going to hurt me… would they? Frank certainly seemed to think it was a crazy idea, but he'd been told to do it. Dr Hawkins had told him to do it. Why? Why was Dr Hawkins making sure I talked to a crazy, unbalanced girl? Was it to show me what I could become, to scare me into cooperating? But I was already cooperating.

I looked at the diary, lying on the floor. I hadn't written about last night, hadn't had a chance. I supposed I could just tell him about it, as he'd arrive in a few minutes. I returned to staring at the wall… wondering… should I? Should I tell Dr Hawkins about the terrors in the night and Charlie's return? My head was swimming again, though it didn't seem to spend much time still these days. I resolved to stay the course. I just prayed that my behaviour last night hadn't persuaded him I couldn't be helped.

There was a gentle knock against my door. I looked up to see him standing there, looking all doctorly and concerned.

"Are you able for a session today, Eoin?"

His tone said it all, he wouldn't push. If I said I wasn't able, he would just walk away. But what would that mean? Would it be a sign that I was getting worse, that I needed to go back on drugs? I just didn't know.

"I think so, Dr Hawkins. Yeah, I should be fine."

He smiled. "Good, good. Well why don't we head to my office?"

He stood back to let me out of the room so I could walk ahead of him, just like the orderly had. He didn't want to walk beside me anymore, I felt myself tearing up as I realised this.

I trudged to the end of the corridor, barely nodding at

Earl as he buzzed us through the door. Dr Hawkins walked a little behind me all the way to his office. He had his hands in his pockets, strolling along as if on a morning stroll, but I knew he was doing it to keep me where he could see me.

I stopped at the door to his office and looked back at him.

"You can go in Eoin, it's open, just take a seat."

Sighing, I opened the door and went to the couch. I'd thought that Dr Hawkins was trying to build trust between us, but now it seemed that he didn't trust me enough to be near me. Although, considering the freak out last night, I couldn't blame him. I was so angry and frustrated I had to stop myself turning to bang my forehead repeatedly off the wall. I couldn't help but think that if I could knock myself unconscious, I might be able to get some brief respite.

"How are you feeling today, Eoin?"

I looked up to find him sitting in his usual seat, with a pad and pen in his hand. At least that hadn't changed, he hadn't even moved his chair further back.

"I don't feel so good Doctor."

"Oh, and why is that Eoin?"

I totally didn't shout "Well duh!" which I was proud of, instead I kept my voice calm.

"I think you know. I'm upset about what happened last night."

"What happened?"

I gave him a look so full of scorn than you could have opened up a scorn mine and sold it in buckets.

"You know what happened, Earl knows so I'm sure someone told you. I freaked out, and when people came in to try and help, I attacked them and had to be sedated."

"I know what I read in the report this morning Eoin, but I want to hear about it from your point of view. What was going on in your mind? What did you think was happening?"

"I... I had a bad dream." It could have been a dream.

"Tell me about it."

"I was riding across a rocky plain on a horse, towards a hill, to rescue… a girl, from dragons."

"Was the girl someone you knew?"

I knew he'd ask. "It was Miranda."

His pen scribbled furiously. "And what happened?"

"The dragons were attacking her, tearing her apart. I was riding my horse towards her but the ground became muddy and the horse started sinking into it. I got off and tried to pull him out but he just kept sinking and then when I looked into his eyes," I faltered, unsure of what to share.

"Go on Eoin, what happened when you looked into its eyes?" Dr Hawkins was smiling, leaning forward in his seat.

Well, I'd come this far.

"They were human eyes, and he spoke to me, in my mind. It was Charlie, the horse was Charlie."

"And what did he say Eoin?" His voice was gentle, careful.

"He tried to warn me. A shadow came over us, and when I looked up it was one of the dragons. It was on top of me and then I woke up, except I could feel it, tearing me apart, slicing me open. I screamed and screamed but it wouldn't go away. And then there were people in the room and everywhere they touched me there was more pain and… and then there was nothing."

I looked up expecting, I don't know, a shocked silence, a concerned face, but Dr Hawkins just sat scribbling away as if he had to get everything down or it would disappear. He talked without looking up.

"And this morning, how do you feel? Any pains?"

"No. I mean I'm a little sore, but a night of nightmares sore, not someone slici…" I grimaced at the memory of my stomach being sliced open searing through my mind.

"And voices, any voices?"

I sat, gripping the edge of the couch, my head and my heart warring with each other. Telling him that Charlie was back felt like a betrayal, but how could I betray a voice in my head?

"Eoin." Now he stopped scribbling. "Eoin, did you hear something this morning?"

I let the words spill from my lips, the barest mumble that felt like it would fall like a lead weight as soon as it left me.

"Charlie's back."

Dr Hawkins' stillness changed. It went from eager and attentive to barely restrained excitement. I could practically hear him vibrating, a stretched elastic band about to snap.

"And what did Charlie have to say?"

He said each word in careful measure.

"He warned me that it was only the start, that they'd return, that I was in trouble."

"Interesting. Did he offer a way out?"

"Well, no, but I didn't give him much chance to. I told him to go away, that I didn't want to listen to him anymore. He agreed to go away until after lunch."

Dr Hawkins seemed confused.

"You told him to go away, and he just did?"

"Well, yeah, he always has. Is that bad?"

"What? No, no, it's good, yes. It shows that you are in control of your subconscious imaginings, at least partly. Have you written about this in the journal?"

"Oh, no, we started so early I haven't had time."

"That's ok, why don't you write about it when you get back? And if Charlie does come back to you later, be sure to write about that as well. Don't be afraid Eoin, it's all helping to make you better."

"Yes, Dr Hawkins."

"And don't be afraid to let Charlie help you. I mean, don't do anything he tells you to do outside yourself without talking to me first, but for the inside of your head, he certainly seems to help you sort things out. Ok?"

"Yes, Dr Hawkins."

"Good, would you like to call your mother before we

finish up?"

"Oh yes, please. I don't have to wait until tomorrow?"

"Let's see if we can give her a surprise."

The call only lasted a few minutes, but it was good to hear Mums voice. She asked how everything was going and I reassured her that things were well. I so wanted to be home with her, to go back to my old tormented life. It was horrible and full of pain but at least I knew what to expect from each day. I didn't tell her that, I couldn't stand to hear her heart break again. I told her I loved her, and that I'd talk to her soon.

After she hung up, I stood with the receiver pressed against my ear, not wanting to give up that connection.

"All done, Eoin? Why don't I escort you back to the ward, lunch will be in about an hour."

I slowly placed the receiver back on the phone, staring at it for a second. Something occurred to me.

"Dr Hawkins." I said, eyes still on the phone "Would Miranda and I be able to spend some time in the recreation room before lunch? I promised her that we could play checkers again today."

He seemed to consider me.

"Did you enjoy your time together yesterday?"

"Yes, I mean, she's kinda out there, and difficult to follow, but it was nice."

"You definitely seem to be a calming influence on her. Tell you what, when we get back to the ward, I'll check up on Miranda. If she seems able for some recreation time, I'll bring you both to the rec room myself. How does that sound?"

It sounded like he was trying to keep an eye on us. Perhaps he thought we'd be canoodling.

"That sounds great, thank you."

24

On the way back to the ward, he walked beside me again, which calmed me and made me feel a bit more human.

Dr Hawkins swiped us into the ward and dropped me at my room.

"Stay here Eoin, I'll check on Miranda then I'll let you know."

I nodded, picking up a book to read, but as I sat on the edge of the bed, I found myself unable to concentrate on the words on the page. I was nervous, which was confusing, I didn't think it was about Miranda. I mean, I knew she was supposed to be dangerous but she seemed fine with me. But then I had just met her the day before, unless you counted exorcising her demons on Friday night, which I didn't. I guess I'd just have to see how it w-

"Eoin!!"

The tackle-hug knocked me off the bed and on to the floor. Miranda gripped me tight around my chest as I tried to pull back in the air she'd knocked from me. Then she removed herself and sat on the floor beside me, bouncing in place.

"Eoin, Eoin, the dark doctor says we can play, and I think you win this time and you came for me and it's so bright bright bright right? Light bright, which is great for those who need it to see, I don't but that's ok, it does make things pretty."

I waved a hand at her as I tried to pull myself up.

"Miranda, slow down, plenty of time, try keeping it to one word a second."

"Oh… hi. Can. We. Play. Now?"

She looked at her hand as she slowly counted the words of on her fingers, then looked at me with a big smile.

I looked into her eyes as she smiled at me, so open, so honest. What else could I say?

"Okay Miranda, we can play."

"Yay!" She bounced up and down again, her shoulders swimming in the baggy blue t-shirt.

She grabbed my hand and pulled me towards the door.

"Come on, it's time to move! why do you never move when it's your time? Your light doesn't look so good, I'm really sorry about the dragons. Did you have orange juice or milk with your toast? I like orange juice better."

I jerked back against her pull.

"Woah! You're sorry about the what?"

"Eoin, I see Miranda found you, she was exceedingly eager to head to the recreation room. Shall we depart?"

Dr Hawkins was standing at the door to my room, waving us out. I let Miranda pull me up off the floor and out the door towards the head of the ward. She was laughing and giggling as she pulled me along.

I expected Earl to be as wary as he'd been yesterday, he did seem to tense up as we approached, but as the sound of Miranda's giggles filled the corridor, he looked at us with a puzzled kind of smile.

Buzzed through the door and into the corridor, Miranda kept a hold of my hand and swung it back and forth as we walked, all the while babbling away.

"Do you like my fishes? There are more today, some of them got eaten but then the ones that were left must have had babies, I think they do it while I sleep. Thank you for showing them to me, they make me feel better. Will I ever have one big, person shaped fish like you? I tried to look and see but it didn't work."

Dr Hawkins followed us, hands in his pockets. I thought he was being careful at first, either with me, or Miranda, or both, but when I looked back I thought I saw the hint of a smile under his moustache. Maybe it was good to see Miranda happy, I know it made me smile, and he wasn't telling us not to hold hands like Frank had.

Miranda bounced and skipped beside me as we turned the last corner before the recreation room. Dr Hawkins had trailed behind, and as we turned the corner out of his view Miranda whirled in front of me, reached up to place her hands on my cheeks and stood on her tip toes to kiss me.

The Earth stood still. Ok, it didn't, it probably kept on revolving at a nine hundred miles an hour, but in that moment when her lips met mine, Everything just stopped, the moment stretching into an eternity. There was only us, our bodies so close together, meeting at our lips. My skin tingled, my heart faltered, my mind melted and my breath caught. She pulled away, looking up at me shyly through lowered lashes and I didn't see the thin, pale, straggly, dark haired waif. Instead her skin glowed with a pale light that filled me with warmth and love and contentedness and made her beautiful. She threw her arms around my chest and laid her head against me, and I heard her whisper.

"I love you, my brave knight."

I opened my mouth, but no sound escaped me. Her words caught me unprepared. I didn't know what to say, much less what to do. As I tried to reassemble my mind into something functional, I heard Dr Hawkins approaching the corner. With a blurring speed, Miranda spun away twirling her hands above her head.

"Doctor birdy pubs is here, truth will flee in future fear. Falsehoods are our only friends, they will save us in the end."

She called out the words in her usual singsong voice, some kind of children's rhyme, as she twirled and danced.

Dr Hawkins chuckled as he walked up beside me.

"It seems your playmate is full of energy today, Eoin."

"Huh? Yeah, I mean yes."

As Doctor Hawkins walked forward to unlock the recreation room, I raised my fingers to my lips. I could still feel her there, like a ghostly memory of affection. I looked up to see Miranda standing looking at me. Completely still for once, she was just looking at me. Her face was open and honest and full of love. It was equally the most beautiful and terrifying thing I have ever seen.

As soon as Dr Hawkins opened the door, Miranda ran past him giggling.

"Aren't you going to join her, Eoin?"

I looked at Dr Hawkins, and tried to remember how to move again. I gave myself a mental shake and walked into the recreation room. Miranda was performing her impression of a dog at a rabbit hole, boxes flying from the cupboard she was digging in until she emerged with the checkers box and ran back to a table. She had the board set up by the time I walked over, her hands a frenzy of movement. I looked over my shoulder at Dr Hawkins as he sat at the desk and picked up a pad and pen. As I sat down opposite her, Miranda looked up and a puzzled expression crossing her face, causing her to scrunch up her pixie nose.

"You said I could go first even though it's your turn."

"Did I?"

She nodded pointedly.

"Yes, I'm sure of it."

"Ok, I guess you can go first then."

"See, I told you that you did!"

She broke into a wide smile and made her first move. There was less talk then yesterday, and more emphasis on the game, but there was something bothering me.

"Miranda?" I said, as I moved to take two of her pieces "You mentioned dragons earlier."

"Oh yes." She replied, taking three of mine. "Thank you, I... I didn't know if you'd come."

She looked down at her lap blushing and started twisting the fingers of her hands together.

"And how did I come?"

She looked up with a puzzled frown.

"Do you not remember? My poor knight, did they cut it out of you? That happens sometimes, but the wound will burn back the memory, it hurts so."

Her voiced was low and frightened now. I could tell she didn't like talking about this, but I wanted answers.

"Yes, it's very hard to remember, can you remind me

what happened?"

She sat looking at her hands in her lap, and when the words did come, it was in a soft whisper that I had to lean forward to hear.

"The darkness tied me to the tree, they do that sometimes. Sometimes they like to chase me, but other times they make me struggle. They started to tear me open, same as always, but it was worse this time, because the light you put inside me made the cuts burn more, made the pain more real. I called for you, I screamed and I screamed until my screams became little birds of pain that flew off to find you."

She seemed to shrink in her chair, trying to make herself as small as possible. I felt a lump in my throat, but I pushed on, needing to know.

"And then what happened, Miranda?"

She looked up and there were tears running down her cheeks.

"And then you came. You rode up on your horse, and your horse glowed just like you. You saved me. The dragons flew away and I slept." She let out a tear filled broken laugh. "I finally slept and it felt so good."

And she was looking at me again, with love in her eyes.

"Thank you, brave knight."

She reached forward and took my hand. Her skin felt cold against mine. I wanted to gather her up and keep her warm, which confused me. I'd only known the girl for a day or two, but I looked up into her pale blue eyes, and I was lost.

"I love you, brave knight, and I will enjoy the gifts you give me, however long they last."

There were those words again. I wrapped one of her tiny hands up in two of mine and tried to be serious with her.

"Miranda, you can't love me, you've only just met me."

She cocked her head to the side, and when she spoke it was in her singsong voice again.

"But I will love you, so if I will love you then I have

loved you and therefore I do love you!"

She smiled as if that solved everything. My brow furrowed as I struggled to deal with this. I wanted to help Miranda, and I really wanted to establish if we were sharing dreams, and why. But I did not want a love sick groupie who made six foot muscled orderlies flinch. What exactly would happen if I rejected her? I sat staring at the board, considering my next move. I had to ensure that Miranda didn't think I was going to return her feelings and stop her piece from advancing up the right side of the board. But how did I do that without hurting her or sacrificing at least one of my pieces? And if she managed to king the piece would that mean I loved her too? But no, it couldn't because I didn't have enough pieces left and soon they would take them all, and all the pieces would be black and it wouldn't matter. And it hurt, it really did, I mean it was only a piece, why did my heart tear so?

I looked up from the board at Miranda, but she was all blurry and swaying. I wish she wouldn't do that, it was probably some kind of distraction, to win the game or make me love her. It wouldn't work, silly girl, besides, how could I love her without a heart? And mine was being torn out, slowly, my flesh tearing until pain had no meaning. Then blurry Miranda made sounds, wavy sounds.

"Eoin... are... something... are you... Doctor! He-"

Did she have to turn all grey and dark? I mean the blurriness was hard enough but if it got any darker I wouldn't be able to see her at all. Best just to sleep now. I think I felt the bang as my head hit the floor.

25

The darkness was like a weight upon my body, it pressed in on all sides, no light, no air. I couldn't breathe. It wasn't darkness, I reached out and felt the darkness crumble beneath my fingertips. I breathed what air I had and smelt the mustiness of earth. I was buried, I was buried alive. I started freaking out, I wanted to scream, but that would just use up oxygen faster. I had to get out, I had to breathe. I closed my eyes, useless anyway, and began to claw at the earth above me. I tried to turn my face away from the falling earth. My lungs burned and my head was starting to hurt. I clawed frantically, making a small hole above me. I pulled myself up, clawing further but there was just more earth, and my head was starting to spin. I was taking quick shallow breaths through my teeth, keeping out the earth, but it wasn't enough, there wasn't enough air! My head felt like it was splitting in half, I couldn't think, I was going to die. I was going to die, buried in the ground, and no one would know.

That's when I screamed. I didn't care that it would kill me quicker, I didn't care about the dirt that filled my mouth, I just knew that I would not go quietly into the dark. As my ragged scream filed my ears, I shoved my hand at the earth above my head and felt it break through the surface. I closed my mouth, swallowing soil, almost choking as I tried to scramble through. Just my head, I just needed my head out. I needed to breathe. My lungs were on fire, desperately wanting to breathe in the loose soil around my face. My throat hurt from where the soil I'd swallowed had scraped it. My eyes were filling with tears.

This could not be it. I had not come this far, I had not fought this hard to die beneath an inch of soil, struggling in vain. I tried, but I wasn't strong enough. I felt the darkness coming, I didn't want it to, but it was. That's when it happened. It was the barest brush of skin. Someone touched my hand. I felt a jolt of electricity rush through me, then it was gone. Only one person made my skin feel like that, Miranda. They had come for her again. I desperately pushed up, reaching for the person above. I felt my hand grip an arm and I pulled with everything I had. With a horrible tearing sound my head shoved through the surface and I took in great gulping breaths, choking as the dust and dirt tried to fill my lungs. Coughing and spluttering, I wiped at my eyes, looking around me.

I was in a cave. It was dark, but dry. There was a rhythmic roaring from the cave mouth and flashes of light. As the next flash came, I looked down at what I'd grabbed. It was an arm, dressed in a black shirt sleeve. The arm led to a body, wearing a black shirt and black pants, lying face down with a pool of blood spreading out to one side. So… not Miranda.

I choked on some dirt and coughed, trying to clear my airway. Once I could breathe, I pulled myself from the earth. It was hard, my shoulder screamed in protest every time I moved it, probably torn from my last desperate pull. But I managed it, finally pulling my legs free and falling to lie on the earthen floor, my blue clothes stained brown, my entire body aching, my head still pounding. I reached out to turn the bodies head so I could see who it was.

It was me. The hair was a little longer, but it was me. I guess I'd died after all. As the cave spun I decided to let the darkness take me, if only for a little while.

26

I remember that the pain came first. It felt like I'd been kicked all over and my head had been smacked repeatedly against metal bars. I was unfortunately in a position to know what that felt like. I groaned softly, and then started talking to myself, in a ragged scratchy voice.

"Eoin, Eoin are you awake? Please Eoin, you have to get up, we don't have much time."

I opened my eyes and waited a few seconds for the cave to stop spinning, then I turned to look towards the sound of my voice. I wasn't talking to myself, the other me was.

"Oh... hello me... I thought you were dead, or that I was, or maybe both."

I looked bad. I had a long gash across my chest where my black shirt had been sliced open, that explained the pool of blood where I'd found me. There was a giant bruise over one of my cheeks and a cut under that eye.

"What happened to me?" I managed to croak out.

He winced every time he breathed, but his voice was getting stronger. "You appeared below ground, you must have been homing in on me."

"No, no... not this me, that me." And I waved a hand at one of the two images of him that were waving back and forth as I struggled to focus. "What happened to that me?"

He looked hurt, emotionally, he already looked pretty damn hurt physically.

"Eoin, don't you... I suppose you wouldn't. Eoin... it's me. It's Charlie."

He chose that moment to swim into focus, and I stared blearily at the me that was Charlie, kneeling down beside me.

"Well score one for Dr Hawkins." I said, breaking into a giggle that turned into a pain filled cough.

"What? What do you mean?"

"He always said that you were just an aspect of me, a positive aspect trying to help me deal with my condition."

"Eoin! I'm not an aspect, I'm real. But we're both going to be screwed if you don't wake up and start making sense."

"I'm not the me that needs to make sense, you are!" I tried to shout it, but it made my throat sore, so I settled for an angry tone.

"Eoin, everything I've done has been to help you, please believe that!"

"Why? Why should I believe me!?"

He looked upset. Well I suppose I would be the person who'd know how to upset me.

"Eoin, I'm not you! It's me, Charlie, I'm-"

I sat up, not caring that it hurt.

"What? My destiny? My way out? My salvation? 'Cause you haven't been much help lately, disappearing while I'm locked in a looney bin."

"What? I nearly died! Again!"

"Again? What?"

"That's what I'm trying to tell you, you pig headed idiot... I'm your brother!"

I'm not actually sure how long I sat there staring at his pain filled face. I mean, I could see it was hurting him just to talk, so why he'd expend so much effort to tell me something so ridiculous was beyond me.

"And you expect me to believe that?"

"Gods, I knew I was the smart one. Eoin, how did you celebrate your last birthday?"

"Mum took me to the zoo, we spent the day there."

"The whole day?"

I thought for a second.

"No, she had to do something in the morning. We went when she got back"

Charlie nodded.

"And the year before that, she had an errand to run as well, didn't she?"

"I don't know, yeah, I think so, so what? She's busy,

she's a single mum, single mums are busy."

Even I could hear myself getting defensive.

"Eoin, don't you think it's a little strange that Mum disappears for an hour on your birthday every year?"

"You're just making stuff up."

He looked down and sighed.

"When's the last time you went to Dads grave?"

"I can't go into graveyards, the whispering gets so bad that I scream. I have a picture of Dad instead."

He fell back from his knees to sit on the ground.

"Eoin, you've never been to Dads grave because Mum never wants to bring you. Because my name is there too."

"What?"

He paused, and turned his head away from me before he spoke again.

"I died Eoin, when we were born. We were twins, I died and you lived. Mum never really talked about me much, but when you started talking to me, she stopped mentioning me at all. Once you went on meds she pretended like I never existed, never mentioned me to anyone. The only time she ever acknowledges me is once a year, on our birthday. She brings flowers to the grave, she cries and tells me she's sorry, and that she'll never forget me. Then she kisses the head stone twice, once for me, and once for Dad. Every year, Eoin."

The anguish in his voice was tangible. I thought about my last birthday. I had been excited about going to the zoo. When I saw Mum's car drive up I had grabbed my bag and almost ran into her as she came in the door. Her eyes had been all red. She had said it was allergies.

I looked at Charlie and I felt myself falter. Maybe he saw it in my face, because he reached for me.

"Take my hand, Eoin"

I took his outstretched hand, and as our fingertips met, a spark jumped between us. It tingled across my skin and up my arm, sliding into my chest, filling my heart. It was a little piece of me that had found its way home. I looked into my brothers eyes, and I wanted to believe.

"But… how?"

"How am I here?"

"No, how do they get the figs in the fig roll, of course how are you here!" I didn't hit him. Instead, I congratulated myself on my self restraint, conveniently glossing over the fact that I could barely move anyway.

Charlie let go of my hand and stood, looking down at me.

"We're twins Eoin, our souls were entwined when we were born, but I didn't make it. Instead of moving on, I stayed bound to you. I grew up with you."

A sad smile spread across his face.

"I've always been with you, every day. We used to play together. You sucked at hide and seek, though it probably didn't help that I could move through walls."

He sat back down beside me, looking me in the eye.

"Mum didn't think too much of you having an imaginary friend, I always told you that my name was a secret, even back then I knew it would upset Mum. But you let it slip, just like this time, we were fighting and you called me Charlie. That put an end to that. Pretty soon you were being medicated and I couldn't reach you anymore."

Charlie reached up and squeezed my shoulder.

"You don't know how long I've waited, Eoin, watching you suffer every day and wishing I could help."

I sat staring at him, struggling to piece together what he was saying,

"Ok. Right. So. Either you're my long lost dead brother come to help me-"

"Twin brother."

"Ok, long lost dead twin brother, OR… you're a manifestation of a mental illness that I have been diagnosed as having by every doctor from here to the horizon. I hope you can see why I'm not exactly feeling very trusting right now. Especially since, even if you're telling the truth, you lied to me!"

He sat back at my shout, holding his hands up.

"What? What did I lie about?"

"Eh… duh! I don't recall you introducing yourself as 'Hi, listen this might sound crazy but I'm your dead twin brother and I've come to rescue you'."

"Would you have believed me?"

"Of course not, that's crazy!"

"Well there you go then. Besides, I didn't lie to you. I told you it was complicated."

"Thereby earning the understatement of the century award."

"Eoin, if I had told you everything, you never would have let me help you, and I did help you, didn't I?"

I thought back over the past couple of weeks. It had been a rollercoaster. There had been good times, but were they real or just in my head? I tried to stand up and the cave spun around me before I fell back to the earthen floor.

"Where are we anyway? Why are we in a cave? Why was I buried alive? Why are you covered in blood?"

When in doubt, start asking questions.

"Truthfully?"

I gave him a look filled with so much sarcasm I think I pulled a muscle.

"Yes Charlie, the truth would be nice for once."

He sighed and winced, reaching for the wound on his chest, though it didn't seem to stop him moving.

"We're in the spirit world. You shouldn't be here but you must have gotten pulled in when they attacked me."

I raised an eyebrow.

"Ok. I'll deal with the impossibility of that sentence in a minute. First of all, who's 'they'?"

"The Furies. You saw them last night, they lured you to them with Miranda's screams."

"Those dragons? They're the Furies, like, the Greek gods of vengeance?"

"Roman not Greek, but yeah. I don't know if they're the original Furies or it's just a nickname, it doesn't matter really. They are big and scary and they want to tear us to pieces."

"Hey, hey… what's all this 'us' business, ghost face?"

"We're both on the hit list Eoin, me for defying the powers, you for your actions and the attention they've drawn."

"What attention?"

"Dr Hawkins. It seems that he has a great interest in people with your abilities, did you think it was a coincidence that you and Miranda were in the ward together?"

I sighed, rubbing at my forehead.

"I haven't really had a chance to think about anything, Charlie."

"I suppose not. Well, the powers can't afford for any evidence of what you can do to emerge, so they've ordered you neutralised."

I remembered him saying that before. Back then I hadn't had a clue what he could be talking about, but now I had an idea.

"That's what happened to Miranda, isn't it? The Furies keep her so wracked with pain that she can't even communicate?"

"That's the plan, yeah. Most people go mad within a month, and are dead within six. They take their own lives or just… stop. They give up the will to live and eventually they just stop breathing."

I thought about Miranda, screaming in the night. I thought about how it had felt for me, the soul destroying pain during the night, the crippling flashbacks during the day. That was her life, night after night, every day. No wonder she thought she loved me, I'd rescued her from hell.

I looked at Charlie and asked the question that was filling my mind.

"How long?"

He paused, confused.

"How long what?"

"How long have they been attacking Miranda?"

"Oh… emm."

"Charlie?"

"Well it's not like I know everything, Eoin, I'm just a normal spook. But, there was talk of someone the Furies had been set on, I mean, if it's the same person, which it might not be-"

My voice cut off his babble.

"How long Charlie?!"

His answer, when it came, was softly spoken.

"Nearly a year now. It's the only reason I even heard anything about it, no one has ever lived this long once the Furies have begun to tear them apart."

I thought about the torment the Furies had put me through last night. I wondered how I'd be after a week, or a month, let alone a year. My mind couldn't comprehend going through that. I'd grown frustrated with Miranda's scattered words and crazy antics, but now I thought it was a miracle she was able to speak at all.

"So, now what? They tear us apart, and once they're done with us they go back to Miranda? Tell me you have a way out this, Charlie. You do have a plan right?"

"Yes. Sort of."

My expression made plain the great confidence his answer inspired in me.

"Eoin, I'm doing the best that I can! I'm alive, or intact rather, which is a miracle in itself after running into those three."

As he finished his sentence a great roar erupted from the mouth of the cave, the soft silver glow that was issuing from the cave mouth was swallowed by darkness. With a smashing sound a shower of rocks flew in from the entrance.

Charlie's face blanched white.

"They've found us."

"What do we do?"

He stood up and looked toward the cave entrance. I could see through the tear in his shirt and his wound seemed to be healing, far quicker than it should.

"We fight."

"Here's this 'we' business again! Charlie, we're in no condition to fight, and two puny humans against three dragons isn't much of a contest."

Charlie turned to face me, and offered his hand, smiling as he pulled me to my feet.

"Not so broken now, are you? How do you feel?"

I let out a short bark of laughter.

"How do you think I feel? I just clawed my way out of the ground, I feel-"

I stopped. I took a deep breath. I stretched out my arms. Nothing hurt.

"...fine... I feel fine. How can I feel fine?"

Charlie's smile quirked a little higher on one side.

"You're in the spirit world now, things are less set in stone and more what you believe them to be. You were so busy arguing with me that you forgot you were injured, so your spirit body reverted to its base state."

I shrugged my formerly torn shoulder, feeling no pain.

"Huh, wish that worked in the real world. Wait, if that's true, why is it taking you so long to heal?"

He reached up to pull back his torn shirt and look at the slowly healing gash across his chest. It was only the length of his hand now, and the width of a finger. A scar line stretched out from either end.

"This is different. The claw of a Fury doesn't just hurt you, it fills you with the memory of the pain, and every time you try not to think about it, you get a full on flash back. You're right back there, being torn open. You literally have to convince yourself it's not there, even through the blinding pain, and that ain't easy."

I remembered the flash backs from this morning.

"I can imagine. They made me believe it was happening, even in the real world."

As I watched, his wound drew together a little more, even as he winced in pain.

"I'll be fine, a few more minutes and I'll have this healed."

The silvery light blacked out for a second as there was another crash of rubble followed by a loud roar. I hoped we had a few minutes.

I shook my head as I stared at the entrance.

"How are we supposed to fight them?"

Charlie's' smile broke into a full on grin.

"Ah, finally we get to the fun stuff. Like I said, the spirit world is shaped by belief and will."

He pointed to the piece of tattered black fabric across his chest.

"You see this shirt?"

I nodded, though it was hardly a shirt anymore.

"See, it's not really a shirt, it's not really anything. It's a projection of how I think I'm dressed. That means if I really, really believe something, like 'The shirt is mended'."

I watched the pieces of fabric drift towards each other and knit together, until his shirt was whole and clean again, not a stain or crease on it.

I reached out, wide eyed, unable to find where the tear had been.

"Wow. Ok, so, what, we really believe the Furies aren't there and they go away?"

"I wish it was that easy. We can't make them disappear any more than you can make me go away, no matter how much you wish it sometimes."

He was wearing a teasing grin. I couldn't help but feel that I was seeing more of Charlie than I had before.

"We can only affect ourselves, and sometimes the area around us if we're really good, but it means we can arm ourselves."

"So, I can wish up an Uzi?"

I was half joking, but the thought had appeal.

"You can try, though it won't do you much good."

"Why not?"

He waved a hand.

"Give it a try."

I closed my eyes and held my hand up, I remembered every Uzi I'd seen in a movie or game, how they looked. I imagined the weight, the cold metal... I gripped my fingers around it, knowing it would be there. I opened my eyes to look at the slick black metal Uzi in my hands.

"Cool!"

Charlie seemed unimpressed.

"Now try and fire it."

With a gleeful smile I raised the Uzi at the cave wall and pulled the trigger, or tried to. It wouldn't move. I pulled harder, knowing that it would move, and it did. There was a click, and nothing happened.

I turned back to Charlie.

"What's wrong with it?"

Charlie gestured at the gun.

"Do you know how a gun works? I don't, not all the little levers and chemicals that all work together. You don't know what's inside the Uzi so you can't imagine a working one."

"Huh." I threw the dud Uzi against the wall. "I suppose that makes sense, but then what do we fight them with?"

Charlie's face split into a grin.

"It's time to get medieval on their asses!"

He held up his hand, the air shimmered and a bright shining sword appeared, longer than my arm and glistening in the half light.

"A sword, is that all?"

"Not quite."

The sword began to radiate a glow, which brightened steadily until the entire blade burst into orange flames. I jumped back.

"Holy crap. Ok, I admit it, that looks bad ass. Will it hurt them?"

"Oh yes, it doesn't damage them as much as their claws do us, but it can definitely put a dampener on their day."

"Why can't you just, you know, shoot the flame at them, all mage style?"

Charlie shrugged.

"I've tried, but it fizzles out within a few feet, I don't have enough influence on my surroundings. It's useful if you're in close range though. I just imagine it shooting out."

"Cool, I definitely want one of those." I held up my hands in front of me and concentrated.

"Eoin, it took me years to be able to conjure a sword so quick, it might take a-"

With a woosh the sword appeared, burning bright and longer than Charlie's. The hilt was black braided leather and the pommel was a silver skull.

Charlie managed to stop gaping after a second or two.

"Wow, I ... I don't know how you did that."

I looked at the sword in my hand, it had seemed so easy.

"Should I not have done it?"

Charlie shook his head.

"No, no it's good. Maybe the fact that you're still alive means you're stronger, try shooting the flame."

I could feel the sword in my hands, lighter than it looked, humming with power. I pointed it at the wall. I imagined that power rushing forward, and a line of flame burst from the sword tip, splashing against the wall and leaving a rough charred circle. Charlie let out a whoop

"Wow! That's, well that's further than I've ever projected. We might actually have a chance after all."

I turned away from my impressive act of destruction and gave him a look.

"You mean we didn't have a chance before?"

"No! No, of course we did, but you know, flamethrowers make everything easier."

We burst in to matching grins.

"Nicely put, I totally want that on a t-shirt."

Charlie turned back towards the cave entrance.

"Good, now armour up."

"Huh?"

I watched as Charlie's clothes rippled into leathers and chainmail, with gauntlets and boots to match.

"Nice. Will it stop them?"

Charlie shook his head a little.

"Not completely, but it'll slow them down. They caught me by surprise before so I couldn't put up much of a fight, it took all I had to hide here."

I took a deep breath.

"Ok, what's the plan? I mean, are we fighting to the death, 'cause I'm not liking that idea. Their deaths I don't mind, but mine, really not a fan of it. Actually-"

I stopped in mid practice swing.

"Charlie, what happens to me if they get me?"

Charlie rested his sword on the ground and gave me a sombre look.

"If they can kill you here, now, while you're ripped from your body, not just dreaming, then they'll take your soul forever and your body will slowly die."

I lowered my own sword until the tip hit the ground.

"Huh, guess you took that blunt honesty thing to heart, aye?"

"No point in sugar coating it."

"And what about you? What happens if…"

He raised his sword again and took a practice swing.

"Same deal, minus the dying body."

"Right, definitely to be avoided. So… plan?"

He shot me a smirk.

"Right, there's a short tunnel to the outside, once we're out they'll be on us, keep moving downhill. At the very bottom, there's a giant oak tree, it's a gateway back to the physical plane. If you can get to that, touch it, think of home, think of returning, think of waking up, it should return you to your body."

"And you?"

"I'll be right behind you, bro."

I smiled, but it faltered and dropped into a frown. Charlie looked at me.

"What is it?"

I looked away from him, unable to face him as I said the words.

"Charlie, how do I know? How do I know this isn't all in my head, and in real life I'm not slaying dragons, but lashing out at people, hurting them?"

He lowered his sword and sighed.

"Well what about Miranda?"

"What about her?"

"Have you talked to her, did she remember the dragons? Or anything else?"

"Yeah, actually."

"Well there you go then, how can it be all in your head if it's in her head too?"

I thought of all the crazy things Miranda had said, about the Furies, about my aura, about everything. I didn't know what to believe. Whatever logic was left in me was warring with my instincts, which were telling me that if I didn't step up, right now, I was going to end up dead.

I looked up as another crash darkened the cave entrance. I raised my sword, thick black gloves appearing over my hands. The darkness flowed up my arms, turning into form fitting body armour. As the darkness finished covering me I swung my sword and looked to my brother.

"Let's do this."

27

We rushed towards the tunnel mouth together, roaring our defiance. Whether it was defiance of the Furies, or the powers that sent them or the truly crappy hands we'd been dealt from day one, I don't know. There was about twenty feet of tunnel to the outside, the silvery light getting brighter as we ran. I stumbled a little as we ran from the entrance, trying to get my bearings. A shining orb hung in the sky, almost as bright as the sun, but its light was silver, its surface mercurial. The sky itself was the deep dark blue of the last few minutes of twilight.

Our cave mouth came out half way up a rock strewn hill, scree rattled beneath my feet as I tried to keep my footing. The landscape was barren and bleak, nothing but rock and gravel all the way down the hill to the towering arms of a great oak tree. Oh and dragons, three roaring pissed off dragons diving straight towards us.

It was the first chance I'd had to get a proper look at them. They were black, like holes cut into the universe, seeming to pull the light from around themselves. They were as big as a single decker bus, but scrawny and sickly looking. They were not majestic, or beautiful. They were slick and foul and twisted. Just looking at them made me want to throw up. The worst were their eyes. I expected them to glow, or have slits like a lizard, but they were human. Bloodshot and distorted, but human. Human eyes filled with utter disgust and hatred. I could feel their hate, surrounding me, pressing in, trying to drown me. I raised my arm, instinctively trying to shield myself from it. I watched as a large round shield appeared along my forearm. I glanced at Charlie to see him manifest a shield with a pointed end, its colour and design matching the rest of his armour.

A loud roar drew my attention as one of the dragons flew low overhead, its teeth dripping with black slime as it snapped at me. I swung the shield up to block its bite, but the blow threw me to the ground.

"Eoin! Get to the tree!"

I scrambled to my feet and made my way down slope, the loose rocks making it slow going. Another dragon made a low swoop, and then came back around in a dive straight for me. I turned towards it, aiming the tip of my flaming sword at it over the top of my shield, and let loose a stream of flame. The flame dissipated into nothing before it reached it, but it was enough to make the dragon turn its dive to avoid it, flying off to my right. I turned and scrambled over a boulder. I was halfway to the tree before

I realised I wasn't being attacked anymore.

I turned and looked up the slope to see the three dragons circling Charlie. He wasn't very far from the cave mouth, he hadn't run at all. He was standing, turning in a circle, fending of the dragons as they took dives towards him. Even as I watched two dived from opposing directions, and as he fended off the first, the second tore open his sword arm with a swipe of a talon.

His scream roared out across the hillside, and laid over it I could hear a hissing. They were laughing. They were taking their time. They were enjoying themselves.

"Charlie!"

Charlie swung his shield to block another swipe and turned to face me.

"Eoin! Run! It's ok! Just run!"

As he was facing me a dragon dived at his back, its claws wrapping around his shoulders and throwing him to the ground where it could land on top of him. The dragon's roar of triumph overlaid my brother's scream of pain.

"Noooo!"

I didn't think. I couldn't think. I just started running. I ran up the steep shifting hillside as if it were nothing, I threw aside my shield, my sword. By the time I was halfway to them I was running in my hospital clothes, the armour forgotten.

The dragon on top of Charlie reared up on its hind legs, and I could see blood on its talons.

"I'm here! It's me you want, me you were sent for! I'm right here, you bastards! Leave my brother alone!"

I stood screaming as a soft rain began to fall. It was ice cold and it stung my skin wherever it touched me. I watched as the dragons three heads swung to look at me. I felt their hate reach me like a blast of hot air, it made my stomach twist and I fell to my knees retching. I could hear their roar as they rose up, feel them moving towards me, flying fast, converging.

I opened my mouth to scream and their hate filled my

throat, it poured inside me, seeking to drown me. Their hate flowed all the way into my very core, and there it found something. There it found my hate. My hatred of the evil in people's hearts. My hatred of the daily hell I suffered. My hatred of the look I caused in my mother's eyes when she knew I suffered and could do nothing to fix it. My hatred of the things they did to Miranda. My hatred of them, and all that they stood for. Their hatred filled me up like a burning acid, and deep inside it found my hatred, glowing like a piece of barely sub-critical uranium.

As I felt the first talon pierce me, I let it go. Every piece of hatred, all the repressed anger, all the screams I'd held back. I screamed them all in a lance of pure . I filled the sky and I watched them burn. Dark against the brilliance of my burning light, they twisted in agony until I incinerated every hateful, nauseating piece of them, their ashes falling to the rocky ground. The light faded, and darkness came swiftly. I didn't feel my head hit the ground this time.

28

My head hurt, a lot. And when it's me saying that, you know it means a LOT. I tried to open my eyes but the light sent searing pain through my head, so I contented myself with a slow body inventory. Legs: present. Arms: at my side, sluggish movement response, but functional. Head: judging by the nauseatingly bad headache I had, still attached, if perhaps not at 100%. Sense of imminent doom: topped up to full capacity. All was normal with the world. I gingerly moved a hand to check my chest. My t-shirt was soaked, but it felt like sweat. My face, when felt, did not turn out to be covered in bandages. So far, ok. I relaxed my squinting eyelids and let some light start to leak through them.

After a while, I could open my eyes and the pain was only terrible. I was in a hospital bed, the side rails were a dead giveaway. I was propped up a little, facing the room, and there was a drip in my arm. It ran up to a clear bag, hanging from the usual metal stand. The sun was shining in through a high window on the opposite wall, glaring and bright. There was a screen on wheels to my right, a wall to my left. The wall had a door, not a swinging double door like I expected, but a metal door with a window in the top half. Across the room from me were two empty beds, separated by a screen. My killer headache was slowly fading into a grievous bodily harm headache, so I tried some gentle arm movements, and eventually sat up. The room didn't like that at all. It let me know this by spinning uncontrollably. I decided that the ceiling was far more interesting than I'd previously thought and deserved my careful consideration. I'm not sure how long it was before the door opened, but I'd managed to triple check the number of ceiling tiles above my bed.

The door opened with a buzz and a clunk, just like the ward doors, which I thought was weird for a hospital. A nurse bustled in, returning a swipe card to her belt. She tucked a lock of her blonde hair behind her ear as she looked down at her clip board. When she looked up and saw me awake she smiled, and I noticed that her eyes were green.

"Well, you gave us quite a scare young man. It's good to see you awake."

"W'ch hsptl?"

"Pardon?"

I swallowed and tried again.

"Which hospital? Which hospital am I in?"

She gave me a confused look.

"Eoin, you're at Dr Hawkins institute. My name is Ceara, do you remember coming here?"

My stomach clenched. I shouldn't still be here.

"Why amn't I in hospital?"

"Eoin, you're here for specialised care, the kind you can't get in a hospital."

"But I'm sick."

"Yes Eoin, and Dr Hawkins is working very hard to help you."

"No! I mean all this!" I waved at the bed and the drip.

"I'm fully qualified to the deliver the care you required after your... episode." There was a slightly defensive note to her voice.

"Hah! Tune in next week for the next dragon filled episode!"

Nurse Ceara took a hesitant step backwards.

"Of course, Eoin. I'm just going to find Dr Hawkins and let him know you're awake."

She smiled again, but this one didn't reach her eyes. She moved to the door, keeping her eyes on me, swiping her card without looking down. I could practically feel the drop in tension as the door clunked closed.

Great, I was freaking nurses out now. After a minute or so I managed to sit up successfully. I leaned forward, trying to peer around the screen.

"Hello? Anyone else in here?"

There was no answer. I pulled myself around to sit on the edge of the bed, slowly letting my brain catch up. I'd either been in the spirit world or going crazy. I had exploded as dragons were beginning to tear me apart or I'd had a delusion that that was happening. I'd woken up in a locked hospital type room, but still in Dr Hawkins Institute, which was strange. If I had fallen and hit my head, which I thought I remembered happening, then surely I needed medical attention? It certainly seemed serious enough for them to put me on a drip. Just how long had I been gone? Maybe they had thought I'd just fainted. But then that didn't explain me being in this room on a drip.

I checked the bag on the drip stand just to be sure they

weren't filling me with drugs, but it just said saline solution. Guess I couldn't dismiss the dragons as a drug dream then. The more I thought about it, the more unreal everything seemed. I had a twin brother who was a ghost? I'd just done battle in the spirit world? If that was reality, how could I possibly be sane? But my thoughts kept coming back to Miranda. She knew. She knew what went on inside my head. I recalled what Charlie had said; how could it be all in my head if it was in hers too? I lowered my face into my hands with a groan of frustration.

The buzz and clunk alerted me to someone entering. Looking up, I saw Dr Hawkins walk in, keeping his eyes on me as he used one hand to close the door behind him. He was dressed in his usual drab manner, though he was sporting a white lab coat as well today.

"Hello Eoin."

I offered him a muffled reply with my face still in my hands.

"Hi Doc."

"You seem to be feeling better."

I looked at him at him over the tips of my fingers while I repeated a soft mantra in my head; 'I must not piss off the nice doctor, I must not piss off the nice doctor, I must not piss of the nice doctor.'

"Better than unconscious, yes. How long was I out?"

"Oh, about 24 hours."

"Huh. Seemed shorter."

It had seemed much shorter. Maybe exploding in the spirit world had kept me unconscious once I returned, maybe time moved differently in the spirit world, or maybe I was just crazy and none of this was real. I'd have to ask the disembodied spirit of my long dead twin brother the next time I saw him.

"It seemed shorter? Were you aware? What's the last thing you remember?"

I rubbed my temples, trying in vain to ease the pain growing behind my eyes.

"I was in the recreation room, playing checkers with

Miranda, and then I think I fainted or something."

Dr Hawkins stood at the end of the bed with his hands in his pockets.

"And after that? You said it seemed shorter, what did you experience Eoin?"

He was calm and reassuring, but there was something off. There was a tension in his body that belied his casual attitude. His eyes bored into me, demanding answers. I stared back at him, wondering what it was he wanted from me, as the air thickened between us

He cracked first, breaking the tense silence.

"The nurse said that you were talking about dragons."

I thought about what Charlie had said, Dr Hawkins didn't want to help me, he wanted to use me. I ran that thought around and around in my head, wondering how much it sounded like the paranoid ramblings of an insane mind. This was the moment, Charlie's reality or Dr Hawkins'. Here or there. Pain or different pain. Which was it going to be?

"I had a bad dream."

"Are you sure?"

I gave him a look. "Well what else do you call it when you imagine dragons attacking you while you're unconscious? Why don't you tell me, Doc? Do my dreams mean something?"

He raised an eyebrow at my sarcasm, but otherwise sought to maintain his taut, casual calm.

"They might. It's certainly interesting that when you were taken away, Miranda told me that the dragons had taken you, and that I had to save you or else you'd die. Curious that she should say such a thing, after you'd been taken away, and then you dream of dragons. How can we explain that, do you think?"

His hands were still in his pockets, but his calm was slowly evaporating. His tone was harder, almost confrontational.

As I met his gaze, my resolve hardened. His eyes were not kind, his voice was not soft. As I took a deep breath and began to center, I could see a trace of aura flickering around his head, an ugly dirty red. I grounded, shakily, staring him down.

"Miranda was babbling about dragons earlier in the day. I'm sure my subconscious picked up on that and decided to torture me with it."

"Is that what you really think, Eoin?"

"Sure, you know what active imaginations us teenagers have."

He stared at me, one eye twitching just a bit. I think he was expecting me to crack, to confess everything and beg him to save me. Maybe I would have, a few weeks before. Hell, maybe I would have the day before, but I'd just killed the Furies. I had fought a bloody battle and won. I had fought harder than I ever thought possible, and I would not be stared down by some doctor with an ego.

He flinched first.

"We'll resume your sessions tomorrow." He reached into the pocket of his lab coat and threw my journal on to the bed. "Write about your dream, we can go through it then."

He turned and marched to the door, swiping his card hastily and almost slamming the door behind him.

So much for not pissing off the nice doctor. I picked up the journal and placed it on the nightstand before lying back on the bed once more. I closed my eyes and focused on my breathing. As my body relaxed, I felt my center tighten and my grounding grow stronger. My shield slid into place. It felt strong, powerful. I had thought I would be weak, but as my shield thickened I felt my headache ease and my body relax.

"I feel good."

You want to feel crap now?

"No, it's just, after what happened, I thought I'd be wiped. It's good to hear your voice by the way."

Good to be heard.

I could hear the smile in his voice, the warmth. This was a voice I wanted to trust.

29

They transferred me back to my old room in a wheelchair. I told them I didn't need it but they insisted. I kept expecting to feel dizzy or weak, but I didn't. After all I'd gone through, I wasn't sure if that was a good sign or not. My arm hurt from where they'd taken the drip out, and the plaster itched.

As the orderly wheeled me up to the door of my room I looked down the corridor. Miranda's door was shut, and no sounds came from that direction.

The door closed behind me with a clunk and a scrape, and I was alone again. The room was as I'd left it, save for the tray of food waiting for me, sandwiches and milk. Just looking at it made my stomach rumble and I realised how very hungry I was.

I had finished the sandwiches and was swallowing the last of the milk when Charlie came back.

Well, at least they're still feeding you. That's probably a good sign.

"Hey, how are you feeling?"

Pretty torn up, but I'm a damn sight better than I would have been if you hadn't pulled that crazy stunt. Which, by the way, I don't EVER want to see you do again!

I smirked up at the air.

"You're just mad because I saved you and now you owe me your life, or unlife, or whatever."

Uh huh, totally, you can't see but I'm bowing down before you as we speak.

I laughed, and it felt good. Everything was falling apart and there was a tiny scared voice inside me screaming that I was crazy, but it felt good to laugh with my brother.

Now that I can talk to you, we have to start getting ready.

"Ready for what?"

Tonight, it's not going to be pretty.

"Why, what's tonight?"

Dude, I know you're new to the whole spirit world thing, but please tell me that you didn't think you could tear the Furies a new one and we would just get off scot-free?

"I've always wondered about that. I mean, why is Scotland freer than anywhere else?"

A scot was an old tax, getting off scot-free meant you avoided paying the tax. Look can we please focus!

"How do you know that!?"

I read over peoples shoulders when you go to the library. It's really boring being a spirit... Focus!?

"Right, sorry, but what's the worst they can do? I mean, I killed the Furies, right? Or at least really hurt them, they're not going to be able to come back tonight... right?"

Those three aren't.

"Wait, what? What do you mean 'those three'? There are only three Furies, I read that somewhere."

Charlie sighed in my head.

OK. Firstly, there were never only three Furies, that was one guy's interpretation that became popular. Secondly, I told you that 'Furies' might just be a nickname.

"So, how many of them are there?"

I don't know.

"How can you not know?"

Eoin, it's not like we have Spiritpedia or anything. All I know about the spirit plane I experienced myself or heard through rumours, which can't always be trusted. But I know there are more than three Furies. Some say there are twenty, some say a hundred, nobody knows for sure.

I felt the blood drain from my face.

"So, what does that mean for us?"

It means we get ready for war, because the Powers will send something, maybe more Furies, maybe something else, I don't know. But we have to be ready to fight or else they're going to tear through both of us before we have a chance to scream.

"So horrible other worldly things are coming to destroy my life and make it hell?"

Pretty much.

"Must be Tuesday."

Actually, it's Wednesday.

"It's a quote from... never mind."

Apparently the standard shield Charlie had been teaching me wouldn't be enough to protect me when the time came, it was time to level up. Charlie had me fold the blanket from the bed on the floor to make a comfortable place to sit, and then started telling me the plan.

"We're going to shield the room?"

Yeah, sort of. It's not like your personal shield, although, it comes from it, it's....

"Hard to explain in four dimensions?"

Right. You know how emotions can linger on objects or places, leaving a trace of what has come before?

"No?"

Sure you do. It's how home always feels like a safe place, and school always feels draining, and the house at the end of the road, well-

"The one that gives me the creeps? I always walk on the other side of the road from it, what about it?"

House fire twenty years ago. A mother and three kids, all dead, one of the kids was only two.

Just thinking about it made my stomach lurch in a familiar way. The house literally made me feel sick when I passed it.

"Well, that makes a lot of sense."

Yeah, so, you can imbue a place with energy, cement that energy into a shield and lock it into the structure of the place.

"So I'll have to lock a shield around my room every day?"

Not quite. You see, a shield that's locked to a location, kept in place with emotions tied to that place, it weathers the dawn far better than other things. You will have to top it up each day, reinforce it, but you'll only have to create it once.

I turned to look up.

"Well then why haven't I been doing that from the start?"

It's not an easy task, Eoin. I was waiting for you to progress, and now you're away from home, it's just going to be that much harder.

"Wait, don't tell me, because... it's easier to shield a place that I have a close emotional tie to?"

I could hear the smile in Charlie's reply.

Exactly, you're catching on fast.

"Well there is an underlying logic to all this, sort of. In the spirit world, willpower rules, and strong emotions reinforce will right?"

Right, except if the emotions become too strong, they can break your focus, and then you have nothing. It's a double edged sword.

"So, am I going to be able to shield this room?"

I honestly don't know. I mean, this is all theory to me, stuff I picked up from other spirits. I can't anchor a shield, so we're just going to have to see if you can.

"Ok, let's do it then."

I sat cross legged on the blanket, facing the door, my palms resting on the knees of my blue bottoms as I listened to Charlie's instructions.

Ok, close your eyes, focus on your breathing. Don't try to change it, just pay attention. Listen to your breaths and feel yourself pulling inwards, into the darkness inside yourself. Feel your center, tight and controlled. Feel the line running from your center into the Earth. Feel your shield separating all that is you from all that is not.

This part was the easiest. I was centering, grounding and shielding everyday now; they were becoming a part of me. When I closed my eyes I could see my shield, a thick blue glowing line, tight against my body.

Now, I want you to imagine a wall of energy right in front of you, stretch it from floor to ceiling, wall to wall. Imagine the wall, fill it with energy until it is full and solid.

Nod when it's ready.

I imagined the wall, it glowed blue like my shield, the beautiful blue of a still, tropical sea. I felt it grip the walls of the room as it filled with energy, felt it flowing from me, making it real. I felt the wall settle, and gently nodded my head.

Good, now I want you to push the wall forward until it is just inside the door. Anchor it in place, then nod your head again.

I imagined the wall moving forward, but it was difficult. It seemed to cling to the room, unwilling to move. I concentrated and felt it slide along until it was flush with the wall in front of me. I gave another slight nod when I was happy with its placement.

Good, we're doing well. Now I want you to do the exact same thing with the ceiling, all the way through, nod when it's in place.

It was easier to do it the second time, though it was tricky to imagine a ceiling just above my head. Once it was secure I nodded.

Good, now, imagine the join between the two walls melding together, until they're one piece.

That part was easy and I gave a more confident nod.

We did the wall to my right and left, then behind me, melding each with the others until there was an upturned box of energy sitting just inside the room.

Now for the tricky bit.

I felt my concentration waver.

Steady Eoin, you can do it. I want you to imagine the wall above you thickening, filling with energy and then splitting, so that it's two walls sandwiched on top of each other.

I struggled, trying to hold all the walls in my mind at the same time. This is why it was important to meld them. It was easier to hold a box in my mind than five separate walls, but now the ceiling of the box became two ceilings pressed tightly together. I struggled to imagine it and hold it in my mind. Once I was sure it was in place I gave the barest of nods.

Okay, I want you to imagine the inner ceiling moving down through the room, pushing out anything that shouldn't be there. Think of my voice and your center, those are the only two things that can pass through the wall. Imagine us sliding through the wall as it passes, until the wall is the floor, and we remain within the room, completely clean and clear.

I imagined the inner ceiling moving down. It moved easily, it seemed to want to sink to the floor. As it moved I thought about my center, the feel of it, I thought about the sound of Charlie's voice. I imagined the wall passing over us, letting us through as it sank to the floor. I felt a tingle as it passed over my center, and, something else. I felt a second tingle, outside my body, a mirroring tingle sitting in the air in front of my chest. As the floor of energy melded into place, I felt Charlie in front of me, no body, all center.

Well that tingled. Good job Eoin, but don't relax just yet, there's one more thing we have to do. I want you to remember happy times inside this room. It's going to be difficult, I know, but you need an emotion to tie the shield to the room. Without it, it will fade.

When I reached for memories of the room I kept getting flashes of the Furies attack, of being curled up and screaming. I tried to push that out of my mind, but the only other thoughts that came were memories of bland meals eaten in sadness.

Try Eoin, for me, please.

I thought of Charlie, of how he made me laugh. I thought how I'd smiled when I'd felt his center mirroring mine, I imagined that feeling as part of the shield.

Almost Eoin, it's wavering, I can feel it. There must be something, try.

My mind sorted through the days I'd spent here, bleak and confused, angry. Away from home, so confused. I felt my concentration waver, a ripple ran through the shield, like wind through hair.

Hair as black as night, and skin as white as snow, a touch that made me feel alive, a secret she won't show.

The thought didn't quite feel my own, but as the rhyme ran through my head I found the happy memories I needed.

I imagined the feeling of Miranda ploughing into me as she hugged me, right here on this floor. I imagined how light her body had felt, and how light her laugh was also. My heart ached strangely, I took the feeling, confusing as it was, and I thrust it at the shield. It reacted immediately, seeming to slam down without moving as the faintest wave of yellow ran through it. The air was still and I was protected.

Wow. Ok, whatever you used it worked, nothing is moving that shield without taking the bricks with it.

My eyes shot open.

"Can they do that?"

Charlie laughed.

Relax Eoin, regardless of the spirit world's power over your mind and soul, they cannot touch reality.

I felt my shoulders relax and my head fall, before I looked back up at the air.

"So, I'm safe now?"

Charlie paused a little too long for comfort.

Maybe not long term, I honestly don't know where we're going from here, but for tonight, as long as you stay in this room, you should be fine.

I pulled myself up and started remaking the bed. Then I just flopped on it, eyes staring at the ceiling.

"How do we stop them Charlie?"

Honestly?

"Honestly would be nice, yeah."

I don't know Eoin. We're going up against the powers here, the beings administering every interaction between the spirit world and reality. I don't know if there is a way to win, but I swear to you that I will fight for a way with every speck of energy that I possess.

I smiled up at the ceiling.

"I know you will, brother."

I thought I felt the room get a little warmer, and I wondered if that was Charlie's version of a hug.

30

Dinner was meat, mash and vegetables, delivered by Mr Grumpy McBroken-nose. He opened the door just wide enough to slide in the tray and then slammed it shut.

"If I didn't know better, I'd think that man didn't like me."

Don't take it personally. He's probably scared that you'll try to bite his fingers off.

"Oh god, was he here the night the Furies attacked? Do you think I actually DID try to bite his fingers off?"

Eoin, relax, that wasn't your fault, you were being torn apart.

"Was he here? Was it him?"

I'm sorry Eoin, I don't know. But it doesn't matter. It wasn't you, and we're gonna make sure it doesn't happen again, right?

"Right."

I rolled over on the bed to face the wall.

What's up, Eoin?

"Nothing."

That doesn't work on Mum and it's not going to work on me.

"Liar, it totally works on Mum."

Just because she leaves you alone doesn't mean that she doesn't know you're lying. What's up?

"... I don't want to die Charlie."

Neither do I, buddy, and that's totally not on the cards right now.

I let the tears start flowing as I stared at the wall.

"No, I… I don't want to die, but I think I'd rather die than let them destroy me. I've spent so many days confused and scared, not knowing what was real, with my own mind tearing itself apart. I can't live like that. I'm not strong like Miranda is, I don't know how she's survived. If they come for me, if the shield falls, if I wake up tomorrow screaming and thrashing and full of pain, I'll end it, I swear I will. I know I shouldn't and I know it's selfish and I know it will hurt Mum, but I don't care. I can't care, because I can't live through that pain for the rest of my life."

The room filled with silence as I felt the pool of tears beneath my cheek.

Eoin… I… I won't let that happen. I'll fight with every breath I might have had.

A shiver ran through me as he said those words, like something was falling into place. I closed my eyes, took a breath and felt myself grow still.

"Do you think we'll see Miranda?"

Probably not tonight, they seem to have you on lockdown. Maybe the Doc will let you go to the rec room with her after your session tomorrow.

"Yeah maybe, and I'll probably get to call- Oh God!"

I rolled away from the wall, looking up into the air in a panic.

"Charlie! Mum! What must she be thinking? What have they told her? She must be worried sick!"

Eoin! Relax! They've kept her informed. She's worried, but knows you're awake and recovering.

"What? Are you just lying to keep me calm?"

No, I was with her when they called her.

"So, you can, go to her?"

Yeah, sorta. I mean it's not reliable or anything, but I have a link to her as well as you. It's not as powerful as the one with you, but I can feel if she's really upset and if I follow that feeling I can go to her. That's probably the best way to put it.

"That's how you knew about her visits to your grave?"

Yeah, her pull is kinda strong those days.

I thought about Charlie, floating near Mum, feeling her pain but not able to do anything about it. Being with me every day, but not being able to help, not even with a kind word.

"I'm sorry, Charlie."

What for?

"I can't imagine what it's been like spending most of your life being ignored by the people you love, even as they struggle to cope with their own lives. Seeing us every day and never being able to touch us. It's as bad as what they put Miranda through. You're amazing, Charlie, I love you."

There was silence, but the room warmed.

I love you too, brother.

"So what's the plan for tonight? Man the battlements and repel all invaders? Will it be like the cave?"

It shouldn't need to be, your shield is pretty damn strong. We'll reinforce it before sunset. I'll handle any damage control on the spirit side, you can stay firmly here. That should keep us safe for tonight at least.

"Why only tonight?"

It would take an army to get through this shield, and no matter how pissed they are at you, I don't think they're gonna send that much so soon. Can't speak for tomorrow though, we'll have to wait and see how they react.

"I guess we'll have to take what respite we can."

Pretty much. Speaking of the shield, I'm not kidding when I say it's anchored really firmly, what memory did you use to secure it?

I thought about not telling him, or lying, but I couldn't lie to Charlie, not anymore.

"It was Miranda. The memory of her hugging me in this room, knocking me to the ground with her excitement, then bouncing up and down, so... happy. She was just so happy to see me."

Wow.

"Wow what?"

You just, light up when you talk about her, on the physical and spirit plane. No wonder the shield is strong.

"I'm not getting you?"

Eoin, you're in love with Miranda.

"Shut the f… no, no I haven't even known her a week. I am so not in love with her."

Fine, you're falling in love with her. Either way, there's a connection there. Don't tell me you don't care about her.

I sat up on the edge of the bed and stared at the floor.

"She kissed me, you know."

What? When did that happen? I leave you for a few days and you turn into Romeo.

The teasing tone of his voice softened the words.

"Outside the rec room, we were out of sight of Dr Hawkins for a few seconds and, she just kissed me."

How was it?

"It was, amazing. I mean, I know I don't have much for comparison-"

Or indeed anything for comparison.

I turned red as I went on.

"Right, but, it was amazing. It made me feel like my skin was tingling all over. It felt like the entire world paused for a second, and if I just tried hard enough I could make the moment last forever."

Ahhh, young love.

"Shut up you! It was, beautiful and wonderful and it made me feel like I could do anything. I swear that when she kissed me I could feel everything that was me and everything that was her as well.

Huh.

"What? Got some other comment?"

No, no, it's just… it's nothing.

He sounded worried.

"It was just one kiss Charlie, who knows, the second one might be crap. And even if it wasn't, it's not like we have much of a future. Even if we can get me out of here, she'll still be inside."

Hmmm, true. Ok, time to reinforce the shield, back on the floor.

I rearranged the blanket on the floor and thought about the way Miranda made me feel. I couldn't help but smile when I talked to her. When I first met her I'd thought she was crazy, but now I realised that she just saw the world through a kaleidoscope. Everything was fractured and skewed, and somehow that made things beautiful. I was so not admitting to loving her, it was too soon for that, but yeah, I guess I cared.

I went through the breathing exercises, finding my center. It glowed bright inside me, stronger than I'd ever seen it. Maybe it was like a muscle, growing because I was using it more, or maybe I was waking it up. I followed Charlie's words, feeding more energy into the shield, hardening it, until it felt as strong and solid as it could be.

"How long till they get here?"

It's about an hour 'till sunset, best to relax. I'll give you a shout if there's a problem.

I picked up a book and tried to read, but it was difficult to concentrate on the words. I just wanted it to be time. I wanted to know if the shield would hold, if I would get to sleep tonight. I liked sleeping soundly, I wanted to wake tomorrow without screaming, without pain, without feeling like my brain was numb and my eyelids itchy.

I suppose it must have been an hour, but it seemed like an eternity. My mind was scattered and my stomach felt sick. But as the last light was fading from the high window, I felt a shiver run through me.

"What was that?"

That was nightfall.

"I can feel nightfall?"

Apparently, I didn't think it was something you'd be able to pick up on, but then you do keep surprising me.

"Are they here?"

It's not like a switch, but if they're coming, it won't be long.

"How will I know?"

When they attack? You should feel it, like a sense of unease, or a thudding feeling inside yourself.

"Inside me?"

Yeah, you know, like when you listen to loud music with a beat and you can feel it in your stomach.

I sat staring at the wall, waiting or something I'd never felt before.

"Will you be able to stay with me when they come?"

Oh I'm staying firmly in this room, don't you worry.

As he spoke I felt a wrench in my stomach.

"That was them, wasn't it?"

Charlie's reply was slow and sombre.

Yeah, they're here.

"You can see them?"

Sort of, sense them really.

"Can I?" I said, feeling a larger twist in my stomach

Are you sure you want to?

I thought about it, as two quick twists make made me feel nauseous.

"Yeah, I want to know what's making me feel like I'm going to throw up."

Ok, sit on the bed, center yourself and try to sense past your personal shield.

I sat up on the edge of the bed, back straight. I concentrated on my breathing. It was difficult to focus with the random twists in my stomach, but I felt my body begin to calm, my shoulders falling, my breathing slowing. As I pulled in to my center I could feel that the tugs weren't in my stomach, but from outside, from the shield. I could see the shield in my mind, a ripple ran through it with each tug. I could feel Charlie in the room with me and when he spoke, his voice was louder than normal.

They're attacking, it's a Fury. I can feel its hate.

I mumbled a reply.

"Can I see 'em?"

Sure. Focus your attention outside the shield. Don't imagine yourself there, just, wonder what might be there, I guess.

I thought about it. I was looking at the wall with the door so the corridor was beyond the shield.

"It's just an empty corridor."

You're being too literal, just relax your mind, let it float and the next time you feel a tug, follow it to where it came from.

I relaxed as he talked, letting my mind float, and then a ripple came and I just pointed my mind towards it and looked. It was horrible. I could only see it through the shield, which softened its outline and blurred it a little. I was glad of that. It was a ball of energy, but big and thick and black, with spikes and tentacles lashing out from it, tearing at the outside of my shield. Its attacks seemed to slide off. It sickened me just to look at it. It was evil, pure malice, it wanted to destroy me and laugh while it did it. I pulled my perception back inside myself before it made me throw up.

"How can the powers use something that wrong?"

It's a tool, fit for its purpose. You have to understand. The Powers aren't good or evil, they just are. They don't care if you've been naughty or nice as long as the veil remains in place and the rules are followed. To them the Furies are perfect for their job, they hunt down their targets and eliminate them with passion.

"Why did they just send one after I took out three?"

They probably expected you to be weak or unprepared, or he could be a scout.

Almost before Charlie finished speaking I felt ripples slam through the shield from all four directions, one at each wall.

Here we go, looks like they're really taking you seriously.

"Is that a good thing?" I grabbed my stomach as the twists started to get to me.

Well, not really, but I suppose you could be flattered.

"Oh good, that'll make me feel better when I throw up dinner."

I covered my mouth, a giant belch escaping as my stomach churned from the attack..

Just filter it out.

"I can filter this out?!" I choked out from behind my hand.

Sure, just imagine a cloth screen around you, like a bubble. When signals hit the bubble, they become muted, lowered, so you'll be aware of it but it won't get to you as much. You really must have tied yourself close to this shield.

"Yeah, woohoo." I threw up a little in my mouth.

"Oh God."

I tried to concentrate on my breathing, it was even harder than before. When I finally managed to calm my mind, I imagined a cloth bubble muffling the signals from outside, dampening them. I wrapped myself up in it and immediately the ripples turned to tiny little tugs, much more manageable.

"Thanks Charlie, I don't know if I could have taken much more of that."

You're welcome, sorry I didn't think of it sooner.

"How long will they keep it up?"

Until they get bored, or realise the futility of their actions, which might take a while. The Furies are not renowned for their intellect. It shouldn't be too long though, they aren't even making a dent in your shield.

"Well that's good to know."

It soon became boring, sitting waiting for them to give up. I lay back on the bed, staring at the ceiling.

"Wanna play a game of I Spy?"

Sure, why not.

We had W for window, that didn't last long. B for book, that took a few guesses, then I chose F for faucet, which caused an argument.

"It's a real word, it counts!" I said to the ceiling as I lay back on the bed, hands behind my head.

No it's not, it's called a tap, it was called a tap when you were growing up and it's called a tap now.

"Hey, it's not my fault I have the bigger vocabulary. Maybe the next time you're reading over peoples shoulders, you should pick someone with a dictionary."

It's no fun if I'm never going to guess.

"I disagree, I find it highly amusing."

You are such a… wait.

"What, you've realised I'm right?"

No, I've realised they're gone.

"What?" I sat up, listening carefully, paying attention to my stomach muscles. No twinges, no ripples.

"Whoop! I guess this round goes to the Murphy brothers!"

I felt the air around me grow a little warmer.

I guess it does. Why don't you try and get some sleep.

"Ok, I'll need it if I'm going to face Dr Hawkins tomorrow."

I slid beneath the blanket and curled up contentedly.

"Night Charlie."

Good night Eoin. Sweet dreams.

31

The rabbit screamed behind the fence. It tried to push through but even its screams couldn't escape the wires. The fence cut the screams up until they fell like painful snow. The snow burned where it touched my skin and it made me realise that I had to wake up, I had to wake up right now because of the screams.

I jumped up in the bed as the sound of terror filled the building. It sent a shiver down my spine with their familiarity.

"Miranda!"

Relax Eoin, there's nothing we can do.

"But they're killing her! They couldn't get me so they went after her right?"

Probably, yeah

I jumped up from the bed and ran to the door..

"So we save her, we've done it before we can do it again."

Eoin, there's four of them, we barely took three. You're locked in this room so if we go after them it will have to be in the spirit world. You know, that place we both almost died... yesterday!

I was up off the bed and at the door now, listening to Miranda scream. Nobody was coming to help her, not even to sedate her.

"Why are they just letting her scream? Why isn't anybody coming?"

Eoin, they're used to it, they've probably been wondering why she hasn't been doing this every night.

I turned to face the room as her shrieks tore through me.

"We have to do something, we have to save her."

Eoin, we can't, it's exactly what they want, to lure us out where they can get at us. Miranda has gone through this every night for nearly a year. I know it sounds cruel, but she can take another night. We can come up with a way to protect her tomorrow.

Miranda's scream ended in a tortured sob. I slammed my fist against the metal door, my eyes filling with angry tears. My body was taut, ready for action. I wanted to hit and scream, I wanted to save her, but I couldn't. I was powerless, her cowardly knight, hiding behind my shield. The next scream broke my heart.

"Eoin! Please! It hurts!"

I gritted my teeth and turned back into the room.

Oh crap.

I pointed a finger into the air.

"You owe me your life Charlie! The Furies would have torn you apart if I hadn't stopped them."

That's true, but I don't see how tha-

"And you're my brother, my twin, we're bound together

for eternity?"

Eoin, you're not thinking clearly, you have to be log-

"Bring me in to the spirit world so I can save her or I will never forgive you Charlie, I swear it."

I didn't even know if it was a bluff, I just knew that it would tear me apart to listen to her suffer. How could I forgive someone that would put me through that?

If you get us killed, I'll never forgive you.

"You don't have to come."

Ha! Like you have a chance without me. Besides, someone's gotta watch your back.

I let out a sigh as some of the tension left my body. "Thank you."

Yeah, yeah, you might not thank me when you're run through with Fury claws. Let's get started if we're doing this.

I ran to the bed, lying flat and getting comfortable.

I closed my eyes, before opening them again as I raised my head.

"How do we do this?"

Get calm and centered, I'll talk you through it.

I concentrated on my breathing, but just when I started to sink into myself, Miranda's screams would break my concentration. I couldn't stop thinking about their claws tearing through her.

Charlie's voice rose as he tried to talk me through.

Eoin, if want to save her you have to focus.

Easier said than done. I tried to let her screams fade into the background. Gathering my determination I whispered.

"I'm coming Miranda."

With that promise I found my focus, listening to my breaths as they slowed. I pulled into the dark inside myself, finding my center.

Good, now, I'm going to send you a tether, it will let you follow me. It should feel like a gentle tug. Don't dismiss it, concentrate on it, hold on to it with your mind.

I felt something pulling my attention, distracting me from my focus. I turned my mind towards it and concentrated, trying to focus on that feeling. As I did I felt it tug harder.

Geronimo Brother!

The world turned inside out, my mind exploded into a thousand burning snowflakes... and we were gone.

32

The light flashed bright through my eyelids, jerking me awake. Lightning flashed once more across the black clouds above me. Not dark clouds, but clouds of pure black. The wind whipped through the grass around me, and when I sat up, the tips of the grasses waved around my shoulders.

"Charlie!"

Charlie's head shot up a few metres away.

"Here!" Charlie said, looking around, "wherever here is."

"What do you mean, wherever here is?"

He got up, brushing dust off his black shirt and trousers.

"Well the spirit world isn't fixed to the physical plane, so jumping into it from the same physical place doesn't mean that you'll end up in the same spiritual place."

"So we've no idea where we are?"

Charlie nodded before taking a look around.

"Yep, but more importantly, we've no idea where Miranda is."

I turned in a circle looking out across the plain until my eyes fell upon a mountain in the distance. As I stared at the foot of the mountain, my heart ached.

"She's that way."

Charlie looked incredulous.

"You sure?"

I thought about the ache I felt, focused on it, and it turned into a stabbing pain that left me clutching my chest.

"Yeah… yeah I'm sure."

"Right, now, how do we get there?"

"You're kidding right?"

Charlie waved a hand at the mountain.

"It's miles away, Eoin. It's not like we can fly, we're constrained by what we believe, and I believe in gravity."

I couldn't let them hurt Miranda any longer. It was my fault they were here, tearing her to pieces, making her scream. There had to be a way to come to her aid, to cut through those beasts and protect her from their hate. Sometimes, from extreme emotion bursts forth great imagination. A determined smile crept across my face as I turned to respond to my brother.

"You know what I believe in, Charlie? Rocket cars."

I held out my hand towards the grass in front of us. I imagined the wheels, big chunky tires to take the rough terrain, good suspension just like a model car I'd built, front wheel steering, not that it would be needed, a solid frame chassis, two big seats with crash harnesses, and the important part, two rockets on the back. I concentrated on bringing up the diagram I remembered from my science book. Two chambers, fuel and oxidiser, mixing together in the combustion chamber. Once the valves were opened and the mixture ignited, the rocket would run until the fuel ran out.

"Wow. Ok I'm impressed, but you can't make it run Eoin, it's just a shell, like the Uzi."

I gave him a smirk. "Don't be so sure. They don't let fifteen year olds study guns, but they do let us study rockets, weren't you watching when I did that big report on them last year?"

Charlie walked around the car before shooting me an incredulous look.

"You think you can make it go?"

"Only one way to find out."

Charlie's face split into a manic grin. "Let's go. But first, suit up."

I held out my hand and gripped my flaming sword as it appeared. I stretched my arms, feeling my body armour appear over my clothes. When I looked up, Charlie was in his leathers and chainmail.

He shrugged his shoulders and swung his sword, neatly slicing a stand of grass.

"Let's do this."

We strapped ourselves in, putting our swords into the sheaths beside our seats. I laid my hands on the steering wheel, looking out at the mountain in the distance. I felt Charlie stiffen beside me, his hands gripping the seat. I realised that I was dragging him into a battle that wasn't his. He would have no stake in this if it wasn't for me.

"Charlie, I'm... I know this is dangerous, but I have to do it."

He smiled and reached up to grip my shoulder.

"I know, I kind of knew as soon as she screamed. C'mon, let's go face terrible danger and possible eternal torment, just to save Miranda and bring her home. And once this is all over, you can explain to me again how you're not in love with her."

I couldn't help but return his teasing grin. Turning back to the face the mountain, I reached for the only switch in front of us.

"Hold on tight."

I threw the switch . It opened the valves in the rockets and set off sparks in the two ignition chambers. I imagined it, I knew every step of the reaction, I could see it in my mind, and I willed it to be.

With a roar the rockets ignited and we shot forward, the acceleration shoving Charlie and I back against our seats. The steering wheel jerked in my hands, trying to turn off course. The landscape rushed by faster and faster, the wind in our faces, rushing into our lungs, making it hard to breathe. There really was only one thing that could be said in such circumstances, and we both shouted it together.

"Yeehaaa!"

I kept us on course as the mountain grew larger. When it filled the horizon the rockets cut out, but we continued on, momentum moving us at blurring speed. The grassland gave way to gravel and the ride got bumpier. I heard the springs in the suspension creak loudly and I hoped I'd imagined them tough enough. Up ahead I could see four winged forms, black as night, quick as death, darting around a rock at the foot of the mountain. I roared out a scream as we approached. One of the Furies landed between us and the rock, rearing up, screeching down at us, its slick oily wings beating the air. It held its arms out, talons curved, its head ready to swoop down and tear us apart. I remembered something extremely important, something you should always remember when designing cars, especially rocket powered ones… brakes.

Charlie's scream joined mine as we raced uncontrollably towards the waiting Fury, the car bouncing back and forth. Looking ahead I saw a wide flat shelf of rock just under the gravel in front of the Fury. It made a slight incline, it just wasn't steep enough for our purpose. As we rocketed forward the last hundred metres, I threw out a hand. I could move things here, I knew I could, I believed it. I believed it with all my heart, but could I move it quickly enough once I was in range? I took my fear and mixed it with my anger, I thought of Charlie and Mum and Miranda, everyone I fought for. I thought of all those feelings and I sent it at the rock, willing it to rise, needing it to rise, believing that it would rise.

I felt my mind strain, it felt like something starting to tear inside my head. I knew the rock was too heavy, it was huge. The doubt made me waiver and in that second Charlie's hand gripped my wrist. I felt his power join mine, sliding around it, joining it, filling every place that it wasn't, being everything that was needed that wasn't there already. In that one moment, the energy was whole, perfect.

The shelf of rock shot up to make a ramp in front of the Fury and I saw why I couldn't move it alone. The shelf spread for at least a hundred feet in either direction. I didn't have the chance to wonder just how many tonnes of rock we'd moved because, through the cloud of dust and dirt we'd just raised, I could see the Fury still roaring as we shot up our ramp.

We launched into the air far above the Fury's head, but it had seen our aim and soared up to intercept us. I'm surprised we didn't run out of screams at this point, though every scream was different, every scream had meaning. To this day I've never been able to recreate that scream that conveyed so succinctly the thought "Ohshitohshitohshit we're gonna hit a dragon".

We collided in mid-air, our momentum knocking the Fury back as we carried on towards the ground. There was a sickening crunch as we landed, the frame of the car buckling as the crash harnesses held us in place, shooting pain across my chest. I looked up to see the body of the Fury sticking out from under the front wheels, a bloody spike of rock protruding through its chest.

Charlie was coughing beside me, fumbling with his harness. As it clicked open, he turned to me and croaked.

"Next time, I drive."

I pulled at the clasps on my harness, my chest aching as I moved.

"Sure thing, let's see you kill a dragon while you do it."

As we fell out of the crumbled remains of the rocket car, I was tempted to wait and catch my breath, but there wasn't time. I looked up as several spine chilling roars flowed across the landscape. That's what it felt like, something heavy, sticky and evil flowing across your skin. The three remaining Furies were circling around an outcrop and I could see a small figure chained to the rock that had to be Miranda.

"Really? Chaining the damsel in distress to a rock? That's the problem with agents of unspeakable evil, no imagination." Charlie's tone was joking, but I could hear the pain in his voice. I wondered which one of us was hurt worse from the crash. He winced as he turned towards me.

"So, plan?"

I tried to look determined and confident, a man with a plan.

"Kill the dragons, save the girl, get back to reality before my body starts to get cold."

Charlie smiled and raised his flaming sword.

"Sounds like a plan to me."

He charged forward roaring defiance, forcing me to run to catch up.

Our shields appeared on our arms as we ran over the rocky ground. Charlie leaped from one rock to another, barely touching one rock before he was flying towards the next. His movements were fluid, controlled, as he bounced across the landscape. I looked at him and remembered how much stronger I'd been fighting the Furies before. I ran after him and jumped as high as I could, knowing that I was stronger here, believing that I would keep up with him. The ground retreated below as I soared far higher than Charlie had managed, over taking him in one leap. I flailed my arms as the ground rushed back up, tumbling as I landed. Charlie sailed over my head as I righted myself.

"Strength isn't everything, hotshot!"

I tried again, focusing more on my balance and aim than raw power. I found that my longer leaps let me keep up with Charlie, even if I didn't quite have his style.

With a sudden screech, a Fury landed between us and Miranda. It stretched its oily wings, draping us in shadow, slime dripping from its maw as it roared at us. I sent a stream of flame at its head as Charlie darted low at its legs. The Fury flapped its wings as it staggered back, trying to avoid my flame, leaving Charlie an opening to slice its leg before jumping backwards, landing in a crouch in front of me as the Fury screamed in pain. It flapped again, trying to keep its balance as it retreated backwards, its leg buckling beneath it. It wasn't flying away though, that didn't make sense, it was almost as if –

I jumped forward, ploughing into Charlie and landing on top of him as I poured energy into a shield, shaped liked a dome, covering us completely. I'd just managed to get the shield in place before the other two dragons slammed into it from behind me, talons scraping at the surface, trying to gain purchase. Charlie struggled beneath me as I tried to hold him down.

"Stay still! There's not much room under here and they're right outside."

"Eoin, we have to move, if we stay under this shield they'll break it down and take us."

As he spoke I felt something slice through the outer edge of the shield and I had to concentrate to keep it in place.

"I know! But if I drop it they'll take us anyway."

I struggled to keep the shield in place as I could feel the three of them tearing at it. Charlie twisted around so he was looking up at me.

"Eoin, do you love Miranda?"

"What? This is seriously not the time for that conversation, Charlie."

"I mean it Eoin, this is important. Do you love her?"

I thought about Miranda, I couldn't help but smile, even as I felt the shield weaken. Thinking of her made me feel warm, content.

"Yeah, I mean… yes, I think I do."

Charlie reached up and grabbed my shoulders, pulling himself up to look into my eyes.

"They hurt her Eoin, they hurt her every day. The pain they put you through is nothing compared to what they've done to her. They've plagued her sleeping hours for over a year, tearing her apart, making her scream, shredding her hope and slowly destroying her will to live. You think they've just cut her? They can do anything they want Eoin, make her suffer unspeakable torment. How many times do you think they've torn her up from the inside out?"

My stomach turned as I realised what he was saying.

"Shut up!"

"They did it Eoin, and they enjoyed every minute of it, savoured every terrified scream. Now they're going to take us and they'll do it to her all over again, only it will be worse, because she's known love now, she's known peace and happiness. The memory of you will torment her every time they take her, the knight that abandoned her in this hell."

I shouted into his face as I felt the shield flicker, letting in the sound of screeches.

"Shut up! Shut up! Shut up!"

Charlie bared his teeth and hissed his final sentence.

"They'll do it all Eoin, unless you stop them, so stop hiding and bloody do something about it!"

I raised my head and screamed. My throat should have been raw, but it wasn't, and the scream came out full and ragged, all at once. It held all my anger and frustration, my love for Miranda, my utter rage at being trapped so close to saving her. I poured that scream into the shield until it was full, and then I started digging deeper into myself. Every time Declan hit me, I screamed that out too. Every time I cried myself to sleep, every time I'd woken up, wishing I hadn't. I poured it all out, tears streaming down my face, until I felt the shield start to shiver, unable to contain it. A gut-wrenching pain seared though my insides as the shield exploded, collecting all the parts of me I'd put into it and tearing the Furies with it. I heard their screeches of bloodlust turn to ones of pain as the explosion tore through them, ripping them to pieces.

An eerie silence followed, no roars, no noise, not even the wind. I collapsed on top of Charlie, my vision starting to darken. I felt him turn us over and lay me down, but it was distant, everything felt numb.

Charlie shook me, his voice panicked.

"Eoin! Stay with me, Eoin. I'm right here, stay with me."

I tried to reach up to reassure him, but my arm wouldn't

move. When I eventually managed to raise it up I could see him through it, like a bad special effect. That wasn't right.

"Eoin! Focus, you have to stay here. Don't fade out on me brother, I don't want to lose you, not now that I've finally gotten through to you."

He was talking like it was important, but there was something, something else we were forgetting.

"...Mir... Miranda... get Miranda."

My voice was soft, whispering.

"Ok. I'll get her. Stay here, don't move."

He scrambled off. I wanted nothing more than to lie there and let the darkness take me, but I had to see, I had to see that she was safe. It took all my effort to pull myself on to my side so that I could look at what he was doing. He ran up to the rock and swung his sword, breaking the chains holding Miranda's arms in place. As he cut the second chain her body fell forward. I gasped, but I saw Charlie dive to catch her, his sword clattering on the rocks. He held her awkwardly, trying to get her to stand. I saw her eyelids flutter before she opened her eyes and smiled. I watched her lean up to kiss him, their lips meeting gently at first, then firmer as he returned her kiss, pulling her close in his arms. As I watched my brother kissing the girl I loved, my heart broke and the darkness washed over me.

33

I remember pain. You would think that after so much pain it would all meld together in my memory, that I wouldn't be able to remember one stab from another. But I remember every little difference, every new twinge of suffering.

This one however was new. Every nerve in my body was in pain, not like it was being electrified, no, I'd felt like that before. This was the dull throbbing ache of the day after a beating, but stretched long and thin and running through my body. It hurt to think, never mind to move, and there were circles of concentrated pain at my temples.

I desperately tried to become unconscious again, not wanting to lie there and suffer. And I was lying down, I could feel cloth beneath me, a pillow under my head. So my sense of touch was working. I was breathing, and I could smell a faint aroma of antiseptic that screamed "Hospital" in my head. Two senses accounted for. There was no way I was trying for sight, not if the throbbing of my nerves was any indication as to the pain light would bring. I strained my hearing.

"It's important to understand that there might not be extensive progress immediately. I'm hopeful that the therapy will lead to some dramatic improvements, but we have to be patient."

The voice was calm, consoling. "Doctor" my mind supplied. "Dr Hawkins" another neuron spat out. The ache in my nerves was fading to a dull agony.

"I know Doctor, I've gotten my hopes up enough times to know that I have to just wait and see what happens. I'm just praying for the best."

"Mum?" Whoops, that was out loud. It hurt to speak but not as much as I'd worried it would.

"Eoin!?"

The sound of concern mingled with relief suggested that I may have been out for a while.

"Careful Mrs Murphy, let him come round, it can be very disorientating."

I felt control slowly return, the awareness of my limbs trickling back to me. I twitched a few fingers, moved my lips. Eventually I faced up to the fact that I was going to have to open my eyes. I let one eyelid slide open the tiniest amount, and when lightning stabs of pain failed to materialise, I opened both eyes.

The light was dim, but I could make out a familiar ceiling, the ceiling of my room at the institute. I turned my head to look at the opposite wall. Two figures were sitting on chairs looking at me.

My voice sounded dry and raspy as I croaked out.

"Mum?"

Mum almost choked on her words as a tear ran down her cheek.

"I'm right here, Eoin."

Her hands rested on her knees. Dr Hawkins was gripping one of her wrists, preventing her from rushing to my side. He leaned forward.

"How do you feel Eoin?"

"Like shit." I croaked.

Mum's retort was swift and shocked.

"Eoin Murphy!"

"Sorry Mum."

Dr Hawkins patted Mums knee, before standing and looking down at me.

"The therapy can be very hard on the body. Do you have any numbness or tingling? Do you remember where you are?"

I shaded my eyes as I tried to look up at him, silhouetted in the ceiling light.

"I'm sore all over and I'm at your institute. What did you do to me?"

Dr Hawkins cleared his throat, and then launched into a flat toned speech.

"While your initial progress was encouraging, I concluded that we had reached a plateau and that any further improvements would need a radical-"

"What did you do!?" I pulled myself painfully up onto my side. Mum was rigid in her seat, gripping the sides, biting her lip.

"I concluded that electroconvulsive therapy offered the most oppor-"

"You gave me electroshock!?" No wonder I felt like crap.

Dr Hawkins clinical demeanour did not waver, he carried on in clipped tones.

"I felt it was the appropriate escalat-"

"You let him give me electroshock!?"

Mum sat frozen, her mouth gaping.

"Eoin, I'm sorry, but Dr Hawkins was sure that it will help you. I just want you to get better."

"So you shot me full of electricity!?"

I couldn't believe it. It had come up in conversation between us before, but Mum had always been against it, she said it was barbaric. How could she have let them do this to me?

Dr Hawkins cleared his throat and for the first time spoke with a human tone, albeit a smug one.

"Eoin, can you hear any whispers?"

"What?"

He smiled, clasping his hands behind his back.

"Can you hear any whispers or voices?"

I stopped and listened for a second. The room was completely quiet, but then it would be, because I was shielded. I reached out with my mind to feel my shield... and nothing happened. I couldn't feel it. It's not that it wasn't up, it was like my mind couldn't stretch out at all.

Dr Hawkins voice, clinical once more, cut through my thoughts.

"Eoin? Can you hear me? Can you answer?"

I closed my eyes and concentrated on my breathing, reaching down to my center, which wasn't there. It didn't make sense. I could concentrate on my breathing, and I felt a bit calmer, but there wasn't the solid grounding feeling I got when I centered. I felt lost, I panicked, I couldn't understand.

A softer voice called out, but it didn't quite reach me.

"Eoin, honey, can you hear me?"

"It's ok Mrs Murphy, patients can often be confused and disorientated upon waking. Eoin, it's Dr Hawkins, can you hear me? Concentrate on my voice."

His words made me want to laugh. They were almost a

parody of-

"Where's Miranda?"

My eyes shot open in time to see Dr Hawkins take a step back. Mum turned to look at him quizzically.

"Who's Miranda?"

Dr Hawkins put on his best empty smile.

"Miranda was another patient of mine. Eoin developed... quite an attachment to her."

No.

"What do you mean 'was'?" My head spun as I pushed myself up in the bed, my body telling me that I needed to lie down, but I didn't care.

"Eoin, Miranda was transferred to a more secure facility before your treatment, don't you remember? She became quite violent. She tried to attack you, it took two orderlies to pull her off you."

I managed to get my feet over the edge of the bed and on to the floor, as the ache in my head began to pulse in waves of pain. I raised my head so that I could shout in Dr Hawkins' face.

"Miranda would never attack me!"

Dr Hawkins removed his glasses and sighed.

"Of course, I'm afraid short term memory loss is a side effect of the procedure."

Mum gasped, rushing towards me, feeling my head as if she could find where the memories had fallen out.

"Memory loss? Is he going to be ok? I mean it's not going to keep happening, is it?"

"Relax Mrs Murphy, he's fine now. You can't hear any whispers, can you Eoin?"

"No." I said, through gritted teeth. I really wanted to smack that smug expression off his face.

"And you can't hear Charlie?"

"No."

"I bet you can't even feel any of that shield or center nonsense, can you?"

I wanted to lie, so very much. But I looked up at Mum and the blood was rushing back to her face as she held my cheeks, looking hopeful.

"No. I can't feel any of it."

Dr Hawkins held out his hands, smiling wide.

"Wonderful, a resounding success. It's my opinion that you should be able to return to a normal life. There will need to be follow ups of course, and possibly repeat sessions, but effectively you're cured."

No. My mind refused to accept that sentence. He couldn't just take it all away, not when I was just coming to rely on it.

"What?"

Mum threw her arms around him.

"Oh Dr Hawkins, thank you so much!"

Why was Mum hugging Dr Hawkins and thanking him for crippling me?

"I'll leave you two alone to catch up. Mrs Murphy, I'll bring along the paperwork for you to sign to take Eoin home."

Dr Hawkins left and Mum sat beside me on the bed, beaming widely, her voice high and manic.

"Oh Eoin, it's wonderful, I'm so happy. I can't wait to bring you home, everything's going to be ok now."

I shook my head, the pain was growing, along with my confusion.

"Mum, I had one therapy session and it caused me to lose part of my memory. How can everything be ok?"

She smiled at me, tears running down her cheeks.

"Because it's a miracle! I can finally bring you home and you can have a normal life!"

The headache was making it difficult to think, and the room was starting to spin.

"I don't think I even know what normal is anymore."

"Normal, Eoin, with home and school and happiness. No voices, no Charlie, no imaginary battles with Furies. Just you and me, in a happy home."

The headache was getting worse.

"That ... it's not..."

"What is it, Eoin?"

I looked up into her eyes, brimming with happy tears, and my heart broke. I managed to get some words around the lump in my throat.

"That sounds nice Mum."

The room wouldn't stop spinning. It was just all wrong, the pieces didn't fit.

I leant forward, closing my eyes, trying to think through the pain.

"Mum, I think maybe you should get Dr Hawkins."

Her reply was bright and chirpy, couldn't she see how much it hurt?

"Of course honey, I'll go sign the papers and take you home."

She leaned forward and hugged me tight. The hug felt wrong, but I was distracted by the pain. She stood and moved towards the door.

"Mum?"

She turned, her face bright and happy.

"Yes Eoin?"

Pain sliced through my mind. I wanted to shade my eyes against the dim light, to lie back on the bed and wait until it was time to go, but I couldn't. There were some things in life that had to be said, and if you let the moment pass you by, it would be too late.

"Mum, how do you know about the Furies?"

"What?" her smile wavered.

"The Furies, fighting them, how did you know about that?"

My head felt like it was splitting in two, it was unbearable, but then I'd suffered unbearable pain too often to count.

She held her smile in place, but it had become forced.

"Oh, em... Dr Hawkins told me of course."

I shook my head, but only once, because it made white spots appear behind my eyelids.

"I didn't tell Dr Hawkins about the Furies, not their name, I never told anyone that."

I gritted my teeth against the pain, gripping the edge of

the bed, staring up at her.

She looked around the room, as if searching for the answer.

"I... I heard you talking in your sleep about them."

I could feel the blade slicing through my head, it was carving me up. It took all my strength to stand up and take a step towards her.

"Which is it Mum, did he tell you or did you hear it?"

The questioned seemed to hurt her, she grimaced as she looked at me.

"The second one? NO! Both! Yes, both, he told me, then I heard you say the name in your sleep."

As I took another step towards her the blade of pain moved to my limbs. My body twitched in response to the feeling of my muscles being torn apart. I needed to scream, I had to let it out. I needed to scream, but there was something I had to do first. Taking another faltering step forward, I reached up and grabbed Mum by the shoulders, gripping her tight.

Her eyes went wide. She tried to pull back, but my grip was too strong.

"Eoin, what are you doing? Please, you're hurting me."

I grimaced as I felt the blade slice open my stomach. But I looked her in the eye, and I said what I had to say, shouting the words into her face.

"You! Are Not! My Mother!"

And then I screamed at her, shaking her shoulders. Her scream mirrored mine, and as my rage built, her scream rose until she was screeching, a familiar screech dripping with malice and hatred. She punched me in the stomach and I felt my flesh tear. I looked down to see her black talons digging into my stomach. When I looked back up I was faced with a beaked lizard head, screeching hate in my face. I gripped its head and sent energy between my hands. I imagined bolts of electricity, frying and destroying everything between my palms. The creature's body convulsed as I shocked it, over and over again. I roared my rage at it until its head melted between my hands and its body fell back.

I reached down, putting pressure on my stomach, blood flowing between my fingers.

"Try that for electroshock."

I stumbled and fell, but I didn't hit the floor, I fell right through into the darkness and the pain.

34

I jerked up screaming, clutching at my stomach.

Eoin! Thank Gods! Eoin! Are you ok?

I thrashed on the bed, gripping my stomach. I could feel the pieces coming apart. I curled up into a tight ball, choking out pain filled sobs.

Eoin, it's ok, you're back. Oh Gods, I thought I'd lost you. It's ok, whatever you're feeling, it's not real. It's not real, focus on my voice, breathe Eoin, breathe.

I didn't want to look at my shredded stomach, I didn't think I could take it. Seeing it would be the thing that finally pushed me over the edge, but it had to be done. Hesitantly, with tears streaming from my eyes, I steeled myself and looked down. No blood. Tentatively, I moved my hands. Nothing... I was fine! I almost laughed with relief. I could still feel the pain, still feel my insides all torn up, but seeing myself whole helped. I concentrated on my breathing and felt the pain slowly begin to recede.

Eoin, talk to me, what's happening?

I held up a finger to silence him, I had to do something first. As my breathing slowed, I reached inside myself and found my center. It was weak and faded, battered and bruised, but it was there. I could feel the line running from it to the earth. My shield wasn't up, but that wasn't really surprising given what had happened.

"Ok. Ok, I'm back."

Eoin, what happened? When you faded out on the plain I thought we'd lost you. Miranda completely lost it, it was all I could do to stop her running off to look for you.

"Really? Well, I'm sure you kissed it all better."

It's hard to say what the dominant expression on my face was, but I'd guess at disgust with a hint of rage.

Ah…

I managed to push myself to my feet as I shouted at the air.

"How could you, Charlie? You've spent all this time trying to convince me I'm in love with Miranda, you used that love to make me tear myself apart trying to save her, and then you kissed her. What the hell where you thinking?"

Charlie's words came quickly, tripping over each other.

Now, in fairness, she kissed me.

"And you kissed her back!"

Yeah, and then she punched me!

"That's no exc… sorry what?"

I'm sorry Eoin, I really am. It's just I haven't exactly had a lot of contact with others in my life, and when she kissed me I kind of lost it for a moment. It was… it was amazing. That's no excuse I know and I'm truly sorry and I won't ever let it happ-

"Hold on, get back to the part where she punched you."

Oh, well I thought you'd seen that. When I started kissing her back, she stopped me and pulled back a bit. She had this confused look on her face and her head was cocked to one side like a bird. Then she just drew back her arm and clocked me in the jaw.

"What!?"

Yeah, knocked me to the ground and left a hell of a bruise. Then she screamed at me that I wasn't her knight and she wasn't mine to kiss.

A tense silence filled the room. It went on for a full ten seconds before I broke it with laughter. I couldn't help it, it just rose up uncontrollably. Within seconds I was bent double, holding my sides as I struggled to breathe, the guffaws still coming.

Hey! It's not fu... well, maybe it's a little funny.

"It's hilarious!"

I had a mental image of tiny Miranda punching out Charlie in all his chainmail and I bent over laughing again. Eventually I regained some control of myself and contented myself with a great big smile and a low whisper.

"That's my girl"

So you're claiming her as yours then? We can drop all this denial crap?

"Yes Charlie." I said, my expression serious "She's my damsel, I'm her knight, and if you EVER kiss her again..."

She'll probably kill me herself.

I smiled up at the air.

"That's true."

So, are we ok?

I thought about it. I could still feel the pain of watching him kiss her, and thinking about it made me want to hit something, but she'd thought he was me and I didn't want to lose my brother.

"You ever going to kiss her again?"

Gods, no Eoin, I promise.

"Well then, keep that promise and we should be ok."

I could feel the tension lingering, maybe it would pass in time.

So what happened? I'd hoped you'd returned to your body when you faded out but you were still gone when I got back here.

"You got Miranda back safe?"

Of course, first thing I did, though it took a while to convince her I wasn't a monster. She's back in her room, probably still asleep.

I felt something inside me relax. "Good."

So, what happened?

I told Charlie about the fake reality where I had been shocked normal. It had felt so real, and yet something inside me was screaming the whole time that it was wrong.

I finished with a description of melting the head of the creature that wasn't Mum as its talons tore through my stomach.

"...ew"

"Yeah, not something I want to go through again. Was it a Fury? Can they do that? Trap you in a dream?"

I don't know. I've heard stories about people trapped in a false world, while all their energy is slowly sucked away. But I don't know if it's a Fury that does it or something else, or if it's just a different type of Fury or a skill some of them have. The stories are always vague, probably because very few people taken like that ever get out. The dream feeds you your deepest desire, it's hard to push that away and accept it's not real.

"So being normal is my deepest desire?"

Isn't it?

Charlie's voice was low and sad, I considered the question.

"It used to be, and for part of me, I guess it still is. But if being normal means giving up you, and Miranda, then I'd rather be crazy."

I imagined Charlie's smile as the room warmed a little.

How are you feeling?

I shrugged, wincing a little.

"Like I've been beaten up for three days straight. I'm also completely drained, I don't think I have anything else left in me."

I'm not surprised given what we went through. Eoin, we-

"I know."

My shoulders slumped as I continued.

"We can't do that again tonight." I stared down at the floor, before looking up again.

"But we can't let them get her either."

I expected an argument, but Charlie's chirpy voice responded immediately.

I'm with you, totally on board with that plan. No way are we letting them get their dirty talons on her, no Sir.

I just have one teeny, little question.

I quirked an eyebrow.

"How are we going to do it?"

That would be the one, yeah.

I sighed, running my hands through my hair.

"I don't know Charlie, I really don't know. But we have until tonight to figure that out."

Breakfast came soon after. I wolfed it down like I'd been starved for days.

Whoa Eoin, breathe between swallows.

I coughed a little, then drank some juice to clear my throat.

"Sorry, I'm starving."

Of course you are, your body can tell how drained it is. Food will help, but you need more than calories to recharge.

"Like what?"

You need sunlight, nature, life, energy, closeness, laughter. All the things that make you feel warm and happy. That's what'll replenish you.

"I don't think I'll get much of that in here."

No, which means you're going to be weak and drained when tonight comes.

"Isn't there anything in here that will get me recharged?"

Well, the fact that I'm here helps. Time with someone you care about replenishes your spirit, gives you what you need to carry on in life, that's true of everyone, not just you.

I sat back on the bed, leaning against the wall.

"So if I could get to see Mum?"

Charlie's reply was slow and uncertain.

Maybe, but I don't think Dr Hawkins has that in the plans for today. Besides, asking Mum for a half hour long hug might make her think you've really lost your marbles.

I let the back of my head fall against the wall with a soft tap. There had to be something else. Something that felt like home. Only one thought occurred and I didn't know if Charlie would laugh.

"What about Miranda?"

Huh... I suppose that might work. You two definitely seem to spark off each other. I don't know if it will get you ready enough, but it couldn't hurt.

I breathed a small sigh of relief that it wasn't a crazy idea.

"So how do I get quality time with Miranda? And even if I do, it won't be enough to let me fight like that again tonight, so how do we protect her?"

You could ask Dr Hawkins?

"To protect her?" I said, sounding puzzled.

To let you have time with her, doofus.

I shook my head as I stood back up and restlessly paced the tiny room.

"I don't know if that would work, I don't think he likes me very much at the moment."

Well it can't hurt to ask, he certainly seems interested in your interactions with her.

I stopped pacing to look up.

"Because she's like me, that's what you said, right? He's interested in people like me?"

Charlie's reply came a little too slow for my comfort.

Yeah, the details are a bit fuzzy but you're not the first spirit sensitive person that's passed into Dr Hawkins' care.

"How do you know?"

Gossip mostly, spirits can't really do much with themselves, so they love to gossip.

It's also why you've not been tormented much, even now while you're not shielded, Miranda's not the first person they've had here that was plagued by the Furies. No spirit in their right mind wants to go anywhere near this place.

I smiled and said so softly that I didn't know if he'd hear it.

"Except for you."

Hey! At no time did I profess to being in my right mind, nor did I indicate that I wanted to go anywhere near the

Furies. They came after me, remember?

"I remember. Thank you Charlie, for not running."

I felt the air grow warmer as he delivered his sardonic reply.

Like I'd leave you to get all the glory.

35

I spent some time meditating, Charlie said it would help me rest and recover. I thought I'd have to sit on the floor with my legs in a knot and my hands making weird shapes, but Charlie said that lying down was fine. That seemed wrong, surely you can't meditate properly unless you're uncomfortable, I was sure that was a rule or something.

As I lay on the bed, my breathing slow, my body calm, my mind floating comfortably in the darkness within, I felt some strength return to my center. At the end of the meditation, I managed a shield. Not as thick as I would like, but it was solid and it was there and it didn't drain me. As I sat up on the bed I felt refreshed, better.

There's some colour back in your cheeks.

"There wasn't any before?"

You were looking a little pale, in the sense that a little means a lot, and pale means ghostly.

I smirked and shook my head.

"Gee, thanks for letting me know."

His reply was swift and glib.

Didn't want to worry you.

I smiled, it was nice to bicker back and forth, it was something I'd never known I was missing. The knock on the door made me jump up from the bed.

"Yeah?"

A familiar voice answered.

"Mornin' kid, Dr Hawkins has you scheduled for a session in about half an hour, I thought you might want to grab a shower and change."

I smiled as I answered. "Thanks Earl, that would be great."

I whispered hastily to Charlie as the door lock scraped and clunked.

"Stick with me."

It was Earl that walked me to the showers. We passed Frank sitting at the orderly's desk, he didn't look up from his paperback, just reached out to buzz us through. I got the feeling that Frank wasn't the most dedicated of employees.

Earl walked side by side with me to the showers, hands in his pockets. I walked along, staring at the floor.

"How you holding up kid?"

I looked up.

"Ok, I guess. I don't think I've hit anyone. I was out for a while, woke up in the infirmary."

"So I heard."

"But I think I just fell over and then didn't move, so no biting this time."

"You hit your head on the way down?"

I put my hand to the back of my head. That hadn't occurred to me. I guess when your fighting for your sanity it's easy to gloss over a possible concussion.

"I don't think so."

"Good, you can really hurt yourself that way. They tell you if they think it's gonna happen again?"

"Oh. No, they didn't say much about it at all. Dr Hawkins just said that we'd start sessions again since I was awake."

Earl cocked his head at me. "Huh."

"Is that bad?"

"No, no, I'm sure Dr Hawkins knows what he's doing."

I let the silence sit a few seconds before I asked about what I really wanted to know.

"Has Miranda been ok?"

He smiled and walked a few steps before answering.

"Frank said she was acting up a little last night, but she quietened down."

I remembered Frank buzzing us out of the ward.

"Frank was on last night as well?"

"Yeah, double shift, we're always shorthanded around here."

"But it's just me and Miranda."

Earl looked across at me as we walked.

"In your ward yeah, but we have a couple of other wards with patients that are less…"

"Crazy?"

He gave me a lopsided smile. "That require less monitoring."

"How come I haven't seen anyone?"

Earl took a second to answer and I thought he must be trying to framing a diplomatic answer.

"Your ward is kept segregated. You get the rec room afternoons, other wards get it in the morning."

I asked my next question in a soft tone that made plain the answer I was hoping for.

"Is it because I'm dangerous?"

We walked a few more steps.

"Do you feel dangerous?"

I thought about it.

"Not right now no, but I did nearly hurt people, and there's no way to guarantee that won't happen again."

Earl frowned.

"Same could be said of a lot of people."

I let out a small laugh. "Yeah, but that's just people with a temper, or something that sets them off, they're not crazy."

"Maybe, or maybe they're a type of crazy that everyone accepts."

It was my turn to cock my head. "Huh, I guess I never looked at it like that."

He held his hand against the shower room door, but before he opened it he looked me in the eye and nodded.

"Something to think about."

36

Earl left me to grab my own change of clothes and towel before I headed around the corner to the shower stalls.

I turned the water on and stood letting the stream hit me. As the hot droplets hit my skin I felt a long weary sigh escape me, as if of its own volition.

Feeling better?

I kept my voice low, hoping the noise of the shower would cover it.

"Lots." I leaned forward, resting my forehead against the tiles and letting the stream hit my shoulders and all the tension therein.

Flowing water grounds you naturally, and washes away any supernatural gunk that's sticking to you. If you imagine it running through your shield, cleansing it, it should help even more.

I paid attention to the water as it flowed across my skin. I reached out mentally to feel my shield tight against me. The water flowed under and through the shield. I imagined the water rinsing through the shield, carrying any specks of dirt down and back to the earth, until my shield sparkled in my mind's eye.

"Eoin, finish up soon or you'll be late for your session."

I stretched in the stream, feeling refreshed and a little stronger.

"Ok!"

Well he seems nicer than the other one.

"I like him," I whispered "He's the only one who isn't

scared of me."

I wonder why that is.

I gave the air above me a look.

What?! I know you're fine but there has been a lot of circumstantial evidence that might persuade others to the contrary.

I leaned against the tiled wall and sighed. "I suppose so."

I finished up, towelled myself dry and put on the clean clothes before returning to Earl, throwing the towel and dirty clothes in their respective hampers.

Earl stood forward from where he'd been leaning against the wall.

"Well you're looking a bit fresher."

"Smelling a bit fresher too."

He gave a laugh that was cut short by the bang of Dr Hawkins barrelling through the door.

"Eoin! There you are, I was wondering where you'd gotten to."

The smile fell from my face. "Hello, Dr Hawkins."

"Earl! Why did you take Eoin off the ward when we had a session today?"

Earl seemed to slouch a little, his smile gone, his voice more polite. "Sorry Dr Hawkins, I was just letting him take a shower, and it's five minutes until his session."

"Well I came looking for him now and he wasn't there!"

Dr Hawkins waved me hurriedly through the door.

"Eoin, come with me. Earl, I'll speak to you later."

Dr Hawkins stormed off. I offered Earl an apologetic shrug and walked after him.

Dr Hawkins marched down the corridor, not even checking to see if I was following. It occurred to me that he was the second person today not to walk behind me as if I needed to be watched, but whereas Earl walked beside me making conversation, Dr Hawkins made me feel irrelevant. He barged through the door of his office leaving it open. As I looked in I saw him sitting in his usual chair by the couch, his elbows on his knees, his fingers steepled in front of his nose as he stared into the distance. I entered, closing the door with care.

"Dr Hawkins?"

He jerked around. "What!? Oh, Eoin, of course, please lie down and we'll begin."

He picked up his usual pad and pen but his eyes still seemed to be seeing something other than the here and now.. I sat on the edge of the couch facing him, but didn't lie down.

"Are you okay, Sir?"

"Hmm?" He looked up and attempted a smile. "Yes Eoin, it's nothing, budgetary worries and such. How have you been feeling?"

He began scribbling on his pad before I answered.

"Fine, thank you."

"Good, good." His hand jerked back and forth across the page, but it scribbled to a stop as I didn't go on. His head raised as his brows knitted.

"That's it? Just fine?"

"Yes, thank you."

"You don't want to talk about the fact that you went into a coma? Or what caused it?"

"I'm sure you'll want to and I'm happy to answer any questions you have."

It was actually entertaining watching his face slowly turn red.

Careful Eoin, we want favours off him remember?

Ah right. I backtracked as much as I could.

"I mean, I don't really know where to start, it's all so confusing. Perhaps if you could start Dr Hawkins, I could try to make sense of it all?"

He narrowed his eyes but seemed somewhat mollified. I'd underestimated how annoyed he was today.

"Very well, let's start from the beginning. What is the last thing you remember from the day you went into the coma?"

"I was playing checkers with Miranda, the room started spinning, and then everything went black."

His scribbling had resumed and he didn't bother to look up as he rattled off his questions.

"And what's the next thing you remember?"

"Waking up in the room where the nurse and you came in."

"What about the dreams? The dragons?"

I nodded and smiled.

"Well yes, but that didn't really happen."

"And have you had any other unusual occurrences since then?"

I licked my lips, I really didn't want to reveal too much to him. I just didn't know if I could trust him anymore. It wasn't just what Charlie had said, his behaviour today was unnerving me.

We're going to have to give him something or else he'll think you're stonewalling him.

"I… I think I had a dream. It seemed real, but it couldn't have been."

He leaned forward eagerly, his face lighting up for the first time since we'd begun.

"Tell me."

"I dreamt that I woke up in my room, but I couldn't move, not even to open my eyes. I could hear voices, it was my Mum and you. You were talking about me, about a treatment. Slowly I was able to start moving, but I was very weak. When I moved you told me that I had been given electroshock therapy, that it had cured me and I was going home with Mum."

His eyebrows arched as I finished.

"Eoin, you know I would never use electroconvulsive therapy in your case? It's mostly used for people with chronic depression that have not responded to any other treatments."

"I know, even in the dream I knew it was wrong, I knew it didn't make sense. I think that shocked me out of it, and I woke up."

He kept writing but shot me a doubtful look

"And this was last night?"

I bit my lip as I answered.

"Mmhmm."

"How very strange. And did you dream anything else?"

I was getting tired of half truths. I needed to steer him towards what I wanted to talk about.

"Not really. I found it hard to sleep to tell the truth, I was worried about Miranda."

"Ah, yes I heard she had a bad night. She quietened down after an hour or so though, did you slept ok then?"

I shook my head and gave him a serious look that I didn't have to fake.

"Just because she stopped screaming, doesn't mean I stopped worrying."

Dr Hawkins gave me a knowing smile.

"Quite."

"Actually, I was hoping I could ask a favour, Sir."

This warranted but one eyebrow.

"Yes?"

"Would it be ok if Miranda and I went to the rec room again this afternoon? I was just so worried, it would be nice to see her safe and well for an hour or so."

Nice, play on the heart strings.

"No, I'm afraid not Eoin."

Of course that assumes he has an instrument.

"Please Sir, I'm doing so well, amn't I? And I hear Miranda is the best she's ever been. I mean we're working so hard, please?"

Dr Hawkins stopped and looked at me. I felt like a cow that he was considering for dinner.

"Is Charlie here, Eoin?"

Shit.

Shit, shit, shit.

I froze, I didn't know what to say. What was the right answer? What would get him to let me see Miranda?

It is easier to deceive with the truth than with lies.

Ok, good advice, even if it sounded like it came from a fortune cookie.

"He is."

A smile spread across Dr Hawkins' face like a flaming oil slick.

"Good. I have an experiment I want to run. If the experiment is successful, you can have your recreation time."

"With Miranda?"

"Of course, with Miranda. Do we have a deal?"

"But if I don't know what the experiment is, how can I know if I'll be able to do it?"

"Eoin, please understand that the illusion of choice is a gesture I am making to aid your comfort."

The tone of his voice was overbearing, heavy. I felt the temperature plummet. I didn't know if it was Charlie or me or all in my head. I looked into Dr Hawkins' eyes and saw nothing but emptiness. For a moment I thought one of the Furies had possessed him, if that was even possible, but then I realised I was just seeing the cold heart that had been inside him all along.

Sometimes I really hate it when I'm right.

"I agree."

Dr Hawkins arched an eyebrow. "Good. We can begin immediately."

He stood and went to his desk, opening one of the drawers.

"It's a very simple experiment, you won't even have to move."

He removed what looked like a slim pack of cards from the drawer before returning to his seat.

Oh shit.

I wanted to ask what was wrong, but I really didn't know if talking to Charlie in front of Dr Hawkins would makes things worse or not.

"Eoin, these are called Zener cards. There are five different types of card, and 5 of each type, 25 cards in all." He started flipping up the cards, they were blank on one side with a shape on the other. "We have a circle, a cross, waves, a square and a star. I'm going to show you the back of a card. I want you to ask Charlie what shape is on the card and tell me what he says. Do you think you can do that?"

Dr Hawkins sat completely still as he awaited my reply, but I could see the tension in his body and in his aura, which practically vibrated.

Eoin, this is a really bad idea, like monumentally bad. I can't begin to describe how catastrophically bad an idea this is.

I turned my gaze up and to my left so that Dr Hawkins would know I was speaking to Charlie.

"Can you do it?"

The silence went on long enough to make me worry.

Yeah, I can, but this is seriously more trouble than it's worth, there has to be another way.

"Well there isn't."

I turned back to Dr Hawkins.

"Ok, we do this and Miranda and I get to go to the rec room?"

"If you do well on the test, then yes."

I looked back up to my left.

Yeah, I get it, no lying.

I sighed and nodded to Dr Hawkins.

"Ok, we're ready."

He moved a small table over beside me and shuffled the cards before placing them in a pile face down on the surface. He sat behind it with his notepad on his knee and his pen poised. I sat facing him, my hands gripping the side of the couch. Dr Hawkins fiddled with something under the table and then we began.

"Ok Eoin, what does Charlie say is on the first card?"

"Charlie?"

It's a circle.

"Circle."

Dr Hawkins eyes lit up as I answered. He placed the card face down beside the pile, scribbling hurriedly in his notepad, before showing me the back of the next card.

"And now?"

I looked up.

Eoin, I don't think you understand what you're doing here, if you'd just let me explain-

"What's on the card Charlie?"

I kept my tone low, but I don't think I've ever sounded more menacing in my life. I knew that Charlie wasn't going to be happy, but I was not missing out on a chance to talk to Miranda before tonight.

It's a cross.

"Cross."

"Good, now again."

"How many times do we have to do this?"

"All the way to the end of the pack, Eoin, that's the experiment."

I bit my lip, but carried on. The next card was a circle, then another circle, then a square. As we moved on Charlie's answers became sullen, but he kept giving them. Dr Hawkins got shaky as we neared the end of the pack. He could barely hold the last card steady, his hand was shaking so much.

"Last card Eoin, what is it?"

Its waves, which is apt since we are going to drown in the shitstorm you've just created.

"It's waves, are we done now?"

Dr Hawkins was deathly pale. He placed the card face down on the table and tried to write on his notepad. After a couple of attempts and a very deep breath he managed it.

"Yes Eoin, we're done."

"How did I do? Can we go get Miranda now?"

"You got them all right Eoin, every single one, from start to finish."

His voice was weak and far off.

"That's good, right?"

Yeah, if by good you mean suicidal.

"I mean that's what you wanted, right?"

"Hmm?" He seemed to notice me again. "Oh, yes, very well done Eoin. Do you think you might be able to do it again tomorrow?"

No!

"Sure, can we go get Miranda now?"

"What? Oh, of course, go back to the ward. I have some phone calls I need to make."

"Can you call the ward first Sir, and tell them we can go to the rec room? Please? You promised."

"Hmm? Yes, of course, your reward." He stood up slowly, leaning heavily on the arms of his chair. Moving to his desk, he sat down again, before lifting up his phone and pushing a button.

"Hello? Yes, Eoin and Miranda will be heading to the rec room once Eoin gets back to the ward, see to it."

He hung up but kept his hand on the receiver, staring at it.

"Will I go now, Dr Hawkins?"

"What? Yes, head back to the ward Eoin, you know the way. I have an awful lot of things to do."

He was very still for someone with so much to do. I walked slowly to the door and let myself out, gently shutting it behind me.

37

Ok, run.

"What?"

I'd never heard Charlie's voice so scared, and we'd fought dragons.

Eoin, are you blind? He's left you completely alone, no escort. Find the exit and let's get out of here.

"Are you crazy?"

I thought I wasn't, but after watching you sign our death warrants in there I think I might have cracked.

I took a deep breath before I tried to talk some sense into

him.

"Firstly, the entrance will have a swipe card just like the ward, so we can't just leave. Secondly, what the hell are you on about and what was with your attitude in there?"

Eoin, I love you, you're my brother, but sometimes you can be so incredibly and unbelievably dense that I want to tear off your head, just so I can beat some sense into it.

"What? What have I done wrong? We did a simple test that we aced, so we get to talk to Miranda and sort a plan for tonight."

Eoin, what is the purpose of the Furies?

"To make life hell for people like me and Miranda so that the world doesn't become aware of our abilities. What's with the pop quiz?"

If the powers were worried enough about Dr Hawkins' interest in you and Miranda to send the Furies, what exactly do you think they're going to do now that you've given him experimental proof of the existence of paranormal perception?

"But it's not like I showed the world, it was just Dr Hawkins. There are hundreds of people going on about ESP and seeing spirits, what makes Dr Hawkins any different? People won't believe him."

Oh I don't know, I mean he did have that controller thing under the table. Didn't you wonder what that was for, or think to notice that there were cameras in his office?. I think that might persuade a few people!

"...Ah."

Yes, ah. He probably has footage of the entire thing. It'll be up on YouTube by tomorrow, but don't worry, we won't see it because every power in the spirit world is going to come tear us a new one tonight.

I stopped in the middle of the corridor, throwing my hands up in the air.

"Would it help if I said I was sorry?"

It'd be a start. I TOLD you it was a bad idea but you just wouldn't listen!

"I'm sorry, but I couldn't see any other way to see

IAN PAUL POWER

Miranda before tonight, could you?"

No, but I still don't think we should have done it.

My hands balled into fists.

"Charlie, if we don't see Miranda, we won't be able to figure out a plan for tonight. We will have to listen as she dies, torn apart piece by piece. Could you live with that? I couldn't. I'd try to save her, and you'd try to help me so we'd probably all end up dead, or deader in your case."

It hurt to listen to the silence.

So instead, you me and Miranda have to figure out how to stand against everything the powers of the spirit world can throw at us?

"Looks like it."

Well then what are you doing standing around in the corridor like a spare plank? We have work to do.

I smiled and relaxed my hands.

"I love you, Charlie."

I love you too, even if you're an idiot.

I laughed and headed back to the ward. I knocked on the ward door when I arrived, since there was no one to swipe me in. Eventually, after a couple of more knocks, Frank opened the door.

"What are you up to kid, did you get away from the Doc?"

"No, he sent me back by myself."

"What?"

I offered a shrug.

"Well get back to your room, Earl is coming to take you to the rec room."

I strolled to my room, throwing myself on to the bed when I got there, staring at the ceiling, hands above my head.

So, plan?

"You don't have one?"

What, you expect me to do everything?

"Hey, only one of us is the other worldly presence here."

That doesn't make me omniscient.

202

"Pity, because I have this history test coming up I was hoping you could help with."

We'll be history if we don't do something, Eoin.

"Noted." I sat up on the edge of the bed. "Ok, Miranda is the weak link. With her open to attack, they can lure us out of any stronghold we create."

Yes, our shield was holding before we charged out like idiots last night.

"So, what if we put Miranda in a stronghold of her own?"

Good idea, but it won't work. You have to be in a room to shield it, and I can't see you sneaking into Miranda's room long enough to pull it off.

"What if we teach her to do it herself?"

What, now? It took you over a week of slow progression to get to the point where you could pull it off, and to be honest, that's about a third of the time I thought it would take. We can't teach her how to do it in one afternoon.

"You said yourself that Miranda has survived the Furies longer than anyone else you've heard about. If anyone can do it, she can. Besides, do you have a better idea?"

You know I don't. Ok, we'll give it a try. Who knows, maybe she'll surprise us.

"Oh if there's one thing she's good at, it's surprises."

38

It wasn't long before Earl stuck his head in my open door.

"Hey kid, I'm just about to get Miranda, you ready to go?"

"Ready when you are."

Earl walked off down the corridor and I rose to follow him. He reached Miranda's door before me and knocked swiftly.

"Miranda, time to go to the rec room darlin'"

He unlocked the door and began to open it, but before he had it half open there was a blur and Miranda was clamped around one of Earl's legs. There was a scrape and clatter behind me and I turned to see Frank running up the corridor, his chair still sliding back towards the desk. Earl raised his hand as Frank ran towards him.

"Frank! No, it's ok, she's… she's just hugging me, it's fine."

He was right, Miranda was sitting on the floor, her arms hugging his leg. She had a wide smile on her face and she seemed to be cuddling into him, chattering as she did.

"Oh thank you, thank you, thank you. I know you didn't have to and you were always the nicest one and never got angry. It will fix everything, or most things at least, and not enough people will say it so thank, thank, thank you!"

Frank had slowed his run but was still moving towards him as Earl gently tried to prise Miranda off his leg.

"Miranda darlin' I haven't done anything, I'm just here to bring you to the rec room."

Miranda quirked her head up at him and loosened her grip.

"You haven't? Are you sure? Because I remember, and all the things I remember happen, even the dragons."

Earl smiled down at her. "I'm sure they do, but do you think you could let go of my leg so we can head to the rec room now?"

Miranda nodded her head before giving his leg an extra big squeeze.

"Ok, but thank you, even if you don't remember."

Earl placed a hand on her head. "You're welcome, Miranda."

Then Miranda saw me and she moved like a blur. Frank, standing between us, jumped to try and intercept her but she moved like water, effortlessly flowing through the space where he wasn't, before ploughing into me. I was prepared this time and managed to remain upright as she cuddled up against me.

"Oh I missed you, you were so brave I'm so glad the big mean dragons didn't eat you. The 'not you' said he didn't know where you were, I was going to hit him again but he showed me how to wake up, he'd better not try pretending to be you again."

Perish the thought.

Miranda giggled. "Can thoughts perish? I suppose they can grow and get lost. What do you feed thoughts to keep them from perishing? Maybe I could perish my thoughts just a little and they might stay in the same place for a while."

I looked up.

"Did she just-"

Ix-nay on the alking-tay in front of the ormals-nay!

Earl and Frank were staring at us, Frank with a frown, Earl with a smile. I looked back down at Miranda.

"Maybe your thoughts feed on attention, so the less you think about them the more they perish, but if you come back to them in time they'll still be where you left them?"

Her face lit up as she looked up at me.

"That's a brilliant idea! I'm going to try that on the thoughts I need, just as soon as I find them again."

Her eyes looked over my shoulder, into the distance, and when she spoke again her words were less frantic.

"Oh, but it's time to pretend to play now, I don't think I like that as much as playing for real but I guess we'll have to find out."

With that she released me from the hug, grabbed my hand and started pulling me down the corridor towards the doors, giggling loudly as she did. I trailed back, letting her pull me along, before turning to look over my shoulder.

"Em… Earl?"

He laughed as he started walking towards us, patting Frank on the back as he passed him.

"I'm coming, see you in an hour Frank."

Earl walked up ahead as a giggling Miranda dragged me up the corridor. I couldn't help but smile and I was laughing myself by the time we reached the door which Earl was holding open. Once we were out in the main corridor, Miranda was content to walk beside me, her hand in mine swinging back and forth.

"You were so brave, Eoin. I could see you fighting you know, and when you hid under the bowl I was so scared but I knew you would be ok. I didn't know you'd 'splode though, you should have seen it, it was incredible. I'm really sorry I kissed 'not you', you'd just 'sploded and it knocked me against the rock and my head was all dizzy, do you forgive me?"

She stopped and looked up at me with wide eyes, biting her lip. She looked so soft and vulnerable. I just wanted to take her in my arms and hold her tight and never let her go.

"Yes Miranda, I forgive you." I reached my other hand up and stroked her cheek. "It was an easy mistake to make and he's promised it won't happen again. Come on, we're nearly there."

I pulled her onwards as Earl sauntered behind us with his hands in his pockets.

"Why is 'not you' so quiet? Is his jaw sore? I hit him really hard, I didn't think I could hit that hard but I was so angry, and he fell down very far away."

My name is Charlie and I'm quiet because it looks bad to other people if Eoin starts talking to the air.

"But you're not there, you're here."

No, not there, the air. It looks like he's talking to himself and we've been trying to avoid people thinking he's crazy.

"Oh, well then why are you talking to me?"

Because everyone already thinks you're crazy.

I coughed loudly.

Ok, ok, I'll shut up. Good luck getting her to do the same though.

We turned the corner and waited as Earl went ahead to

unlock the rec room door, holding it open for us as we went inside. I led Miranda to the games cupboard as Earl pulled up a seat at the desk in the corner.

"Why are we going to the games? You don't want to play any."

"No, But I do want Earl to think we're playing a game."

"So making Earl think we're playing a game, is the game?"

I couldn't help but smile. "I suppose you could look at it like that, yeah."

I took the checkers board to the table furthest away from Earl. He looked up but didn't object.

"Ok Charlie," I whispered as I set up the board, "how are we going to do this?"

Well, since we now know she can hear me, I suppose I can try to talk her through it myself.

"Can other people not hear you?" Miranda was making a tower out of her pieces, each piece perfectly placed on top of the one below.

No Miranda they can't, up until now we thought only Eoin could.

Miranda stopped balancing her pieces and looked at me, her face a web of confusion.

"So how did you know you weren't just crazy?"

As she asked the question I realised that I had never known for certain. No matter how much I believed in Charlie and everything that had happened, there was always some small part of me shouting that I was crazy, that it was all in my head and that I was going to spend the rest of my life in a place like this, screaming at the walls.

Even now, talking to someone who I knew was real, and who could also hear Charlie, part of me was waiting to wake up and realise that it was just a dream.

I let my hands place the checkers pieces and spoke to the board, my voice a little weary.

"I guess none of us can know whether we're crazy or not. We just have to do the best we can."

"I do."

Her reply sounded so solemn, I looked up to see her sitting up straight with her hands in her lap, looking into my eyes.

"Do what?"

She dropped her gaze, but kept her solemn tone.

"I know I'm crazy. I have to be, I decided that a long time ago. But then I thought you must be crazy because you're in my crazy. I thought you might be just another part of the crazy."

She looked back up, cocking her head to the side.

"But you take the crazy away, so how can one part of crazy make the other crazy better?"

I thought about Dr Hawkins' early theory, that Charlie was an aspect of my psychosis that helped me control the rest of it.

"I think you'd be surprised how many people might think that could happen."

She shook her head and resumed playing with her pieces.

"Well I don't, it's silly, and not giggly silly, it's determinedly ungiggly silly. But when you were here with the other non-crazy people then I knew you couldn't just be mine, except you are mine, aren't you?"

I looked up into her smiling face and was lost.

"Yours as long as you'll have me."

She smiled, her eyes lighting up, and I felt my heart melt in that moment. She reached across the table and took my hand, her voice shy and timid.

"Can that be forever?"

Sure, after all that's only going to be about another 6 hours.

"Charlie!"

Look I hate to intrude on your moment here, I actually do, but we don't have much time.

I sighed and took my hand back.

"You're right."

I'm always right.

I quirked a smile. "Don't push it. Miranda I want you to listen to Charlie, he's going to try to teach you how to shield yourself."

Miranda's tower of pieces fell rattling to the table. "No! I got lost last time, you said I couldn't but I did, please don't make me!"

"That won't happen again Miranda, Earl's not going to pull me away like that. This is really important, or I wouldn't ask you to try again. Those things are going to come back tonight, and there's going to be more of them. Charlie and I won't be able to protect you from that many, we have to teach you how to protect yourself."

She turned one of the checker pieces around and around in her fingers, staring at it.

"If I try, will you hold my hand again?"

I smiled, reaching across the table to take her hand in mine.

"Of course I will. We'll be right here, we won't let anything happen to you."

Miranda squirmed in her seat, nibbling at her lip.

"I'll try then."

I gave her a smile and saw her blush, which only made me smile more.

"Charlie?"

OK Miranda, did Eoin show you how to breathe and calm yourself and look inside you?

"Yes, before I got lost last time, I could see the grey mist around me with the yellow fishies in it."

Eh, right. Well, concentrate on your breathing and go to the same place as before.

Miranda closed her eyes, her hands gripping tight around mine as she did, relaxing as her breathing slowed. She spoke, her voice low and soft.

"It's difficult, my head is so full. I try to think of breaths but when I do I think that breaths are just air and air is everywhere, so that means that my breaths are Eoin's breaths, and it makes me want to kiss him."

She blushed bright red, squirming and gripping on to

my hands. I wanted nothing more than to lean forward and kiss her in that moment, but there was no time.

Gods save us from young love. Try hard Miranda, don't reach for the calm, let it settle. This is your natural state, before the world and other people start poking you, just let yourself fall into it, slowly, gently.

She breathed in and out a few more times, her rhythm regular now, two seconds breathing in, two breathing out, over and over. I felt her grip on my hands relax a little, her shoulders fall slightly.

Good. Now, can you see your aura Miranda?

"Or a what? A what or a Miranda?... silly Charlie."

Her voice, so soft, moving up and down in her sing song way, was like a lullaby. I felt myself relaxing just listening to it. Her face had settled into a happy smile.

The mist around you Miranda, it's called an aura, can you see it?

"Oh yes, it's yellow! It's yellow with grey fish now! The greys are still too big though." When she pouted her lips she looked so adorable my heart ached. I couldn't help but worry if this was normal. It's not like I'd had any experience with these feelings, or had someone I could talk to about them. Part of me was worried that my feelings for Miranda were just a symptom of everything that was happening, but then I remembered that kiss.

Ok, now I want you to imagine hugging the mist tight against you until it's a thick blanket all around your body.

"Mmhmm." Miranda twisted a little back and forth, snuggling in to her imaginary blanket. As she did I thought I could see a faint yellow light around her head.

Good. Now you have to make the blanket harder, so that things can't get you. Make it form a shield around your skin, protecting you.

Miranda's brow furrowed.

"Can't, mist's too slippy, won't go where I want it to."

Ok, ok. Imagine you're a tree.

"Can I be gumdrop tree?"

There's no such... sure, be a gumdrop tree.

I had to hold back a laugh as Miranda wiggled happily and then began swaying gently back and forth in her seat.

Ok, now a tree has hard bark on the outside to protect itself, but it's still able to move and sway in the wind.

"Sway sway sway, stay sway stay." Miranda mumbled to herself as she moved gently back and forth.

Can you feel your bark Miranda, can you feel the rigid coating surrounding you?

"Yes, it's all thick and knobbly, feels funny."

That's ok, just make sure it completely covers you Miranda, from head to toe.

That got another brow furrow.

"Of course it does, it's bark, I'm a tree."

Of course, silly me. Now whenever bad things come for you Miranda, whenever you feel attacked or threatened, all you have to do is be a gumdrop tree and your bark will protect you.

"Yay!!" She bounced a little before resuming her swaying with a dreamy look on her face.

"Will that protect her tonight?"

For about ten minutes, but it's a start, and come nightfall, every second is going to count.

The door to the rec room burst open and an agitated Dr Hawkins rushed in.

Oh crap.

"My sentiments exactly. Miranda, come back to me now, just come back from the dark inside and open your eyes."

She was humming something to herself as Dr Hawkins headed over to Earl. I was worried she wouldn't hear me, but she turned her head to face me and opened her eyes, her face lighting up when she saw me.

"I feel wonderful."

I smiled and stroked a thumb over the back of her hand.

"And we'll try to keep you feeling that way. It looks like I'll have to go, but I'll try to talk to you again before tonight.

"Ok, I think you'll do more than talk though." She

dipped her chin, looking up at me through her lowered lashes as she blushed.

Well you're totally in there.

"Charlie!" I just about strangled the shout into a hoarse whisper.

"Oh!" Miranda sat, her face lit up with wonder. "I'm still barky!"

And you'll stay barky until tomorrow morning. You'll have to be a gumdrop tree again then to fix your bark, if we live that long.

Dr Hawkins hurried over, Earl followed looking decidedly unhappy.

Dr Hawkins was wearing a somewhat manic smile and rubbing his hands together.

"Eoin, Miranda, good to see you enjoying yourselves."

Miranda stood up and waved her arms up in the air, moving in an unseen breeze.

"We're being gumdrop trees! Well I am anyway, Eoin has his suit of armour so he doesn't need bark."

Dr Hawkins' smile grew forced

"Well doesn't that sound fun? Miranda, I have to talk to Eoin about something very important. Earl will take you back to your room."

Dr Hawkins tensed up, waiting for her to react.

"Ok! Can I hug him goodbye or is that still bold? The other big man was very scared when I hugged Earl."

With a relaxing of his shoulders he waved her towards me.

"I'm sure a hug will be fine, just say goodbye now."

Miranda came around the table and hugged me tight for what seemed like an eternity, yet it was too short. Before she let go she whispered in my ear.

"Don't forget your toothbrush!"

With that she skipped off, grabbing Earl's hand as they left, surprising more than just Earl. I could hear her chattering away to him as they left.

"Have you ever been a tree? It's very relaxing, I think I'll be a tree from now on."

Dr Hawkins stared after them as the door closed.

"Well you've certainly had an effect on Miranda."

I stood, folding my arms.

"Or she's had an effect on herself."

He nodded half heartedly.

"Perhaps, perhaps. Eoin I have something very important to talk to you about."

He's repeating himself, this can't be good.

"There's going to be a meeting of some very important people tomorrow. I want you to do the Zener card experiment for them, just like you did for me today. Do you think you can do that?"

NO! No way, no how!

"I don't know Dr Hawkins. I mean, maybe I just got lucky today."

He patted me on the shoulder.

"Now Eoin, we both know that's not true."

Just like we both know you're not going to do it again.

He gripped my shoulder and looked me in the eye.

"Validation of the experiment will mean a lot to the institute, Eoin."

Validation will only get us killed quicker!

"It could help us secure funding to continue to help Miranda and others like her."

By which he means he wants to make money off you.

Dr Hawkins gave me what he probably thought was a warm smile.

"I know you wouldn't want to see Miranda hurt just because you wouldn't do something."

You evil, conniving, manipulative snake in the grass!

"I want to sleep with Miranda!"

I had just enough time in the shocked silence that followed to realise it was me who had shouted that.

"What?"

What!?!?

"No! I mean, yes but not like that. I want to sleep in the same room as Miranda tonight."

"Eoin, I really don't think that's appropriate."

Eoin, you're a genius!

"We won't get up to anything! Separate beds, you can have the room monitored, cameras, whatever you want. I don't want Miranda to be alone tonight, I don't think I could stand to hear her screams again. I'd be up all night and in no state to do any experiment."

Bam! Take that, Dr Evil!

Dr Hawkins stood with his hands in his pockets, pursing his lips.

"Well, Miranda does seem to be quieter around you. Ok, we'll move Miranda and you to the infirmary for observation tonight. There are cameras there for monitoring purposes so we'll be able to ensure you behave yourselves. But in return , you'll perform for our visitors tomorrow and answer all their questions."

"Deal."

I take it all back Eoin, we might actually... wait we're not going to do that tomorrow, are we?

Dr Hawkins pulled the pack of Zener cards from his pocket.

"But first, let's run through the experiment again. Then I'll make the arrangements."

We ran through the full pack, with Charlie giving me all the answers. Dr Hawkins didn't shake quite as much this time, and he wasn't taking notes. I think he just wanted to see me do it again, so that he knew he wasn't crazy. He made me go through the pack twice, shuffling between each run before he was finally satisfied. He sat with a faraway look on his face.

"Ok Eoin, dinner should be ready, head back to your room. I'll make the arrangements."

"We need to be there before it gets dark."

Dr Hawkins stopped smiling down at the deck he was shuffling long enough to acknowledge me.

"Hmm? Yes, of course, that shouldn't be a problem."

I rose to leave, but realised I was locked in.

"Emm... Dr Hawkins, the door?"

"Yes? Oh, right, let me walk you back to the ward."

34

He walked beside me this time, but it's like I wasn't even there. He whistled quietly to himself, occasionally letting out a bark of laughter, making me look like the sane one. When we reached the ward, he swiped his card and walked through immediately, almost letting the door hit me as I followed. Then he just stood near the orderly's desk, staring off down the corridor and making Frank nervous.

"Dr Hawkins? The arrangements?" I said, nodding my head towards Frank.

"Oh yes, silly me, just so much to think about. You head back to your room, Eoin."

I walked off, looking back over my shoulder. He started talking to Frank, and from Frank's confused reaction I trusted that he was keeping to his word.

Brother you are a genius! Getting him to let you sleep in the same room as Miranda, brilliant!

I smiled as I walked into my room and stretched out on the bed.

"It was one of my better ideas. Will it work?"

Maybe. I mean you can shield the room and we can all stay inside, but after what you pulled today, and what's coming tomorrow, I honestly don't know what they're going to send against us. But at least now we have a good chance of seeing tomorrow. Speaking of which, you're not actually going to perform like a monkey for him, are you?

I sighed and closed my eyes.

"I don't know. I'm just working on getting through tonight Charlie. We'll deal with tomorrow if it arrives."

Dinner sat uneaten on the floor. I knew I should eat but nervousness had chased away my appetite. I lay on the bed, jittery and anxious.

"What if I can't do it Charlie?"

I think this is more of a talk for Mum than me.

My brow furrowed until my brain caught up. "Charlie!"

I threw a pillow at the ceiling, not that it would affect him in any way, but it made me feel better.

"I meant what if I can't protect her, protect us?"

Then we'll all suffer through eternal torment. So, you know, no pressure.

I let out a nervous laugh.

"You really know how to bolster a guy."

It's a skill. Once we're done here I'm thinking I should do seminars.

"I wish Mum was here."

There was a tense silence before he replied.

Me too.

"Why haven't we seen her? I thought she'd be at my bedside if I was in a coma, no matter what Dr Hawkins said. I'm definitely surprised she didn't come to see me when I woke up. She hasn't even called."

That we know of, she could be calling every hour and they're not telling you.

I looked up in disbelief.

"He wouldn't!"

Eoin, right now we don't know what he would or wouldn't do. He's not the benevolent doctor that Mum thought he was, he wants to exploit you.

"First, we'll battle the army of the spirit world, THEN we'll figure out how to get around the manipulative doctor who has me locked away. Priorities, brother."

40

It was only an hour or so before Earl knocked on the open door of my room.

"Hey kid."

"Hey Earl."

He hesitated before leaning into the room and speaking softly.

"Listen, the Doc says that I have to bring you and Miranda to the infirmary for the night. Are you not feeling well?"

"Something like that, we heading now?"

He nodded, but looked suspicious.

"I guess so, if you're ready. I'll have to see if Miranda, well if she's-"

"Currently sane enough to transport?"

Earl made a face.

"Yeah, but I have to say, she's been like a different person since you came along. I wish I knew what the secret was. There's a lot of young people that could use some of the changes I've seen in Miranda."

He was looking me in the eye and his tone held more than his words. I felt as if he was waiting for me to open up and tell him my secret for curing crazy girls.

"I think Miranda just needs to know that there's someone else who understands what she's going through, that she's not alone."

Earl kept eye contact with me until I began to feel uncomfortable, then nodded.

"I can see how that would help. Anything you want to bring along with you for tonight?"

"Sure." I grabbed a couple of books and headed towards the door. "Let's get Miranda."

As we walked up to Miranda's room, Earl stood to the side and gestured at the door.

"You want to knock kid? I think she'll respond better if you let her know what's happening."

I smiled and stepped up to her door, fist raised, when I heard her shout from inside.

"I'm ready! If you'd open the door instead of asking silly questions we could go already."

"Miranda?"

"Oh! That's me! Isn't it? Yes it is. Who's there? Eoin and Earl and Charlie?"

"Who's Charlie?" I ignored Earl and kept talking.

"Yes Miranda, it's us, we're going to-"

"But I don't need firming."

I smiled, I was getting used to keeping up with her replies now.

"It's not because you're sick, it's like-"

"Oh, will there be pillow fights and...other stuff? I don't know what happens at sleepovers."

"Well we can tell stories and practice being trees, would you like that?"

"I've never slept in a tree before!"

"Well there's a first time for everything. Earl is going to open the door." I waved him forward.

Earl unlocked the door and slowly opened it. Miranda was sitting cross legged on her bed facing us, with a folded towel in front of her on which sat her toothbrush and toothpaste.

"Ah." I said, looking up at Earl. "I'll have to get something from my room before we go."

Miranda burst into a fit of giggles.

"You never listen!"

41

We stopped to pick up my toothbrush and headed out of the ward, past a terminally disinterested Frank. Miranda skipped ahead as Earl walked beside me. We watched her skip and spin, dancing from one side of the corridor to the other.

I looked up at Earl as Miranda took another turn without having to be told. "She's never been to the infirmary, has she?"

He shook his head. "Not that I know of, but she might have been there and I don't know about it."

"You think that's the case?"

He stared thoughtfully at her as she pirouetted in the middle of the corridor. "No, no I don't think it is."

I nodded to myself. "Don't worry about us Earl, there are cameras in the infirmary and we'll be monitored, Dr Hawkins said so."

Earl narrowed his eyes.

"Did he now? What else did he say?"

I looked at my feet. "Nothing, just that everything would be fine."

Earl tried to keep his questions casual, but he couldn't hide his concern.

"Did he say why you and Miranda had to sleep in the infirmary?"

"No, maybe it's just easier to keep an eye on us there?"

"Yeah, maybe"

He sounded far from convinced.

Up ahead, Miranda was bouncing up and down in front of the infirmary door.

"We're here! That was a fun trip, can we do it again? Oh, but we'd have to do it backwards, maybe doing it backwards would suck the fun away, what do you think?" She looked up at Earl.

"I think you need to step aside darlin' else I won't be able to get the door open."

"Oh ok!"

Facing forward, Miranda took two large deliberate steps to her right, counting aloud as she moved. She then looked up expectantly.

"Was that aside enough?"

Earl laughed softly.

"That'll do, yeah."

He swiped the door and held it open for us. Miranda burst into the room and ran straight to the second bed on the left.

"Bagsies! My bed. That one is yours." she said, pointing to the next bed down.

Earl smiled down at me.

"Guess that's you told."

I would have argued, but I couldn't stop smiling.

A look of concern washed over his face. "Listen kid, if anything happens, if you... need a hand, use the phone." He pointed to a handset mounted beside the door. "Just press 9 and you should get put through to an on duty orderly, ok?"

Earl's concern felt genuine. It was nice to have someone worried about me without an agenda.

"Ok, thanks Earl."

He reached up and squeezed my shoulder. "You're welcome kid. See you tomorrow."

He swiped his card and opened the door. "Bye Miranda."

Miranda looked over from where she was bouncing up and down on her new bed. "Bye Earl! Thank you again for tomorrow!"

Earl's face took on the look of slight befuddlement that I was beginning to see a lot around Miranda.

"Eh, you're welcome, I guess."

And with that he left, the clunk of the door lock sealing us in.

What the heck was that? Why didn't you just tell him

you asked to sleep here with Miranda?

"Don't know, but it seemed important. Groundwork maybe"

For what!?

"It just seemed like the right thing to say in the moment. Look, can we focus please? We have to lock this place up."

Ok, but I think Miranda is starting to rub off on you.

"Would that be so bad? Don't answer that."

I turned back towards the sound of bouncing.

"Miranda, grab your pillow and come here."

I tried to duck but I wasn't fast enough and I took the blow full force in the face.

"Pillow fight!"

Man, that girl could throw. I opened my mouth and felt my jaw.

"I thought pillows were supposed to be soft."

Suppose it depends on how hard you throw them.

I approached Miranda, who was standing on her bed giggling as she swung another pillow, keeping me at bay.

I tried to sound serious, but it was hard not to laugh.

"Miranda, no, it's not time for a pillow fight right now. We have to make the room a tree, would you like to help?"

That got her attention.

"Oh yes, that sounds like fun! I want to sleep in a tree!"

"Ok, well then grab a pillow and come sit on the floor over here."

I made sure we were sitting in view of one of the cameras, I didn't want them sending in someone because they thought we were up to something. Of course there might be no one watching, but I wasn't taking any chances. We sat on pillows on the floor, facing each other. I took her hands, one in each of mine, gripping them gently.

"Ok, Everyone ready?"

As I'll ever be.

Miranda nodded.

"Yep!"

"Ok Charlie, anything different this time?"

Not much, it's a bigger room, and a bigger threat. I'll

add any juice that I can and if we can incorporate
Miranda's energy that would be good too. Oh and try to
keep the shield around the bathroom down the back, you
don't want to end up getting torn apart just because you
had to go.

I gave the air a smirk. "Good point. Ok Miranda, are
you ready to breathe with me?"

She squeezed my hands tight and looked me in the eyes.

"I've always been ready for you Eoin, it's not my fault
you took so long."

You try not blushing in response to that. Lord knows I
failed.

"Ok, just focus on your breathing. Listen to Charlie,
he'll lead."

I closed my eyes, focusing on my breathing and trying
not to get distracted by the feel of Miranda's hands in
mine. As my breathing slowed I focused inwards, finding
my center. It felt a lot better than this morning, pulsing
with energy. But it still wasn't as bright as it could be. I
felt my concentration waver as a wave of doubt ran
through me. Genius as this plan was, it would be useless
if we didn't have enough energy to pull it off.

Ok, deep breaths, nice and calm. Pull into the darkness
inside yourselves, feel your shields, I mean eh, your bark.
We're going to place a thick layer of bark all around this
room to protect us, ok Miranda?"

"Mmhmm" she replied. Her voice had gone soft again,
and she was trailing her thumbs to and fro over the back
of my hands, causing swirls of sensation.

Ok, now I've put a wall of energy up along the wall
with the door, reach with your minds and see if you can
feel it.

I tried to, but Miranda's touch was too distracting.

"Found it! Oh, your wall is blue, can I poke it?"

No Miranda, not yet. No, don't! Eoin, can you keep up
here? Miranda, what are you doing?

"I'm playing with the wall!"

I coughed, trying to focus, reaching with my mind. I

could sense the wall, but it wasn't flat, it was rippling in places.

What is she doing?

I shrugged my shoulders and tried to stay focused.

"You're asking me?"

I felt along the wall with my mind as the ripples spread and started to harden into ridges.

"Is she..."

I think so. Quick, add your part before she finishes.

I took a thread of energy from within and let it flow into the wall, filling it up. As I did I felt the wall harden, the outside covered in curving ridges, I could even feel knots of energy in places.

As I pulled back with my mind, I let out an awed sigh.

"She made it into bark."

That she did. What's more, she made it strong. I don't know how she did it but those ridges are acting like wave breakers, they're dissipating any energy sent in before it can get to the shield.

"What? How?"

I told you, I don't know!

Miranda started giggling and when I opened my eyes she was bouncing on her pillow. "That was fun, let's do the roof!"

Slowly we shielded the infirmary. It was a much bigger space than my room and took a lot longer, even with Miranda working her crazy mojo. Within about an hour we had the entire infirmary encased in Miranda's bark shield, backed up with extra energy from me and Charlie. When we were done, Miranda stretched and yawned.

"I'm tired now."

I'm not surprised, that was some seriously good work Miranda, well done.

"Thank you! I go to sleep now. Eoin, you tuck me in, which is nice because I've never been tucked in before."

She hopped up into the bed and pulled the covers up over herself.

I looked around the room, I could feel the shield in place,

but it still seemed so vulnerable a place.

"Should we be sleeping?"

Definitely, might be your last chance to dream. Don't worry, when they come you'll wake, and I'll be here.

I stifled my own yawn. "Ok."

I went to Miranda's bed and tucked her covers under her mattress as she giggled. As I smiled down at her, all tucked in, something occurred to me.

"Miranda, do you know if everything works out ok?"

"Oh definitely! Everything works out and we're all very happy."

I felt my heart lift.

"Either that or we all die tonight, but it's definitely one of those two!" She said, nodding her head emphatically.

My smile faltered but I kept my reply cheery.

"Well, good to know it's definitely one of them."

I stroked a strand of hair away from her face and she turned to nuzzle my hand like a baby animal.

"Thank you Eoin, for everything. I love you, I'll always love you, even if we all die."

I leaned down and placed a delicate kiss on her forehead, before whispering "I love you too, Miranda."

I stroked her head before turning to climb into my own bed. I pulled the covers up and lay watching Miranda.

I told you so.

"Shut up you!" I retorted, but I was smiling as I said it.

42

I dreamt. I don't know if it's the only dream I had in the institution, but it's the only one I remember. Miranda and I were having a picnic in the park, under a tree. A big red blanket set the scene, with food from a wicker basket served on little plastic plates. Miranda was sitting in a yellow dress. She looked, different. Her black hair wasn't tangled, it flowed over her shoulders like silk. Her skin was still pale, but a milky pale, that seemed to glow in the sunlight. Her eyes were the brightest I'd ever seen them, and as I stared into them I got lost in a tropical ocean of blue.

"Whatcha looking at?"

Her voice was the sweetest song in the world.

"You, you look so different."

She wiped a crumb of cake from the corner of her perfect, pink lips.

"Am I?"

"You're beautiful. I mean, you're beautiful anyway, I just mean-"

Her giggle cut me off. That at least was the same, but then that was perfect to begin with.

"Silly knight, I've been here the entire time. You just needed to know how to look."

The ground beneath us shook and the leaves began falling from the tree. She leaned in, throwing her arms around my neck and kissing me. In that moment I didn't ever want to wake up. She nuzzled my nose as she pulled back.

"They're here, it's time to earn our future."

And with that she faded away, leaving nothing but the shaking.

43

I was startled awake by movement, grabbing at the sides of the bed to hold myself steady, but the bed wasn't moving. As the next tremor hit I realised that it was all in my head, literally. It felt like my head was being shaken about, but none of my other body parts felt anything. Each tremor sent waves of pain through my brain, and as I placed my head in my hands, I heard a soft keening.

Miranda was sitting up in bed holding her head in her hands, whimpering softly. I scrambled across to her bed so that I could hold her. She threw her arms around me and rested her head against my chest.

Her words came out in a pain filled whimper.

"It hurts Eoin, it hurts when they roar."

"I know, it's ok, it'll be ok." I stroked her hair and looked up.

"Charlie?"

We're in deep shit, Eoin. There are so many attacks on the shield that I can't keep track of them. I honestly can't tell how many Furies are out there, but it's more than we can take. And there's something else out there, something I've never seen before, it's big and powerful and it keeps charging into the shield.

My head shook as the next tremor hit. Miranda squealed and grabbed at my t-shirt.

"Is there any way to stop the pain?"

You need to filter the feedback from the shield, like before.

I nodded, closing my eyes, imagining the vibrations in the shield flowing into my head, imagining them arriving smaller, quieter, like a gentle murmur. When the next tremor hit, it felt a fleeting second of dizziness, but Miranda still squeaked.

"Is there any way we can help her?"

Not really, she's tied to the shield tighter than either of us. Unless you can get her to dampen the signal herself, there's not a lot we can do.

I lifted Miranda's face from my chest so that I could look her in the eye. She resisted, squirming closer against me.

"Miranda, Miranda it's ok. It'll be ok, you have to listen, can you hear me?"

She nodded to me, tears running down her cheeks.

"You need to imagine a wet towel, wrap it all around your head so that everything is muffled. You can still hear the roars, but they're all quiet, can you do that for me? Wrap it all around your head."

She nodded her head and closed her eyes. When the next tremor hit she screamed but kept her eyes closed, her hands gripping at my t-shirt. With the tremor after that she let out a whimper, and the one after that, nothing. Finally she collapsed back against my chest, breathing heavily. I cuddled her close, stroking her hair.

"Charlie, how are we holding up?"

Not too good. To be honest, I'm surprised we've lasted this long. The shield Miranda made is amazing, it's turning aside the Furies' attacks like they were pebbles, but whatever it is that's causing the tremors is weakening it. I don't know how long we can hold up.

I looked around the infirmary, looking so peaceful in the night, and yet I was terrified.

"How long until dawn?"

I could hear the fear in Charlie's reply

Too long, far too long.

My mind reeled, but I couldn't give up.

"Ok, we hold the shield as long as we can, and when it falls, we fight them off until dawn."

There was a pause before Charlie's incredulous answer.

You're serious?

"You have a better idea? Because I'm open to suggestions."

Ok, shore up the shield down the door end, I'll take the other end, we'll do what we can.

I looked down at Miranda, curled up against my chest.

"What about Miranda?"

Let her rest, it looks like the attack is taking a lot out of her.

I tucked Miranda back into bed where she curled up into a ball. Her breathing had calmed though, and she seemed to be asleep. I grabbed a pillow and sat in the middle of the room facing the door. I calmed my breathing and tried to focus inwards, ignoring the shivers and tremors from the shield. Once I was calm and centered, I sent my mind out, probing for weaknesses.

With each tremor attack, the entire shield seemed to tremble, it was difficult to tell which direction it came from. I could feel the shield weakening around the edges as it slowly began to shake apart. I poured energy into the seams, imagining them thickening. I could feel Charlie working behind me, using his own energy. Where the seams ran through the middle of the room, our energy melded. We worked well together, pouring just enough energy in to keep everything secure without tiring ourselves out. For the first hour I thought it might work, I sat in meditation, completely focused on the task, keeping everything balanced. But after the second hour I could feel myself beginning to flag. I just wasn't used to concentrating on a task for this length of time, and I was starting to run out of energy. As the cracks began to spread through my half of the shield, I knew we were losing the battle.

As a particularly bad attack sent a spike of pain through my mind I called out.

"Charlie!"

I know, get to Miranda. I have a plan, it's a long shot, but it just might work.

I climbed on to Miranda's bed, gently shaking her.

"Miranda, I'm sorry, it's time to fight."

She looked up at me and her face was paler than ever before.

"I'm scared, Eoin."

I hugged her close and stroked my fingers through her hair, comforting her.

I wanted to say something calm, confident, but in the end, I had to settle for honesty.

"I know, I'm scared too."

I felt the shield start to collapse, cracks appearing and spreading fast. And I could feel Charlie pouring energy into it, but not to repair it, it seemed like he was making it worse. I heard Charlie roar as the shield shattered, flaring in a blast of energy that had Miranda and I screaming as the world faded to black.

44

I regained consciousness to the sound of an explosion, flame and stone shooting through the air. I could hear angry screeches and roars as well as some disturbingly wet meaty sounds that I didn't really want to think about. But none of this was happening nearby.

I was huddled around Miranda, we were both still in our t-shirts and bottoms, and there was utter calm around us, all the noise was moving away.

"Take that you spineless parasites! Didn't see that coming, did you!?"

I turned to see Charlie standing triumphant in his chainmail and leather, his flaming sword raised high as he stared out at a field of carnage. As I looked around I realised that we were in the center of a ruined building. Multiple stone walls surrounded us, none more than a few feet high and many burned black or crumbling. Outside the walls on every side I could see rubble and flaming bodies. The building had exploded, tearing through anything that was near. I looked out past Charlie to see the largest ugliest worm in all imagination. Its body was thicker than a train tunnel, and its circular maw held rows upon rows of teeth. I would have crapped myself but for the gigantic shard of stone that had pierced it just behind the head, pinning it to the ground. Despite that, I flinched every time it twitched. I turned to my brother.

"You did this?"

The manic grin on his face worried me.

"That'll teach them! I got the idea from your shield blast last time. I blasted the shield out as it collapsed. It tore right through them, they never saw it coming."

A screech like nails on chalkboard multiplied a thousand times ripped through the air, making me clutch at my ears. Charlie grabbed me and moved me back towards Miranda.

"Suit up, here come the rest of them."

I looked out to see movement on the horizon.

"Aw crap."

I'd known it was too good to be true. For a moment I'd really thought that Charlie had saved us, but at least he'd bought us time. I stretched out an arm and felt the grip of my sword beneath my fingers through the armoured gloves. Black body armour spread over my limbs and chest and I stood, defiant and ready to fight.

The tiny whisper shook me.

"Eoin… Eoin where are we? What happened?"

Miranda was sitting on the stone floor looking around.

She looked up at me, her brow furrowed.

"Are we safe yet?"

I knelt down, reaching out my shield arm and stroking a gloved finger along her cheek.

"Not yet, just shield if you can and stay behind Charlie and me."

She shook her head in confusion.

"But this is a dream, how can I be a tree in a dream unless the dream says so?"

I stood and smiled down at her.

"We're not-"

Charlie's shout drowned me out.

"Eoin! Incoming!"

I twirled around to a Fury diving in, one side of its black snout burnt away. Obviously Charlie's explosion hadn't taken out all of the initial attackers.

It screamed its hate at us and a sick twisted feeling washed over me, making me gag. Behind me I heard the sound of retching as the scream reached Miranda, but there was no time to look after her, the Fury was diving straight for us. I fell to one knee, aiming my flaming sword over the top of my shield.

"With me, Charlie!"

As Charlie dropped beside me I angled my sword towards his, he caught on, moving his sword until they met at the tip. As the Fury closed the flames at the tips of our swords grew hotter and brighter, joining together into a dense ball of fire. I gritted my teeth as the Fury was almost upon us.

"Wait for it….wait for it."

The Fury roared again, turning its mangled head to look at us with its one remaining eye. It would be on us in three seconds… two.. one.

"Now!"

We both roared as we sent our ball of fire shooting straight into the Fury's body. There was a thwump of hot air that knocked us on our backs. The smell of burnt flesh filled the air as our ears were treated to the sound of wet meaty chunks hitting the ground around us. I got to my feet, Charlie was doing the same, Miranda was staring at a piece of flaming Fury meat.

"Eww! I don't think I like this dream, when can we wake up?"

I shot a questioning look at Charlie.

"Not for hours" he answered. "I don't know exactly how long till sunrise, but it's not soon."

"There's no way to just, wake up?"

Charlie shrugged.

"Sure, but without a gateway it takes time and meditation in complete calm, which I don't think we're going to get anytime soon. If there was an easy way back we would have used it before."

A long drawn out screech rattled through the air, it seemed to come from every direction. Miranda whimpered and my heart ached. I looked at Charlie.

"We're gonna need some bigger weapons."

I held out my hand, fingers spread as I slowly turned in a circle. Crossbows, I knew how they worked. They could have electric motors to wind them. I'd done a project on electric motors, it was all about the magnets. Combine that with a hopper to feed new arrows and we had machine crossbows. I concentrated hard, forming eight of them around us, then a wall of spikes and barbed wire surrounding them. With hoppers full of arrows, we were ready for battle. Charlie turned, staring at it all.

"Eoin, this is amazing, but will they even work? The arrows will disappear once they get away from you."

"The car didn't."

He raised an eyebrow.

"What?"

"The rocket car, it didn't disappear when we left it, it stayed. I didn't have to concentrate on it, it just was."

Charlie thought about this for a second and then broke into a grin.

"Hold on."

Charlie ran to the nearest crossbow, which was six foot across and almost the same long. Wires lead from the mass of gears and motors along the shaft to a car battery underneath, I'd mounted the whole thing on a swivel to make it easy to aim.

Charlie grabbed the grip and turned it on the swivel, aiming it at the worm carcass in the distance.

Charlie pulled the trigger, he closed the circuit, powering up the motor that pulled back the drawstring until it locked in place. The drawstring locking dropped an arrow from the hopper. The arrow landing in the groove set off a gear by the drawstring which turned once, giving the arrow time to settle before firing. The arrow shot up in an arc before landing in a patch of earth nowhere near the worm.

Charlie shot a smile over his shoulder.

"Well I'm a lousy shot, but it works."

As the next screech tore through our heads, Miranda threw up. I knelt beside her, stroking her back.

"I'm so sorry, I'll keep you safe Miranda, I promise."

Her whimper of pain made my heart ache.

"Incoming!"

At Charlie's shout I spun in a circle. There were Furies coming in from the one side, but there were also dark shadows in the distance in the opposite direction.

"Flying threats first!" I ran to a crossbow on that side and threw my sword blade first into the ground beside it. I swivelled the bow up and fired off an arrow in a long arc to find my range. They were still a few seconds outside of it. I didn't know if they saw the arrow but they didn't slow, tearing through the air towards us. Eight of them flapping towards us on greasy black wings. I looked across to Charlie at the next crossbow.

"Three more seconds, then let them have it."

I counted down in my head.

Three.

Miranda whimpered softly behind me.

Two.

I could see their dark hides glistening.

One.

I would not let them touch her.

The arrows flew and with each one we adjusted our aim, angling in. Within a few seconds we were raining arrows into the line of Furies, moving up and down the line. When the arrows hit their bodies they just flew on, roaring defiance, but a few arrows hit wings, tearing through the oily membranes. The Furies started to drop, trying to fly and heal at the same time. Before they had gotten halfway to us, we had sent them all crashing into the landscape.

Charlie and I shouted out our victory, but the answering roar from behind us made us pale.

The shapes moving along the ground were clearer now. Like some demonic hybrid of ape and wolf, they charged towards us pounding the ground with their knuckles as they leaped through rubble. Their skin glistened darkly like the Furies, but their screeches, issued from fang filled snouts, held not hate, but a thirst for blood.

Charlie and I ran to the other side of the circle and grabbed the crossbows, letting off a stream of arrows. Charlie got one of them in the eye, sending it screaming to the ground, but the other arrows just stuck in their hides, or worse bounced off, as the six remaining figures charged towards us.

Charlie abandoned his crossbow and shouted across to me.

"Eoin! It's not working!"

"I know, I know!"

I held out my hands and felt the hose materialise between them. I could sense the bulk of the oil tank looming behind me, and knew instinctively that the hose was joined to this supply. I could even hear the noise of the pump, struggling to maintain the pressure.

I pulled the trigger and sent the stream of oil in a high arc, until it splashed down over a hundred feet away. I moved in a wide turn, the oil streaming out under enormous pressure, drenching a line of earth and rubble in the slick mess.

I dropped the hose and went to reach for my sword, which wasn't there. I had left it stuck in the ground beside the crossbow on the other side of the circle.

"Eoin! Whatever you're doing, do it now!" Charlie had resumed firing arrows, for all the good they did. The were-apes were advancing quickly, and had almost reached the oil-soaked earth.

I extended a hand out towards my sword. My sword was forged from my will, so it would bloody well do what it was told. In an instant, the sword flew across the circle into my outstretched hand and I spun, sending a stream of flame out into the oil, thin and bright and hot. It was further than I'd ever sent it before, but I knew it would work, I believed it would work because it had to.

The flame just reached the edge of the oil. I watched as it flickered, seemed to die, and finally caught. A wall of flame rushed along the line of oil, just as three of the were-apes jumped into it. They fell screaming, rolling through the thick wall of fire until they emerged as thrashing flaming balls of pain. The other three roared from behind the wall of flames as their comrades died.

Charlie ran over and slapped me on the shoulder.

"Way to go, Eoin!"

"Don't celebrate yet, there's still three left."

Charlie wiped his brow with the back of his glove.

"Yeah, trapped behind a wall of fire!"

There was a loud crash of splintered wood and I barely pulled Charlie aside as a large metal cog flew past us. Charlie turned and I could see the crossbow he'd been standing by smashed to pieces by a huge jagged rock. Charlie looked out through the wall of flames to where the were-apes were picking up more rocks.

"Shit!"

"Told you so!" I said, turning to face a piece of rubble heading straight towards us. I held up my sword as it turned into a giant, oversized, flaming baseball bat. I swung at the rubble, getting a solid hit and sending it flying back towards the were-apes as I was sent flying onto my ass. As I shoved myself back to my feet, pain shot through my leg.

"Ow!"

Charlie smirked. "Yeah, physics is a bitch. Brace yourself next time."

Charlie followed my lead, but stood with one foot planted on a piece of ruined wall, bracing himself each time he swung.

I found my own patch of wall, but as I hit the next rock it shattered, slicing up my cheek as the shards flew past. I cried out, clutching my face, but the scream of pain I heard behind me made my blood run cold.

I turned slowly, not wanting to see but unable to stop myself. Miranda lay on the ground, the blue of her t-shirt slowly turning black as the blood spread from the shard of rock impaled in her stomach. Her hands were either side of it, clutched against her stomach, perhaps afraid to touch the rock itself. Tears were running down her cheeks as she screamed, the pain so jarring that she struggled to catch her breath.

"Eoin!"

I ran to her, falling to the ground beside her, forgetting everything else that was happening around me. I took her head into my lap, stroking her cheek and whispering softly to her.

"Shhhh, it's ok, it's ok. I know it hurts, but you can heal it. It's not like the real world, you can make it better, you just have to concentrate."

"Eoin! I can't hold them, they're coming!"

I could hear Charlie's pleas somewhere in the distance, but they weren't important. I stroked Miranda's hair as she sobbed.

"Miranda, please concentrate, you can make the pain go away here."

"No!" she sobbed "It's a dream Eoin. They always take me in the dream, they always hurt me, there's nothing I can do!"

"Miranda, you're not in a dream, you're in the spirit world. We can control what happens here, watch." I held my hand out to a crack in the stone beside Miranda's head. I tried to concentrate as Charlie shouted in the background.

"Eoin! They're through the fire. Eoin I need help!"

Slowly, a little shoot of green emerged from the crack. It twisted as it rose, filling out, sprouting leaves, then a bud, until a beautiful flower with purple, blue and yellow petals burst forth, a flower never seen on earth, a flower of the mind. I picked it and placed it on her chest.

"We can be anything we want to be, your imagination is the limit."

She looked up at me with her wide eyes. "I can be a tree?"

Her eyes were my whole world as I answered. "Yes, you can be a tree."

She closed her eyes and smiled. Her skin began to change, it grew thicker and brown, with ridges forming on her cheeks. The change spread down her body, and when it reached her stomach the shard slid out, falling to the ground, and I could see thick uninjured bark through the hole it left in her t-shirt.

"Oh thank God" I held her close, crying softly, as Charlie screamed in pain.

I jumped up, spinning towards him as a giant hand grabbed my body and lifted me into the air. They had looked huge and ugly from a distance, but were even worse up close. Its teeth were rotten in its snout, the stench as it roared in my face was unbearable. I could see black ooze streaming down one leg where it had been burned. Its massive hand gripped me harder, and I felt my ribs creak as I struggled to breathe. I tried to call my sword but I couldn't think through the pain. As I struggled I could see over its shoulder, where even more monsters were charging across the ruined landscapes, all shapes and sizes, everything from our deepest nightmares coming to get us.

Charlie was fighting off the other two were-apes, but one of his legs was torn open and he couldn't move fast enough to stay out of their reach. That's when I knew. I knew that even if Charlie could kill the two were-apes attacking him, he could never save me. And even if he could somehow save me, there was no way we could stand against the monstrous horde that was about to reach us. It was over, I was going to die. I didn't mind so much, I really didn't. The tears that fell weren't for my death, or even for the pain as my ribs began to crack, they were for Miranda. I had promised to protect her, I had been her knight, I was all that she had and I hadn't been good enough.

You hallucinate before you die, right? I'm sure I've read that somewhere. That's what I thought was happening when the branches slid up and around the were-ape's face. They were moving too fast, they couldn't be real. But then the were-ape lurched up in the air, its hand opening, letting me fall. As my landing was broken by a bed of flowers, I thought maybe that was what death felt like, falling in pain, but landing in flowers.

I turned my head and saw something truly beautiful. Miranda stood tall, her skin brown ridged bark, her hair the darkest black moss, her feet anchored to the ground with roots. One brown arm was stretched out, the end turning into a twisted mass of branches that spread out to wrap around the were-ape. As she spoke her eyes flared with bright blue light.

"Get your paws off my boyfriend, you dirty, wolf ape!"

She swung the roaring were-ape down, smashing him into the two who were attacking Charlie. As they lay sprawled on the ground, roots shot up from beneath the earth, more and more, until a mound of twisted brown wood covered the place where the three creatures had been.

The branches withdrew into Miranda's arm until it was a normal arm with a hand and five fingers, albeit covered in bark. She wagged a finger at the twisted mound.

"Bad puppies!"

Miranda stood with her arms outstretched, her clothes gone, her body covered in ridged bark from head to toe. She stood on her tiptoes with her eyes closed, reaching out to the world around her, and it answered. Grass sprouted from the cracks in the stones, followed by flowers, then trees, growing years in the space of seconds, their roots spreading out, cracking and engulfing the flagstones. When she let herself rock back from her tiptoes, we were standing in a grassy meadow surrounded by trees. She looked at me with shining eyes and giggled, hugging herself with bark covered arms, and I could breathe again.

"Hey! A little help here please!?"

I looked up and saw Charlie half way up a tree, his chainmail caught up in its branches. His leg still looked torn up, but it had stopped bleeding. Miranda put her hands to her mouth and laughed.

"Charlie! Whatever are you doing up that tree? Come down!"

"What a good idea Miranda, why didn't I think of that?

Unfortunately though, I'm a little caught up!" He thrashed, trying to get himself loose, which only caused Miranda to laugh harder.

"Silly boy! Here, let me help." She held out her hand and the tree Charlie was stuck in creaked and moved, the branch he was hanging from bending low to the ground before gently unwinding from his mail. Charlie dropped a foot to the ground, landing a little awkwardly, but staying upright. He used his sword as a walking stick to hobble over to us.

"Thank you. Miranda, this is all very impressive but we have to get ready. I saw a horde of monstrosities bigger than imagination on their way to tear us apart."

Miranda waved away his comment.

"Oh those, yes they're at the edge of the grove, my trees don't like them much."

I jumped up and joined them.

"They're here?!"

I grabbed Miranda's hand

"We have to run, we're too drained to fight."

My eyes searched the clearing.

"Maybe I can conjure something to get us away."

Miranda cocked her head at me, causing her neck to creak in a very disconcerting way.

"Why would we need to run, the trees are keeping them out."

"What do you mean?" I looked around, thinking that the trees, though sturdy, were not going to hold out anything for long.

"Oh I'll show you, it'll be fun!"

She threw out her arms and trees round us rustled. Branches reached down and curled around us, lifting us into the air.

"Hey! I only just got down!" Charlie said, waving his sword around as he tried to get enough balance to cut the branch away.

"Charlie!" I held my hand out to him. "I really don't think that would be a good idea."

The branch that was holding me passed me to another branch from a neighbouring tree. From tree to tree we were passed until we'd moved up and out from the clearing. Finally we were all deposited on top of a tall tree with wide flat branches that twisted together at the top to form a platform.

As we landed I felt the platform rise a little and I realised that it had just finished growing that way to give us a perfect place to stand. I looked out across a small forest. It was almost a perfect circle and must have been the length of five or six football fields across. We were just out from the center, our platform a good ten feet above the leafy canopy.

Miranda walked to the edge of the platform, she seemed to sway as she moved, reacting to a wind I couldn't see. She held up a hand, pointing out to the edge of the forest and turning her head back towards us.

"There, the bad things come, but my trees will have none of them."

I looked out to the edge of the forest and saw cloud of dust, the trees at the edge swayed and swung as if in a hurricane, twisting about. As I watched, a black figure was flung from the tree line, back out into the dust cloud.

I heard Charlie's sword drop as he walked out to the edge of the platform.

"But how? How are you doing this? The power it must take, how are you splitting your attention between all the trees?"

Miranda smiled, showing teeth like polished wood.

"Charlie, I've spent years with all the past, present and future in my mind, trying to figure out if what I was remembering was now, then or might not even come to pass. Splitting my attention between a couple of hundred trees is child's play by comparison."

I walked up to her, reaching for her arm.

"Miranda... you're-"

"Coherent? Cohesive? No longer kooky?"

"I was going to say you're amazing, but sure."

She reached up to wrap her arms around my neck, looking up at me with those glowing blue eyes. The colour was deeper now, like dazzling sapphires.

"I'm in my nexus Eoin, the center of my being, you unlocked it for me. I will never be as connected as I am right now. It's not something that you can stay in, not for long."

I reached up to stroke her cheek, her bark felt smooth and warm.

"Does that mean... when you wake... will you..."

"I might not remember everything that has happened here, nor will I be as bad as when you arrived, Earl has seen to that."

"Earl?"

"Oh Eoin, we really don't have much time, please just shut up and kiss me."

She smiled again and words caught in my throat. There really wasn't anything I could do but bow my head and let my lips meet hers. It was a beautiful moment, one I never wanted to end. And then Miranda breathed into me and our breaths were one, and with it our minds were one, and I was everywhere. I could feel the trees battling at the edge of the forest, I could feel the tree that we were standing on, shifting its strength to keep us balanced. I could feel every other tree in the forest, growing and swaying and rejoicing in being. But most of all I could feel Miranda, her heart sang out in joy and mine answered, until I felt it would burst from my chest to be closer to hers. Just as I felt I could take no more, as my mind was on the brink of breaking, she broke the kiss, pulling back with a mischievous grin. As I stood, trying to catch my breath, she caught me with her sapphire eyes and whispered.

"Some things deserve more than words."

There was a discreet cough.

"Eh, guys, I hate to interrupt but, what the hell is going on? I mean, Miranda has gone all Jean Grey Phoenix and saved our asses, cool, but where do we go from here? Are we just going to hide in the forest every night?"

Miranda turned to face Charlie, leaning back against me, her head resting on my chest.

"Oh I won't be able to do this again tomorrow. Who knows if I'll ever find this place again? But don't worry, I won't need to, Eoin is going to fix everything."

"I am?" I realised I had unconsciously put my arms around her, pulling her against me. It was a little weird that I'd done it without realising. Not weird enough for me to let go or anything, but still.

She arched her neck to look up at me, reaching up to stroke my neck.

"You really should have more faith in yourself, my love."

Her blazing eyes faded for just a second.

"Oh, are you my love yet?"

Her face twisted in confusion as she pulled away from me.

"It's... I'm not supposed to... because it can scare."

I spun her around and reached for her face, I could feel her bark skin growing colder.

"Miranda, are you ok? What's wrong?"

She grabbed at my shoulders, steadying herself. Her eyes were screwed shut and her voice came out through gritted teeth.

"I'm slipping out, so difficult to balance, hurts a little, like tiny red hot icicles."

I shot Charlie a panicked look.

"What do we do!?"

He held up his hands.

"You're asking me? This is way beyond anything I've even heard about."

Miranda closed her eyes, took a deep breath and let it out slowly. As she did, I felt the tree beneath us shudder. She pulled my hands away from her face and kissed my fingertips, before opening her eyes. The bright blue light flickered, but it was there. Holding on to one of my wrists she turned to Charlie.

"Take my hands, both of you, it's time to go home. We

have to go now, before I forget how."

Charlie came and stood on the other side of Miranda and took her hand. She closed her eyes and began to murmur softly to herself, over and over. I couldn't make out the words but it went up and down like a nursery rhyme. The light from the twilight sky grew brighter. I looked around and realised the light wasn't coming from the sky though, it was crystallising from the air around us. Yellow and green lights appeared as specks, moving and waving in the air, meeting and merging, flowing until we were encased in a ball of shimmering light. Miranda opened her eyes and looked up at me.

"I love you Eoin, with all that I am and all that I will ever be. Remember that for me, even if I don't." She leaned up and kissed me as the world exploded.

45

I was sore when I woke. I almost didn't want to open my eyes for fear of what wounds I would find. I breathed tentatively, fearing cracked ribs, but the sharp pain I was expecting was absent. I opened my eyes to find myself sitting up against a pillow at the head of Miranda's bed. Her head was in my lap and she was making contented noises in her sleep. I stretched my back and heard it crack. Wincing, I stretched my arms out, looking around the room. The first light of dawn was showing through the high windows. We'd made it.

"Charlie?" I whispered, not wanting to wake Miranda.
I'm here. Man that was a wild ride.
I smiled. "Yeah, but we made it through."
For now. Dr Hawkins is still expecting you to jump and prance for him today, and those monstrous hordes will just come

back tonight. Even if we refuse to do the experiment, the fact that Dr Hawkins is investigating both you and Miranda is enough to make you a target.

I nodded, smiling to myself.

"It is a dilly of a pickle."

Did you hit your head on the way back?

I leaned my head back against the cold metal of the bed frame.

"We're alive, we made it through the night, and my girlfriend is a superhero, allow me some levity."

I'd be more willing to if I thought you actually had a plan to get us out of this.

That's when the idea came to me. It was like Charlie said, you didn't reach for the calm, you just let it settle. My mind was relaxed and then amid that relaxation came the idea. I trusted that I would know what to do, and then I did. It all seemed so obvious.

Miranda stretched in my lap and yawned like a kitten.

"Is it breakfast time? I hope there's orange juice, much better than milk."

I stroked her hair and she leaned up to nuzzle my hand.

"Do you remember what happened, Miranda?"

She closed one eye and considered the question.

"We made the room safe but then it shook, and I was scared. Then I was in a dream and it hurt."

A bright smile spread across her face.

"But then you told me that I can be anything I want in dreams, so I became a tree, and my roots spread so deep and so far that I was everywhere and everything."

Her smile grew secret and a soft blush filled her cheeks.

"Oh and then you kissed me, because... because of something important. Oh! Because I saved you maybe? That must be it! Did I save you?"

The last was said in a serious tone, with her eyes upturned.

I leaned down and whispered into her lips.

"Yes, you saved us all, my heroine."

I felt her lips smile against mine and I pulled her tight against me to deliver a kiss worth fighting through the night for, or so I thought. Instead she pulled away, biting her lip and pushing herself out of my embrace.

I let go, my voice full of concern.

"Are you okay? Is something wrong?"

She winced, looking up at me, and whispered confidentially.

"No, I just need to pee"

I sighed in relief, holding my hand up to my face to hide my grin.

"Well, off you go then."

She ran off towards the bathroom at the end of the infirmary, shouting back over her shoulder.

"Stay there, I don't want to lose you!"

I smiled, turning around to look at the infirmary in the dawn light. I looked up at one of the cameras and wondered why they didn't come in when we had fallen asleep in the same bed. Maybe nobody had been monitoring us after all.

My concerns were forgotten when the bathroom door opened and Miranda skipped out wearing a toilet paper headband, tied in a bow.

"I found a hat! Do you like it?"

She twirled and posed, showing off her new attire.

"It is magnificent. Truly you are a lady of taste." I bowed and held out my hand to her. "Would you care to dance?"

She curtseyed with a dress that wasn't there. "Of course, kind Sir."

I placed one hand around her waist and held her hand out from her body with the other. I began to hum softly as I twirled her in circles. She kept up admirably, laughing and giggling as I whirled her around the floor. I stopped as I saw Earl leaning against the wall by the door with his arms folded. Miranda carried on twirling when I stopped, pirouetting off on her own.

Earl held up his hands and smiled. "Don't stop on my

account."

Miranda called out as she twirled towards him.

"Earl! Isn't my hat pretty!?"

"That it is, darlin'."

He looked to me and gave me a wink.

"When you've finished dancing I have to take you back to your rooms, breakfast will be ready soon."

As we grabbed our things I noticed the stubble on Earl's chin and the bags beneath his eyes.

"You ok, Earl?"

He stifled a yawn as he replied. "Yeah I'm fine kid, everything go ok here last night?"

I looked back at Miranda as she spun, trailing a length of toilet paper where her headband was unravelling.

"Yeah, everything was great."

46

Miranda insisted on holding Earl's hand on the walk back to the ward. He didn't seem to mind and spent the walk smiling down at her as she skipped beside him. We arrived at the ward and for the first time I could remember, there was no one at the orderly's desk.

"Earl, shouldn't someone be here?"

He shook his head.

"No need, you guys weren't here last night. Frank should be on duty in an hour, I'll hold the fort until then."

Miranda stood picking pieces of toilet paper from the tangles of her long black hair. She turned to us, her face lighting up.

"We should have breakfast!"

Earl nodded. "It'll be here in about 20 minutes, Miranda."

She shook her head.

"No! Together, the three of us, we should have breakfast."

Earl seemed to consider this, before a smile spread across his face. "You know what? I think that would be lovely."

While Earl phoned down to the kitchen for an extra breakfast, Miranda and I went to our rooms. Earl thought it would be better if Miranda was out of sight when the meals arrived, apparently her reputation reached further than the ward. Once Earl called the all clear, we grabbed pillows from our rooms and sat in a circle by the orderly's desk.

Over a breakfast of eggs, toast and orange juice, Miranda laughed and giggled and told Earl a story about a heroic young girl who had set out to find her lost knight in a magical forest. The trees themselves had moved against her and so she ran across the canopy to find him. When she finally tracked him down, they had shared a kiss so powerful, that it broke the curse that kept them apart.

Earl smiled tenderly at Miranda while she told the story, weaving her hands in the air as she described the girl's quest.

"That is quite a tale Miranda, I'll have to remember it. I have a girl, younger than you, but she loves stories."

Earl looked at his watch.

"Ok, Frank will be here soon, you two should head to your rooms."

Before he could get up, Miranda jumped up and kissed him on the cheek.

"Thank you for breakfast Earl, it was nice not to have to eat alone."

Earl seemed stunned for a moment, and he raised a hand to his cheek. When he found his voice, it came out serious, but far from sad.

"You're welcome Miranda, you're very welcome. Best get to your room."

She skipped away singing a song about seeds not

knowing what they'd be as she disappeared into her room, closing the door behind her.

As Earl began picking up the trays, he gave me a sideways glance.

"Doc has the big wigs coming in this afternoon for a meeting."

The remark was casual, but the way he looked at me was not.

"I know. He wants to show me to them."

He raised an eyebrow. "I thought he was going to show them Miranda. Her progress has been amazing."

"Yeah, but that had nothing to do with him." Both his eyebrows were up now. "I mean, well he's a really good doctor, but-"

Earl took pity on my stammering.

"Well maybe we'll never know why she's getting better."

I smiled and nodded, but he kept going.

"So why does the Doc want to show them you? Not that you're not doing well, you seem good."

I bit my lip, I trusted Earl, but my gut was telling me that now wasn't the time to confide in him.

"It's complicated, I'm not really sure how it will go."

He considered me for a second longer than was comfortable. I waited for him to speak and break the silence.

"Well I should be back in time for it, so I'll see you there."

The thought that Earl would be there made me feel better about it, though I wasn't sure why.

Earl waved me away as he turned back to the orderly's desk.

"Ok, get to your room and I'll talk to you later."

47

The day was tense, sitting around waiting to be shown off. I tried to read, but after reading the same page three times and still not taking it in, I gave it up as a lost cause. Just after lunch, Dr Hawkins stopped in for a visit. He seemed agitated, fiddling with a loose button on his white doctor's coat.

"Our biggest benefactors are coming in to see you, Eoin. When they see the experiment, we will have no problem securing funding to... help even more children."

Well, he's lying his ass off.

It was getting easier not to react to Charlie's sarcastic commentary. Dr Hawkins made me run through the Zener cards again. Charlie was reluctant, but he played along. Dr Hawkins calmed a little after a complete run of right answers. He stood and smiled down at me in what he probably thought was a friendly manner.

"Good, good. The meeting will be in about an hour, I'll send someone to get you."

As he turned to go, I felt myself jumping to my feet.

Now was the time, this was the moment on which the future depended.

"Dr Hawkins?"

"Yes Eoin?"

I hesitated, when I tried to think what to say, the words wouldn't come. I took a deep breath and relaxed. I didn't reach for the words, I just let it happen, and I knew what to do.

"I want Miranda there, for the experiment."

He folded his arms, his face growing stern, all traces of friendly doctor vanishing.

"What? Impossible, you can't just bring an unstable patient al-"

"Except she's not unstable."

My interruption was quiet, but firm, I looked him in the eye as I took a step towards him.

"She's better than she has been since she got here. Think how impressed the benefactors will be when they see this formerly psychotic patient sitting, happily having a conversation. She's still a little strange, but she's not violent in the slightest, it's a testament to your skills."

Dr Hawkins' eyes narrowed.

"What are you up to, Eoin?"

I kept my hands by my side. I maintained eye contact, my face was open and calm, my voice steady.

"I want Miranda there Sir, and I can't see how it's anything but a good thing for you."

He paused, and the silence stretched between us. I knew he would be the one to break it.

"Fine, but there will be an orderly on hand at all times. If she's the slightest bit disruptive, she'll be removed immediately."

He looked harried and grumpy, which made me smile inside, though I tried not to show it.

"Thank you, Dr Hawkins."

He frowned, as if trying to figure out what he'd been tricked into, but he left.

Charlie piped up as soon as Dr Hawkins was out the door. His voice bewildered.

What was that all about?

"Miranda has to be there. She's part of it."

Part of what?

"Part of what happens."

Dude, cryptic much?

His confusion was understandable, but I didn't share it. As I replied, my words came with a calm surety.

"It will all work out. There's a plan, but if I think about it too hard it will disappear, I have to settle into it. Can you trust me?"

He sighed loudly.

Ok, I'll trust you. But I want you to know it's only because you're my brother, and there's pretty much nothing I can do to stop you. Also... I haven't got any better ideas.

I laced my words with the appropriate amount of sarcasm.

"You're unwavering faith in me is heart warming"

48

I lay on the bed for the next hour with butterflies in my stomach. I could practically hear Charlie not bugging me with questions. The truth was that I had no clue if I was going to manage to pull it off, but I had to trust that when the time came, I would know what to say.

I was concentrating on my breathing, trying to keep calm, when the knock at the open door made me jump. When I looked up I saw Earl leaning against the door, looking clean shaven and bright eyed.

"You ready kid? It's time."

I sat up and nodded, taking one last deep breath before standing.

"Let's go."

I walked out of the room and headed towards the ward door, waiting for Earl to call me back, which he did.

"Wait, we have to get Miranda, Doc wants her there too."

I turned, raising my eyebrows.

"Oh." I said "Why?"

Earl shrugged.

"Dunno, maybe he just wants to show her off like I said."

I walked along after Earl.

"Do you think she'll be able for it?"

He stopped to let me catch up, shooting me a thoughtful look.

"You tell me kid, you know her better than any of us."

As we approached Miranda's door, Charlie's indignant voice filled my mind.

What the hell Eoin? What kind of game are you playing here?

I waved my hand behind my back, hoping he would get the hint and shut up.

When Earl opened the door, Miranda was sitting on the edge of her bed, which was neatly made. Her hands were folded in her lap. Her long, black hair was shiny and sleek. Her blue t-shirt and bottoms were crisp and new. She looked at me and her eyes were no longer the pale blue tinged white they were the first time I'd seen them. Instead she met my gaze with brilliant blue sapphires.

All I could do was stare, the awed silent seconds stretching out, before I managed to stammer a few words.

"Miranda, you look, wow."

Earl chuckled. "I had one of the nurses bring her for a proper shower and clean up. Took some bribery, but worth it, right Miranda?"

She took in my reaction, her lips curling a little, before turning to Earl.

"Definitely, thank you."

She turned back to me and gave me a wry look that stole my heart, before turning her head from one side to the other.

"I've been trying to decide which is my best side but they both look the same."

I held out my hand and answered with utter sincerity. "That's because every bit of you is perfect."

"Liar" she teased, but she jumped up and took my hand. Earl lead the way, holding the ward door open for us before walking ahead. He seemed content to let us hang back and follow him from afar..

Miranda swung my hand as we walked. "So, do you think you'll remember your lines?"

I squeezed her hand. "I'll remember them when I have to, I can't remember them before then or else I might forget them."

She lifted my hand so that she could twirl beneath it.

"That's true, but I have faith in you."

What? Sorry what? Did you crack her code or just become cracked?

"Shhhhh, don't get so agitated Charlie. Just remember, when the experiment begins, tell me what's on the cards. Don't try to lie to me, it's important."

But I thought you had a plan for how we wouldn't have to do the experiment? I've been waiting all day to find out what it is.

"I didn't say I had a plan not to do the experiment, I said there was a plan that would make everything turn out alright. Really Charlie, you should listen more carefully."

"He's quite silly sometimes" Miranda chimed in.

Eoin, you better know what you're doing.

"I don't, but I will do, I know I will."

Up ahead Earl stopped at a door and waited for us to catch up, and as we approached I could hear Dr Hawkins voice through the door.

"I know that what I am about to demonstrate is miraculous. However, I hope that when you see it with your own eyes, you will believe, as I do, that we are on the brink of a major breakthrough. The implications are simply astounding-"

Earl knocked and peered into the room, before opening it wide and waving us in. A line of five men in suits sat against the wall on the right. Dr Hawkins stood before them, next to a small table with two chairs. A pack of Zener cards sat in the center of the table.

"Gentleman, this is Eoin, the boy I've been telling you about. Oh, and Miranda, another of our patients."

The second man in the line leaned forward in his chair.

"I know that girl, isn't she… I mean, is it safe to have her here?"

Dr Hawkins dismissed the query with a confident wave of his hand.

"Of course it is, Mr Dunne. Miranda, say hello to the nice man."

Miranda curtsied with a dress that wasn't there, looking

up through her lashes at the objecting man. "Hello, I like your tie! Doesn't it restrict you though?"

Mr Dunne reached up to straighten his tie and nodded thoughtfully. "I suppose it does sometimes."

As Dr Hawkins exhaled, I realised he'd been holding his breath..

"Miranda is just one of the amazing successes we've been having lately. Earl, why don't you and Miranda have a seat while we begin?" He waved to two chairs against the wall opposite the men. As Earl and Miranda went to sit, Dr Hawkins went to the table and pulled out the chair facing the men. "Eoin?"

I sat down, feeling my heart beating fast in my chest. I concentrated on my breathing, finding my center. I felt the line that grounded me. I knew my place and I was in it.

Dr Hawkins moved around to the opposite side of the table.

"I know you are all very busy, so we'll begin immediately."

He sat opposite me with his back to the men and lifted up the first Zener card, high above his shoulder so that the men could see.

"Now Eoin, please tell me what shape is on the card."

I concentrated on the back of the card, waiting for Charlie to tell me. I fidgeted as the silence lengthened.

"Take your time Eoin, just tell me what shape is on the card." His words were calm, but his face was growing red.

Where was Charlie? Was he abandoning me? It was vital that I knew what was on the card or everything would fall apart.

It's a circle.

"Square." I said.

Dr Hawkins spluttered but recovered, laying down the card and quickly picking up another.

"And this one?" he said, glowering at me.

Eoin, what are you doing? I said circle! This one is waves, what is going on?

"Hmm, triangle I think. No, a cross!"

Dr Hawkins turned in his seat to address the frowning men. His voice growing in pitch.

"Just a small case of nerves I'm sure gentleman, we just need to warm up a little."

He turned back, whispering to me. "What are you doing, Eoin?"

I let tears well up in my eyes. "I'm doing my best, Sir."

Dr Hawkins spoke through gritted teeth as he held up the next card.

"Well, do better!"

We got through 20 cards in all, I guessed every single one wrong. It was Mr Dunne who called a halt, standing and waving a hand.

"Dr Hawkins I think we've seen enough. I'm sure you brought us here in good faith, but the boy obviously has no clue what is on those cards."

Dr Hawkins jumped up, knocking over his chair. "But he can do it, the video. You've all seen it, he did it only yesterday."

Mr Dunne turned to me. "Eoin, is this true? Did you guess all the cards correctly yesterday?"

"Yes Sir."

I stood as Mr Dunne's brow furrowed in thought, .

"But the lighting is different today Sir, so I couldn't see the reflection in Dr Hawkins glasses anymore. If he leans forward a bit and holds the cards lower, I could try again."

Chairs scraped across the floor and banged against the wall as the rest of the men jumped to their feet. Shouts filled the air, most of them directed at Dr Hawkins, who backed up in the face of the wave of angry words.

Dr Hawkins edged closer to the exit waving his hands placatingly at the group as the commotion intensified. His words came out in short panicked bursts, trying to address the various shouts aimed at him.

"But he can't have cheated... Of course I never told him to... No, Gentleman please... please listen, it's all down to his imaginary friend."

Brother, have I ever told you that you're a genius?

"Multiple times" I whispered, "but no need to stop."

Mr Dunne poked the doctor in the ribs. "Doctor Hawkins, I'm afraid that I'm going to have to seriously reconsider my patronage of your institution!"

I caught Dr Hawkins' eye as he backed away, and if looks could have killed I would have been a smoking crater. The look lasted less than a second, and then his face resumed its projection of innocence.

"Mr Dunne, please, you know we do good work here, just look at Miranda. No one was able to approach her safely before and now she sits there all prim and proper."

Miranda stood when Dr Hawkins pointed in her direction.

"That's very true Sir, I feel much better."

I saw Dr Hawkins relax a little as he tried to herd attention towards Miranda and away from me.

"There you are, surely you don't want t-"

"Ever since Earl said I could stop taking Dr Hawkins pills, I've been feeling more like myself again."

At Miranda's words a hush spread out through the room. All eyes turned towards the meek, neatly presented girl in the corner.

Mr Dunne walked towards Miranda, pushing Dr Hawkins aside. As he crossed the room I could see his fists ball up with tension, and I didn't need any special senses to see the anger running through his frame. But when he approached Miranda I saw the tension slowly subside, and when he spoke, his voice was calm and gentle, though I could still detect a trace of anger, held by iron self control.

"What did you say, Miranda?"

Dr Hawkins tried to protest but Mr Dunne silenced him with a look.

"Ever since I got here I've been given pills every day. Dr Hawkins said that I had to take them if I wanted to get better. But I never felt any better, only worse. A few days ago, Earl said that I could stop taking the pills. He's been helping me flush them down the toilet. Now I feel much better, and it's all thanks to him."

Earl sat in the chair, head down, hands folded in his lap. He was perfectly still.

"Earl, is this true?" Dr Hawkins' indignant shout hurt my ears..

Earl stood up and faced the men, holding his left wrist in his right hand.

"Gentleman, it was my belief that Dr Hawkins was over medicating Miranda, and that he knew that she was overmedicated. What his purpose was in this I don't know, but he has had a lot of private sessions with her. I've also seen Dr Hawkins using patients for what I can only assume are his own experiments, including letting Eoin and Miranda sleep in the same room together unaccompanied, even though at the time he still believed Miranda to be dangerous to others."

Mr Dunne turned on Dr Hawkins, flabbergasted. "Eugene, is this true!? This is completely unethical!"

Eugene? You've got to be kidding me.

"Hey." I whispered, moving a hand up to cover my mouth. "Everyone's got to have a name."

Dr Hawkins had reached the babbling portion of his defence. "Yes, well no, I eh, in NO way harmed Miranda, and any insinuations… and I was sure Eoin would be safe in the room with her, she's been much better since he got here. Not that that's due to him! It was quality care, provided by myself, and …"

Mr Dunne pointed at Earl. "You Sir, get these children back to their rooms. As for you Eugene, I believe we should all retire to your office to discuss this further."

The men were curiously silent as they filed out, leaving the three of us alone. Well, four.

Dude, you could knock me down with a feather, were I in fact capable of interacting with solid matter. How the hell? Did you know the whole time you were going to do that? I mean-

"Ix-nay!" I said through gritted teeth, glancing at Earl who was currently being hugged by Miranda.

Oh, right.

"Thank you, Earl!" Miranda was trying to hug and bounce at the same time. "I knew it would all be ok, you are the bestest, most wonderful person who isn't Eoin ever!"

Earl's deep laugh joined mine and the last of the tension that had filled the room was dispelled..

"C'mon kids, let's get you back to your rooms. Then I have to go find out if I still have a job."

I reached up, placing my hand on his shoulder. "Thank you, I know you risked a lot to help Miranda, to speak out. It means the world to us, thank you."

Earl reached up to where my hand gripped his shoulder and gave it a rough squeeze, while giving me a satisfied nod. Then we lured Miranda back to the ward with the promise of ice cream.

49

Mum came later in the day, with a court order authorizing my release. It seemed that ever since I fell in to the coma, Dr Hawkins had been denying her access, saying that I had taken a bad turn and that contact would only make me worse. She was on the phone with a lawyer by day two. I heard her shouting for me as she ran down the ward, but I hardly had a chance to move before she burst through the door of my room and started hugging me. She held me tight against her then pulled back, holding my head, looking into my eyes, making sure I was real and whole before hugging me again..

"Oh Eoin, I'm so sorry! I trusted him and he lied to us, I'm so sorry, I'll never let anyone take you away again!"

She sat down on the edge of the bed, holding my hands

as I sat beside her. She took a deep breath, laughing a little as she tried to get her words out.

" I was talking with Mr Jenkins, the orderly."

"Earl?"

"Yes, he said that Dr Hawkins has been overmedicating other patients, that it might not have been a placebo he'd given you at all."

Ah.

I felt the moment stretch and the roads diverge before me.

"Who knows Mum, all I know is that I haven't taken a single pill in days and I'm fine."

Good call.

"Oh my baby, I'm so happy to see you. We're leaving this awful place right now, we're going to get you dressed and then I'm getting you some proper food, you look so thin.."

Mum stood and gently pulled at my arm, but I shook my head.

"Mum, I can't just go, what about Miranda?"

Mum opened her mouth to dismiss my objection but then a look of confusion crossed her face.

"Who?"

"She's another patient here, the only other patient on this ward. I can't just leave her."

"Eoin…."

Her confusion only deepened.

"I mean, it's wonderful that you can show such compassion, but this girl isn't your responsibility."

"She's right, Eoin." I turned to see Miranda standing in doorway, hands behind her back, biting her lip.

Mum looked at Miranda and then turned to look at me, raising an eyebrow in a way that was far too knowing for my comfort.

"Oh, you must be Miranda then."

Miranda stepped forward and offered her hand, which Mum took. "It's very nice to meet you Mrs. Murphy, you're very pretty."

Mum blushed and tucked a strand of hair behind her ear. "Well, thank you Miranda, I must say you're very pretty yourself. Are you friends with Eoin?"

"He's my…"

Oh no.

"…very good friend, yes. Do you like trees?"

I let out the breath I'd been holding.

Mum took the change of subject in her stride.

"Why yes, I love trees. I love going for walks in the park, especially now the leaves are falling."

Miranda looked at Mum with that far away gaze in her eyes, and her words came out in a dreamy whisper.

"I think if you were a tree, you'd be a rosewood tree."

Mum smiled but I could see her wondering where this was going.

"Oh, well that sounds pretty."

Miranda came back to the here and now and her face lit up.

"They are, but they're also one of the strongest woods on earth, almost nothing can break them."

Miranda turned to look at me.

"Go on Eoin, I'll be fine."

And for the first time that word didn't make me cringe, because I knew in my heart that it was true. She would be fine, not fine leave me alone, or fine for now, she was really going to be ok.

Miranda hugged me tight. I'd like to say our hearts merged, or that our thoughts were one, or that it felt like so much more, but it was just a hug, though one I didn't want to end. She let me go, smiling, and went back to her room.

50

Mum didn't even wait to get me home to feed me, bringing me for a burger as soon as we left. As I bit down into the meat and the gorgeous juices filled my mouth I realised how bland the food had been in the institution. As we ate, we laughed and joked, not talking about school or her work or what had happened. We just... enjoyed ourselves.

We got home and Mum continued to hover around me, constantly looking around to check that I hadn't disappeared. After the fifth yawn she realised how tired I was and suggested an early night. She followed me up and tucked me into bed, which she hadn't done in a very long time. It was embarrassing, but I let her do it. It was a small price to pay to see her so happy.

When she left I was so tempted to just turn over and go to sleep, but there was something important I had to ask.

"So, how badly are we screwed?"

Well you're out of the nuthouse and Mum loves you more than ever, and seems to be sweeping my very existence under the proverbial rug, so I think you're doing ok.

"On this plane maybe, what about the other one?"

I've been up there listening to the gossip, to be honest they're painting you as some kind of hero.

"What?"

Yeah, the boy who faced the Furies and lived.

I let the pride build a second before I came back to reality.

"But that was because of Miranda."

Regardless, the spirits speak highly of you. But the most important thing is that I've found out that the Powers called off the Furies.

"Seriously? I can actually go to sleep without worrying I'll wake up dead?"

You can't wake up dead, actually maybe you could manage it. The main point is that, since you discredited Dr Hawkins, there's no longer a threat to expose the spirit world and the Powers can't move against you.

I'd talked with Charlie too much not to spot the careful wording.

"But they want to?"

Let's just say that when you destroy over half of their army, they tend to hold a grudge. But as long as you keep your head down and don't risk exposing the spirit world, you should be safe.

I'd be safe, but it wasn't just about me.

"What about Miranda?"

Same deal, though hopefully she manages to get out of that nut house.

I thought of her, all alone on the ward now, no nightmares, but no knight either.

"Yeah."

You ok?

I rolled over to face the wall, unable to get the image of her out of my head. I wondered how long it would take for the image to fade, until I no longer knew what she looked like.

"Yeah, I just, I'm tired. I just need to get some sleep."

Ok, sleep well brother, I love you.

I closed my eyes letting the one tear that had managed to build up get soaked up by my pillow.

51

Mum let me take the rest of the week off school, which was a relief. I wasn't looking forward to going back as the crazy kid who attacked Declan Byrne and then disappeared for a week. I was doing some make up work that Mum had picked up from the school when the knock came at the door. Mum put down the saucepan she was holding and went to wipe her hands.

"I'll get it." I said, jumping up to save her the trouble.

I opened the door and there she stood, with sapphire eyes in a bright yellow dress, her jet black hair making her face seem even paler. Only the coat around her shoulders and the pink in her cheeks from the cold let me know that I perhaps wasn't dreaming.

"Hello, you must be Eoin, is your mother in?"

The voice came from over Miranda's shoulder, where stood a red haired woman with a warm smile.

I turned back into the house. "Mum!"

She walked up, wiping her hands on a cloth. "What is it Eoin? Oh, Miranda, how lovely to see you again."

The red haired lady held out her hand. "Hello I'm Catherine, Catherine Moore. I'm Miranda's aunt."

Mum shook her hand in return.

"Lora Murphy, it's nice to meet you."

Catherine hesitated, looking from Miranda to Mum. Mum took pity on her and broke the awkward silence.

"Well it's good to see that Miranda out of that horrible place."

Catherine nodded, wrapping an arm around Miranda tenderly.

"I'm sorry to call unannounced but Miranda insisted that it had to be this afternoon."

Mum waved away the apology.

"Not at all, I'm glad you did. How did you get our address though?"

Catherine looked down at Miranda.

"Miranda directed me, she couldn't remember the street name but she knew exactly where to go. I assumed Eoin told her."

Miranda smiled and gave me a wink.

"Oh, yeah." I said, sounding not at all convincing. "I must have."

Mum stood back from the door and waved them in.

"Come on in the both of you, will you stay for dinner?"

Miranda skipped into the kitchen as Catherine demurred.

"Oh, I wouldn't want to put you out."

Mum took Catherine's coat and ushered her through the hall.

"Nonsense, we've been wondering how Miranda was doing, come in and tell us all about it."

Over dinner the whole story came out. Catherine had tried to visit Miranda after the fire that killed her parents, but she was always told that Miranda was too dangerous to have visitors. Earl had found Catherine's contact information in Miranda's file and phoned her on the afternoon that I'd left. She'd visited the very next day, and after a few days of Miranda acting relatively normally, an outside psychiatrist judged her to be no danger to herself or others and Catherine brought her home.

"It's been wonderful having her back. She looks so like her mother, my sister was always a beauty." Catherine looked at Miranda and I saw a touch of sadness fill her eyes.

"Well" said Mum, clearing away the plates. "I'm just so glad both of them are out of that terrible place. My lawyer tells me that Dr Hawkins has been fired and the institution is being placed under a non-medical administrator. He said Mr Jenkins is helping to run the place until everything is sorted."

Miranda lit up. "Earl? Oh good, I knew it would work out for him. He's very good at his job, I'm sure everybody will be a little less crazy."

Mum smiled back at her. "Yes, well he's got his work cut out, there's an official investigation by the health department and apparently there are all kinds of irregularities. Have you gotten representation, Catherine?"

Catherine looked up at Mum's inquiry, shaking her head slowly.

"Representation? For what?"

"Well, to sue the rotten ba... blighter. My lawyer thinks that his malpractice insurance company will likely offer to settle before the month is out."

Catherine, looked to her side where Miranda was drawing designs in spilled salt.

"Oh, I don't know, I'm just so happy to have Miranda, I don't know if I should."

Mum looked back over her shoulder as she lifted the steaming kettle towards two mugs.

"Let me show you some of the paperwork, I think it'll be worth your while. Kids, why don't you play outside for a bit?"

Catherine bolted upright. "Is that wise, I mean they... they could get in trouble."

Mum smiled and put a mug of tea in front of Catherine. "They're kids Catherine, of course they'll get in trouble, but at least now they're getting in trouble within earshot. Go on you two."

I grabbed Miranda's hand and ran out to the front garden with her. As soon as the door was closed behind us, I leaned down and stole a kiss. It didn't shatter my world, but it did make my heart skip a beat.

If you two are going to start making out in the front garden I'm going to be sick, metaphorically, as it were.

Miranda pulled back. "It's lovely to see you too Charlie. Metaphorically, as it were."

So you're not crazy anymore?

Miranda turned her head to the side and considered the air.

"Oh I was never crazy Charlie, merely overwhelmed by para-sensory input across multiple time space matrices."

Para-sensa-what now?

Miranda giggled. "I have no idea, it's something I said to myself in a dream, I think. It's difficult to remember all the words, they slip away like little fish if you grip them too hard."

Ah, now you're sounding more like your old self.

The rough shout cut across our moment.

"Is that your girlfriend Murphy? Aww, aren't you two sweet!"

I looked across the street. A group of boys were walking along, one had stopped to shout at me. Billy Harrison, one of Declan's hanger-ons.

I turned to face him, standing tall and offering a shout in return.

"Yeah Harrison, it is. What's the matter, jealous 'cause you can't get one?"

That threw him, I wasn't supposed to answer back. I watched his face turn red as a few stray laughs escaped from his friends. Harrison gripped his hands into fists and shouted even louder.

"Oh yeah? Well I wouldn't want one like her anyway, you probably picked her up in that mental asylum you were in, she's just another nutter like you!"

I didn't see red, I think that's just a thing people say, but I felt the anger flash through me. I'd destroyed evil spirits that would make this sorry little imbecile shit himself, I wasn't going to let him talk about my girlfriend like that. I took a step forward only to find Miranda had stepped in front of me and was walking towards him. She didn't shout, she just spoke, but her words seemed to cut through the air, demanding to be heard.

"I'm sorry, I'm very, very sorry."

Harrison smirked. "For what love, being so ugly?" This got a titter or two from his pack, but they were slowly moving away, bored.

Miranda continued, her voice full of concern and understanding.

"I'm sorry that you have to hit out to feel safe. But don't worry, in a year, maybe two, you'll stop wetting the bed and things will be a lot easier for you."

This caused his pack to erupt in laughter, pointing at Harrison and jostling each other, before turning to walk off. Harrison erupted, screaming across the road at us, turning from us to his friends.

"That's a lie! You take that back! She's lying, no listen guys, it's a lie. It just happened once, I swear, I just had too much coke before bed, it's not like... stop laughing!"

He ran after his friends, still shouting. Miranda turned to me with a mischievous grin, curtsied in her pretty yellow dress, and said "Would you care to dance m'lord?"

I bowed as gracefully as I could. "It would be an honour."

And so I took her waist in one hand, her hand in the other, and I twirled her around the garden, with Charlie humming some tune or other, rather badly. And as I danced with Miranda in my arms, I had a moment of clarity. I saw our future. There were many paths it could take, light paths and dark paths and short paths. But on every path I saw, in every choice that could be, there stood the three of us, Miranda, Charlie and I.

'The Other Whisper'

Book One in 'The Other Series'

By Ian Paul Power

www.WolfpackPublishers.com